A SEQUEL TO THE DIANA STRAIN

MANI'S
DAUGHTERS

JOSHUA CONVERSE

DEDICATION

To Anne Rice, for the first encounter.

CONTENTS

ACKNOWLEDGMENTS

The author gratefully acknowledges his first readers, particularly Guy Swalm, David Villani, Elle Otero, Marysia Kosowski, his wife Amy, Durell Duran, Bradley Walker, Elizabeth Thomas, Bill Easton, Ryan Huber, Professor Henry Marchand, the Creative Writing Program at Monterey Peninsula College and the MPC Library, his editor Carrie Glenn, and all readers whose patience and insight that brought this novel into being. All errors are my own.

THE BROTHERS CROW

October 2016

Bill Crow didn't need to be an FBI investigator to know something was up with his brother. Bill had climbed in the Bureau to become special agent in charge of the San Francisco field office, just as Frank had climbed the ranks at the Monterey County Sheriff's Office to become a homicide detective.

Frank had gone silent for months at this point—ever since the Big Sur murders. Before that, Frank, his wife Lela, and Bill came together at least twice a month and sometimes more to go to a ballgame or just have a few beers. Now nothing. Bill had called, emailed, even sent written letters in the mail. No answer. Something was badly wrong.

And so, one night after his work, Bill drove to Monterey to find out what why his big brother had ghosted him. It happened to be Full Moon.

Bill knocked on Frank and Lela's front door for the better part of thirty minutes before Frank finally cracked it open, a hard expression on his face.

"Not a good time, Bill."

"What's going on, Frank?"

"Bad time, Bill. Talk later, okay?"

"No, it's not okay. You've been off since that thing in Big Sur, whatever that was. What's going on? Talk to me. I'm your brother."

Frank considered, pushed a breath hard through his nose and then opened the door, gesturing him inside.

The second Bill was inside Frank closed the door behind him and locked it. The house was dark, and there was a faint smell that Bill recognized as the sour stink of fear.

"What's happening?" asked Bill, almost wanting to reach for his weapon. Something was way off. Lela hated a dark house. "Where's Lela?"

"First of all, lower your voice. It will agitate them," said Frank quietly, leading him from the foyer to the shadowy living room and beyond to the kitchen where the drapes were shut against the night.

"What? Who?"

"Have a seat, Bill," said Frank, flicking on the kitchen light.

They both sat down at the kitchen table and Bill got a good look at his brother. He looked pale with dark circles under his eyes. Frank took out a pack of smokes and offered one to Bill, who declined with headshake

"So, let's have it…"

Frank took a deep drag and looked at his brother, sighed, and said, "Bill, you wouldn't believe me if I told you. You'll have to see it for yourself."

"See what?"

"Lela was bitten by a werewolf last summer. She changes with the Full Moon, and when she does, she can't control herself. It seems to be getting better, her self-control, but it's still very dangerous for her to be free during these times. I... she's in the basement."

Bill's face was impassive and neutral by long habit. He kept his voice low and even, but his mind was racing. Had Frank lost his mind? Was Lela locked in the basement because he was having paranoid delusions? His brother was a dangerous man, and more dangerous if he'd gone around the bend.

"Let's go down and see her," said Bill coolly. "You lead the way," he added, not wanting his brother behind him.

Frank nodded wearily.

"You should know there are two of them."

"Two?"

"Yeah, Aria was infected around the same time. She's staying with us since...since it all happened."

"I see," said Bill, still utterly neutral in his bearing but growing more concerned by the second.

Frank put the cigarette in his mouth and rose, gesturing for his brother to follow. He had no illusions about how crazy it all sounded, or about how his FBI-trained brother was being careful not to react to any of it. Frank would have done the same once. He led Bill to the doorway of the basement, opened it slowly, and an animal smell like the lion house at the San Francisco Zoo wafted up into the hall. Lela and Frank had liked this house in part because it had a basement in a state where basements are few. It reminded them of being back East. Now it was coming in useful, Frank mused darkly.

Bill nodded, "After you, Frank."

"Sure, Bill," said Frank, and walked down. Bill followed. When they reached the bottom of the stairs, two animal roars sounded as one so loudly that Bill had to clutch his palms to his ears.

There across from the two men were great steel lion cages with bent and chipped bars and inside were two huge wolf-women baring their fangs at him with animal hunger in their eyes. It was all Bill could do not to run screaming up the stairs, but he steadied himself and breathed for a moment, his eyes silver dollar wide.

They both began to scratch and rip at the weathered bars, growling and grunting loudly. Adrenaline surged through Bill's shaking hands and caught his breath. Frank nudged him back up the stairs.

"Let's go before they really get excited," he said.

They did, and Frank closed the door behind him, muffling, at least in part, the terrible noises coming from below.

"Obviously I couldn't put this in the police report," said Frank.

Bill looked at his brother, his stomach in free-fall, and said, "What are we going to do?"

"You're going to go back to San Francisco and forget this happened. I'm going to wait out the night and tend to them in the morning," said Frank.

"I can't just walk away. You're family. This change happens every month? Once a month or…?"

"This happens for three nights when the moon is fullest every month. They can change on other nights if they want to, but on these full moon nights, they *have to* change. On the full moon nights, they have less control than when they shift by choice. I don't know why," said Frank, leading him back to the kitchen and stabbing out the cigarette in an ashtray by the sideboard.

He took two rock glasses and a bottle of bourbon and poured a snort for each of them. Bill drank it like a shot and was grateful as it washed over his nerves.

"Are there, uh, experts about this kind of thing? People who can help?" asked Bill. "Someone must know about it."

"There was a big Norwegian, Nob, a shaman, I guess. He knew about this stuff, but he disappeared after he killed the werewolf that did this to Lela. He came as a bunch of crows at the end. I don't know why or how. There's magic in this, or something."

"A guy turned into a bunch of magic crows?" asked Bill.

"I know how it sounds. It happened, though."

"This is all a little much, Frank. Magic crows now?"

"Well, what do you want? You asked me to tell you what's happened. This is it."

"Where is this Nob guy now?" asked Bill.

"I don't know, man. I haven't seen or heard from him since that night, although every time I see a crow now, I wonder," said Frank.

"This is insane," said Bill, pulling loose his suddenly constrictive tie.

"That's a word for it," said Frank, pouring himself another shot.

"So, just live like this, then? That's the plan?"

"The ladies have been talking about trying to trace it back. Find a cure, maybe, at the source. I've been against it. Too risky to be out in their condition."

"Jesus," said Bill.

A ragged howling came up from below them, and in the silence afterward both men shivered.

"There's some church group that hunts them. Lorne Hutchins killed one of them. I think they'll want payback, and they'll kill both Lela and Aria if they find them. Been thinking about going off-grid. If you don't hear from me, that'll be what happened. Probably."

"A church group knows about this? What church?"

"He was a Roman Catholic priest. Father Giovanni Santa Ana. You can look him up. He was a hunter."

Bill scratched his chin, then stood.

"I'll find out what I can, and I'll be in touch. We can figure this out. You're not alone, Frank."

Frank smiled bitterly and said, "Sure, Bill. Sure."

"I'll head back to the office now and make some discreet checks. I'll call you in the morning."

Frank nodded, "Thanks, Bill."

There was an awkward moment where affection might normally have been exchanged. Bill punched his brother's shoulder and made for the door.

Frank sat in a circle of light, wreathed in cigarette smoke, and listened to the groaning of steel below him long into the night.

CHAPTER 1:

THE WOMEN AND THE ROAD

Near Dusk. Night of the Full Moon.
Friday, 09 June, 2017
Somewhere in the Arizona Desert

They rode out into the desert well before nightfall, these curious women. They had been a day on the road. One was small and perhaps twenty-three with dark hair and colorful tattoos of vampish ladies down her arms. There were tattoos of dove's wings across her shoulders that seemed to flap and flutter under the straps of her white tank-top as they drove the black Caddie fast with the top down. The other woman was in her late thirties, dark of hair and bright of eye, and she usually drove, just as she was driving tonight. Periodically, she eyed the gold ring on the third slender finger of her left hand, then looked ahead with a nearly imperceptible wag of her chin, tight and tense: Left.

Right. The younger woman saw it once from the corner of her eye, then again because she was looking for it.

"It's for the best," said the girl as the tined sagebrush and red rises and low green pines whipped by under a darkening sky. The evening was by now the color of cobalt being slowly suffused with ink. The heat of that summer day was still roiling up from the black asphalt in waves, and the air was thick with it.

"Mm," said the older woman softly. Irritation passed like a fast-moving cloud across her face and was gone.

"I'm sorry," said the girl.

"Wasn't you," said the woman.

"I know, but—"

"Let's just find someplace, okay?" said the woman with finality. They spoke no more.

They both knew instinctively when they could go no farther, and pulled off onto a rutted dirt trail without a word, raising the top of the Caddie, locking it, walking away into the night together without a flashlight between them, without a bag. The older woman, who was taller, wore a skirt with a magenta and gold arabesque pattern and a white cotton blouse. Her hair was in a white bandana of the sort often sold at roadside gas stations. The sun was setting behind them as they walked due east away from the car and up the rutted trail and the moon was rising in that same east. The fall of one celestial body would mean the rise of that pale other in a span of sixty seconds. They felt this in their bodies, as a moonflower knows to open to darkness—in their bellies and thighs and in the stirring of their restless calves and the tensing of their toes on the Earth, the women *felt* the coming of the moon. They found a tall saguaro cactus in a low and empty streambed and they began to strip, neatly folding their clothes, setting them together into one pile and placing an egg-sized stone on top. They stood in their nakedness and then crested the hill in their bare feet, unheeding of rock, stone, nettle, or scorpion. They watched, hand in hand, with hungry eyes as the first sliver of pale light crested the horizon. Then they began to change.

CHAPTER 2:

DETECTIVE NO MORE

Before Sunrise
Sunday, 11 June, 2017
The Big Sur Wilderness, California

Frank Crow woke alone in the cabin deep in the forest near China Camp and felt for Lela on the cold side of the small camp bed. She was, of course, gone. He could not quite work up the will to count the days, so he willed himself out of bed instead. The morning was chill, and the hard planks of the floor were frigid on his bare feet, but he stood, pulled on a sweater, jeans, socks, pistol, and boots, then began to minister to the banked fire in the pot-bellied stove.

When the fire was growling, he checked the peepholes on the four sides of the house, then shouldered the rifle he kept by the bed and slid the heavy-duty bolt back on the steel storm door of the cabin. The light of morning was beginning to send pink fingers of dawn over the horizon, and Frank scanned the tree line with the rifle, making a circuit as he checked for tracks in the dust around the cabin. Raccoons had been there in the night, but no men. No wolves. He watched the trees as the light filled them, then slipped back inside with barely a whisper of sound from the greased hinges of the storm door.

He made a quick meal of eggs and a rasher of bacon, black coffee, and a rather dry English muffin, sans butter. After a visit to the bathroom, he began his morning exercises: two hundred pushups, two hundred sit-ups, and then a three mile run (with pistol) through the forest path that made a rough oblong circle centered on the cabin.

The cabin itself was situated in a clearing about fifty yards from the tree line in every direction. It had one front door facing east, and good-sized windows (though he had boarded them up but for the peep holes) facing north and east. Frank panted heavily as he made his way back from his run, checking his watch. Seventeen minutes, forty-five seconds for three miles wasn't bad for a man pushing forty-five years old. A pace like that along the rough-cut trail through the forest was enough to push away thoughts of Lela, what had happened to them, and the terrible price he had paid for taking the case a year ago. That case had resulted in the deaths of Father Giovanni, the author Billy Hatfield, and many others, including the serial killer and origin of their misery,

Lorne Hutchins. Hutchins was the werewolf that had infected Billy and, as it happened, Frank's wife Lela.

He made a wide circle around the cabin, looking in the dust for sign even as he eyed the house and the trees front and rear, then made a slow circuit toward the cabin itself. He checked the thin hair he had left in the door-jamb, found it undisturbed and flailing in the light breeze of the morning. The sun had crested the trees by then. It made him feel safe, and yet he checked the feeling; he was not safe. Frank would not *be* safe. Ever.

He went inside, bolted the door, checked each room carefully and systematically, and then splashed water on his face from the basin he kept in the kitchen, changed his sopping wet shirt for a fresh one, and poured himself a second cup of coffee. Lela's face came to him, and he turned, physically turned, away from the memory of her. Instead, he went to the small table in the kitchen where he generally had his meals; it offered a three-sided view of the clearing outside the house. He plucked up the dog-eared paperback on the table and began to read, pencil in hand. It was, in some sense, this book that had caused much of the trouble. It was a piece of historical nonfiction entitled *The Hutchins Murders*, penned by Billy Hatfield, and it was this book, about Lorne Hutchins' first steps down the path of becoming a serial killer in the town of Hutchins, Nebraska, that had caught old Lorne's attention and invited his dark retribution. He had infected Billy with the werewolf virus and Billy, all unknowing, had killed four people his first Full Moon. That was a year ago. Both of them were dead, but Lela and Aria, Billy's unfortunate onetime-lover-made-werewolf, had fled the California coast in hopes of finding the origin of the disease and discovering a cure.

About midday, a man Frank did not want to kill came out of the woods, and he was put to a decision about shooting him and did not shoot. Instead, he put the rifle just beside the steel storm door, put on his faded peacoat to cover his holstered pistol, and stepped onto the porch.

"Morning, Ingalls," said Frank. Ingalls had been the sergeant in charge of Homicide at the Monterey County Sheriff's Office. Frank was sure he'd been promoted since; despite being in his late twenties, Ingalls had all the earmarks of a future office-holder.

"Frank," said Ingalls, stopping ten yards off the porch and at an angle from where Frank stood. Tactical. His tone was friendly, but his eyes were wary.

"Nice day for a walk," said Frank. "Guess you were in the neighborhood?"

"It's a five-mile walk from the road, Frank. You couldn't have found someplace more remote?"

"I could've," said Frank with a wry grin. "But five miles is far enough to walk with groceries under each arm."

"I guess it would be," said Ingalls with a chuckle. Neither man's smile touched his eyes.

"I'd invite you in, but I'm not going to invite you in," said Frank.

"Okay," said Ingalls. "But I came as a courtesy."

"Oh?"

"Yeah," said Ingalls. "Paperwork came through. You're officially retired. I thought you should know. You're not even provisionally associated with the Sheriff's Office anymore, Frank. I wouldn't want you to get into any trouble claiming to be something you aren't anymore."

"I see," said Frank. "Funny. I don't remember submitting a retirement packet."

"The Sheriff thought this was best."

"Why would that be?" asked Frank.

"You know why," said Ingalls. "Whatever happened last year down here, your reports were clearly not the whole of what happened. That becomes a problem when people are dead or missing."

Frank fought down what he wanted to say, then said, "Okay. Thanks for the heads up."

Ingalls sighed, "Look, you're a good man. A good cop. I'm sorry this went down as it did. I'm sure you have reasons for why you've played things this way."

Frank scratched a grizzled gray chin and said, "Ingalls, why are you really here?"

"I told you."

"Bullshit. Why are you *really* here?"

"You were a person of interest in the investigation. You've been cleared. Having said that, if you want to help explain what happened to Nob Haraldson or Father Giovanni, it would help us close a file."

"My report stands," said Frank. The Sheriff's Office was, as far as Frank could see, just awfully unlikely to accept lycanthropy and ancient Norse magics as a viable explanation for very much at all.

"Fine," said Ingalls. "I'll take your badge."

Frank considered throwing it, set his jaw and drew it from his pocket, marched off the porch and put it in Ingalls' hand.

"Don't come back here, Ingalls."

"Whatever you want, Frank."

Frank watched him disappear back into the trees, then stood for a long time under the clear morning sky. He was not a cop. He was not a husband. He was a man who knew something the world would not accept, living at the fringes. Frank spat, cursing his self-pity into retreat, and began to consider relocating to someplace more defensible. When *they* came, and Ingalls' visit was surely a sign they were coming. He would be ready.

CHAPTER 3:

THE SAFE HOUSE

Evening
Sunday, 11 June, 2017
Carmel-by-the-Sea, California

It should never have happened, thought John Marion, the Archbishop of the Carmel Diocese, as he drove through the dark streets and heavy fog toward the safe house. The loss of a member of the *Gladius Dei*, the Roman Catholic Church's last Holy Order dedicated to directly combating the forces of the Enemy with flame, sword, silver bullet, and Holy Cross, was a loss to the Church itself. What made it worse was that it had been one of the finest of the Order's Crusaders: those few warriors for God who directly engaged the Unclean. Father Giovanni's mysterious murder while he was hunting the werewolf that bedeviled Big Sur last year had been bad enough, but the *Gladius Dei* took it more than somewhat personally and they didn't just send a Justice to investigate. Instead, they had purchased the Flanders Mansion from the city of Carmel-by-the-Sea, established it as a safe house, and moved an entire investigative team in to learn the truth of what had happened those twenty or so miles south, in the dark woods of Big Sur.

Archbishop Marion pulled into the long driveway and parked before the Flanders Mansion's red door. It was a relatively large house for the little town, with its seven bedrooms, five baths, kitchen, dining room, basement, and a great room. It had been built in 1927 in the Tudor Revival English cottage style, and was sur-rounded by 33 acres of woodland. And now, the Arch-bishop mused, it was host to one of the most secret and sophisticated Orders in the world. Archbishop Marion knocked at the door and waited. When the door opened, there stood a tall, slender and clean-shaven man with a thinning head of salt-and-pepper hair, almost totally bald on top. He wore a gray lambswool sweater and twill charcoal slacks, and his brown eyes were large for the rest of his face.

"Good evening, Joseph," said the Archbishop.

"Good evening, your Excellency. Please come in," said Joseph in an American accent subtly salted with Italian.

They stepped through a foyer and into the great room. There was a good fire going in the old fireplace, and a very fit man in his early thirties sat in a leather armchair dressed in a faded red Stanford University sweatshirt, navy blue jeans and well broken-in hiking books. He stood when the Archbishop entered.

"Archbishop Marion, thank you for coming." His voice was deep and rich, but with that trace of California ease.

"Hello Gregory," said the Archbishop, "I got your message and came straight away, although I'm not entirely sure why it could not wait."

"It's a formality, I'm afraid, but a time-sensitive one. Please, have a seat. Would you care for a cup of coffee? Tea?"

"Tea would be lovely," said the Archbishop, sitting across from Gregory.

Gregory nodded to Joseph, who slipped away without a sound.

"We have reason to believe that part of the reason Father Giovanni was lost was due to the interference of a witch named Nob. This witch disappeared around the time of Father Giovanni's murder, and he owned a store dedicated to the occult, particularly occult lore. The collection of this shop is probably worth two million or more. It is about to go up for auction as it is unclaimed. The Order believes this witch was involved, and my Inquisitors would like a chance to parse this collection for clues as to what this witch was up to and where he might be now. One does not abandon such a thing lightly. If he is dead, well and good. If not, we want to ask him some questions," said Gregory.

"Yes, all right. I assume you want the Diocese to bid on this collection of blasphemies and heresies because the Order does not want its fingerprints on the check?" asked the Archbishop.

"Something like that, yes. In exchange, I am authorized to make a donation of double whatever the collection ends up costing the Diocese. Anonymously, of course," said Gregory.

"And then?"

"And then we will take possession. There is a cool, dry basement here of sufficient size. Our people will begin with a thorough inventory."

"I understand your Order has one of the finest occult libraries in the world, Gregory. Is this necessary?"

"It is necessary to help us find the witch called Nob, wherever he might be. We thought he might have returned to Norway, but we could find no record of his leaving the country, and he did not pass through customs there. He has not been seen in his town. We know he is a traveler, but he hasn't shown up on anyone's radar, and we have ears and eyes almost everywhere. This witch, I am convinced, knows something about Father Giovanni's death and may in fact have been abetting the werewolf or werewolves that were loosed on Big Sur last year. He has much to answer for."

Joseph returned quietly and set the Archbishop's tea on a small round table beside the dark red leather armchair.

"Very well," said Archbishop Marion, taking the tea with a nod of thanks to Joseph. "We can bid on it if you feel it's important, but I have misgivings about using the Mother Church's funds for heresies and blasphemies that may end up being of no use at all in finding the truth."

"It's an imperfect world, Your Excellency," said Joseph. "All we can do is to follow God, and pray for His Divine Guidance as we hunt His enemies."

"Amen," said Gregory.

"His enemies lay many false trails. This business has been costly in the extreme. This mansion and its furnishings are no mean purchases."

"And the Order has deep pockets," said Gregory. "This is why we exist, after all. We hunt monsters. It costs what it costs, in silver and in blood."

"May you find what you are looking for, then, Gregory."

"Amen, Your Excellency. And God help us all."

CHAPTER 4:

THE CROWS IN THE SKY

Indeterminate Time
The Sky-Cave
The Spirit World

In the darkness, there were feathers. Nob felt them rushing by his face, and then for the first time in a long time, he became aware he wore a face. A man's face. The face that had been his before the bargain with Crow. His shape had been that of the crows for what felt like a lifetime of lifetimes. His eyes had been a thousand dark eyes, his mouth a thousand sharp bills, his flesh the ropy gristle of dark, hungry carrion birds. He crouched in a frigid and immense cave, and above him the sound of winds howled angry and malevolent. He felt his way along the walls, shivering, and found himself in half-light, then as he moved toward an opening in the cold gray stone, he came to a steep cliff that looked down on a thick carpet of roiling clouds far below. The wind bit at his skin and tore at his beard, beckoning him into the Blue.

Nob turned his back on the sky and groped his way back into the darkness of the cave. The passage opened out on the left, and Nob followed it carefully, cautiously, mindful that the floor might drop out from beneath his man's legs with each half step. The wind was deafening; mournful, and voracious above him in the cracks and mouths of the great cave above the world. By and by, he entered a chamber half-lit from a hole in the great ceiling hundreds of yards above.

A Gothi of the northmen in my Hall, said a sharp, rasping voice, *a Gothi with a Crow's shape*. A black silhouette emerged from the darkness. It belonged to a tall, gaunt man with sallow cheeks wearing a cloak of long black feathers pierced him with eyes as black as oil on a midnight sea.

"This is the Spirit World," said Nob. "And here I seem to be a man again."

This is my Hall. Here many things are not as they seem.

"I am here because you called me here, in this shape because you wish it."

Yes.

"Why? I expect nothing more. A deal's a deal."

You wanted to kill a Child of Fenris and so you have, yes, but I am not finished with you yet, Nob Haraldson.

"What would you have of me, Father Crow?"

I have eaten many a dead man's eye. I know rot on the wind when I smell it. Fenris is not finished trying to eat the world, and his children are not as few as they were.

Crow-that-was-a-man gestured. The cave began to grow lighter as fires blazed in great braziers.

That Old Wolf is not as old-fashioned as some of the Old Gods. He has a new plan. I'm sending you back to thwart him.

"What plan?" asked Nob.

Crow-that-was-a-man raised a black-clawed finger toward the fires as they began to dance. *Look. And be afraid.*

Nob looked. Nob saw. And Nob screamed. He screamed for a long time in that dark place above the world.

CHAPTER 5:

A LADY LOSES HER TEMPER

Evening
Monday, 12 June, 2017
Mike's Roadhouse, Las Cruces, Arizona

"We really shouldn't be here," said Lela as they sat in the gravel parking lot.

"I want a drink," Aria said with an edge in her voice that warned she was tired of having the conversation.

"You know we shouldn't be near crowds. We should stay away from people as much as we can."

Aria looked at Lela sharply. "Who can live like that?"

"We've been over this. We don't know who is looking for us. We don't know if the Church has hunters on our trail. We don't know how easy it is to transmit the disease. We need to know more before we start taking risks for no reason."

"Not no reason," said Aria. "I. Want. A. Drink. And, you know, like, I can't just live my life with you as the only person to talk to forever."

"Yes, but—"

"No," said Aria as she stepped out of the car. She slammed the door and stomped away, her feet crunching over the gravel toward the doorway of Mike's Roadhouse. The parking lot was better than half full of pickups, old sedans, and a handful of newer cars, including one candy-apple red Camaro.

Lela sighed as she watched Aria go, then checked herself in the rearview mirror. She fixed her sunglasses, pulled down her hat, and stepped out of the car.

Aria pushed open the door and was met by a blast of *Lynyrd Skynyrd*. Inside, an even mix of working men drinking off their shifts, troublemakers looking for trouble, good old boys out for a good old time, and bored girls looking for the kind of excitement only cut-and-shoot bars can offer them. All were spread between tables, booths, the dance floor and the bar.

Aria, who had broken their rule about wearing a hat and sunglasses (a measure against facial recognition technology), had also decided to stay in her thin tank-top, but had neglected to put on her bra when they stopped. This meant, of course, that her tattoos were on display; another rule to prevent identification that she now had broken. It felt good. It felt powerful to break Lela's rules, to live on her own terms, if only for a little while.

She felt eyes move over her with interest and envy as she slipped lightly onto a stool at the bar. Aria was lithe, graceful, clean-limbed and long-legged. Time spent bartending and away at college had taught her the effect she had on men (and, occasionally, women) but sometimes she got the sense, since she was *changed*, that her sex appeal was stronger when she wanted it to be.

This sexual power was probably the reason Billy Hatfield, that poor, dead, sweet writer, had managed to get her into bed in the first place, which was, she mused, how she came to be this thing, this hungry, angry wolf in a woman's skin, this *shapeshifter*. Aria shook off the memory of Billy's touch with a shiver and ordered a whiskey sour. The bartender was a tall man with gray eyes and an easy smile. Late twenties to early thirties, blonde, fit, with a dark t-shirt stretched over his well-muscled arms and chest.

"Got some ID?" he asked genially.

"Sure," said Aria, producing the fake ID they had purchased in California before the trip.

He glanced at it, gave her the drink, and asked, "Do you want to start a tab and stay awhile?" She smiled at him and laid down enough cash to pay for the drink and a generous tip.

"We'll just see how it goes," she said, her eyes a dark undercurrent of thirst. She realized she wanted him, or wanted to hurt him. Or maybe both. He lingered for a moment as if he wanted to say more, or just wanted to swim in her eyes and smell the heat rolling off of her skin in waves. Someone called him down at the far end of the bar, and he moved on down the line with a nod to her.

Lela sat down beside her and said, "You should put on more clothes. People are gawking."

Aria stifled the growl in her throat, set her jaw, and downed her drink in one go, then stood.

"I'm going to dance," she said.

"Aria, please. This is dangerous," said Lela in a rushed whisper.

"Good," said Aria with a dark smile.

Lela put a hand on her arm, "You're not yourself. This is... This is something else. You have to get some control and not let it ride you."

Aria shrugged off Lela's touch and said, in the older woman's ear, "I'm fine. Really. I just want a drink and a dance. After that we can go, okay?"

Lela tried to say something else about the cameras over the bar and the entrance, about being recognized, about the hunters looking for them, but Aria was already moving, swinging her hips to the beat as she advanced on the dance floor hungrily.

Lela felt the anger rising, the aggression. Visions of ripping, rending, growling, flaying bloody strips from flesh slid red and hot over her eyes. She shook her head, feeling her temperature rise. It was tempting to take off her bulky sweatshirt, join Aria on the dance floor, or to leap for the nearest throat and start biting, but she fought it down for a long moment, finding a silence and still-ness inside, even as the music blared over her.

Not for the first time, Lela reminded herself that the Change is dangerous, Full Moon or no. She could sum-mon the Wolf here, now, and start killing until she wore only blood. And so could Aria. She needed to keep the younger woman calm, keep her from snaring someone and infecting him by taking him to bed, and get them both out of here without losing her temper.

Lela ordered a glass of water from the handsome bartender and drank it down, then ordered another, letting the cool sweat of the glass soothe the rising heat in her hands. The *Skynyrd* ended and a slow, sad honky-tonk song came on the old-fashioned jukebox. Lela stood sharply, as if she'd been kicked. On the dance floor she saw three men, a big-shouldered flannel-and-denim sporting trucker, a young, dark-haired townie in a Letterman jacket, and a black biker in a Mongols motorcycle cut, asking Aria for a dance and eyeing each other without a hint of good-humor.

Aria looked around at the three of them, half surprised, half bemused. The Mongol was saying something to the trucker. The Letterman kid was answering back. Lela made her way over in time to hear Aria say she'd be around long enough to dance with everyone and take the biker's hand.

"No, we should go. You said one dance," said Lela, trying to keep her tone low, but to be heard over the music.

"Are you her Mama?" asked the trucker.

Lela levelled the full force of her gaze at him and said, "Back. Off."

He did, moving away from her with hands upraised. "Sure," he said. "Sorry, lady."

The young Letterman kid started to laugh, until Lela looked at him, "You too."

The kid, who she realized was probably here drinking on a fake ID, retreated from Lela like a frightened pup.

When Lela turned to talk to Aria, she found her attached at the lips to the biker, barely dancing but grinding slightly.

"We need to go," she said to Aria, a little more loudly than she meant to. This situation was getting away from her and they needed out now, before they infected a man of violence. Lela seemed to remember reading that the Mongols were one of the most dangerous and notorious criminal biker gangs in the country, the big rivals and sworn enemies of the Hells Angels.

Aria didn't break the kiss, but raised a middle finger in Lela's direction.

Lela hissed in irritation, then advanced, even as she felt the eyes, many eyes, watching them. "Do you want to do to him what Billy did to you?" Lela said.

Aria broke the kiss then, her face pink.

"No. No," she said. "Of course not."

"Then we need to leave."

"Is this bitch your girlfriend, baby? She can join us," said the Mongol.

Lela snapped her teeth together and grabbed him by the throat, lifting him an inch off the ground. She felt rather than saw the bouncers dislodging from their perches on either end of the bar and heard the crowd's gasp. She felt herself squeezing his windpipe and imagined it as dry kindling she could snap between her fingertips, but Aria put a hand on Lela's shoulder.

"Okay," she said. "You're right. Let's go. I'm sorry. Let's go."

She dropped the man, who fell in a heap on the floor, gasping, choking, and clutching his neck. How long had he been without air? Not more than a few seconds, surely. Lela was not certain.

A thickset bouncer approached saying, "Ma'am, we're going to need you to l—"

"We're leaving," said Lela, and she and Aria slid briskly out of the bar and into the desert evening.

As Aria slammed the car into gear and peeled out of the parking lot, she saw a crowd drifting out of the bar to watch them go.

"You were saying about a low profile?" said Aria, watching the rear view mirror nervously.

"They had cameras in that place," said Lela. "I don't know if they caught it on camera. God dammit."

"You looked like you meant to kill him," said Aria.

"And if you had infected him, we might have had to. An outlaw like that with this much power? What's wrong with you?"

"I . . . Okay, I'm sorry. I don't know what I was thinking," said Aria. "No more bars."

"Damn right no more bars, Aria, for Christ's sake. Now we need to change vehicles, or at the very least change plates."

"I'll do it this time," said Aria. "I'm sorry, Lela."

Lela took a deep breath and took off her hat, smoothed her hair and face, then said, "We need to get off this road and find a place to switch cars."

"Okay," said Aria. "Okay. I'm sorry."

"Me, too," said Lela, pulling a map from the center console. "We need to be a lot more careful, or we'll be a lot more dead."

CHAPTER 6:

OUR SORT OF PEOPLE

Morning
Tuesday, 13 June, 2017
The Arbor Room Seasons, Washington D.C.

When they all sat down with Senator Freedman, the Senator ordered coffee and the apple butter oatmeal, explaining that his wife had him on a strict diet after his heart attack last year, but that on no account should they, as newcomers, miss the Eggs Benedict here at *Seasons*. The Arbor Room was private and had its own entrance for the sake of discretion, which was always in short supply among the power brokers of the Capitol. The matters they were to discuss required nothing less, and even so, the Senator assured them he had the room swept for listening devices. Each man had switched off his phone and put it in a Faraday Bag in an outside closet.

After the wait staff had come and gone and each man's order was steaming before him, the stately, silver-haired Senator Freedman began.

"The people in this room ought to know each other, and I'm glad I could help it happen." He gestured to his right, at the graying man in a priest's collar and cassock. "This is Cardinal Donovan Frye, attached to the Archdiocese here in Washington."

"Cardinal Frye," here Senator Freedman gestured to his left toward the bony, sharp-angled man with high cheekbones and green jade ice chips for eyes in a blue Brooks Brothers suit and yellow power tie.

"This is Armand Weynman, formerly of Blackwater and now heading up a Biotech outfit called ProGen Global."

Weynman and Cardinal Frye shook hands, and Weynman gestured toward the fourth man at the table.

"And this, I'm sure you gentlemen know, is Dr. Robert Lannon, our Senior Researcher and probably the most preeminent geneticist on the planet." Lannon was lanky and slightly disheveled in an off-white button down shirt, wrinkled slacks and off-the-rack gray herringbone sports coat. He wore round spectacles that seemed to fall perpetually around his nose. His eyes were blue and vastly intelligent.

They stood and shook hands among themselves, exchanged pleasantries, and sat.

"Gentlemen," said Senator Freedman, "I am so glad we could come together this morning to put in motion a project that very well may revolutionize modern warfare, medicine, and bioengineering." He looked at Cardinal Frye, "Cardinal Frye, why don't you start us off?"

The elder man bowed his head in acknowledgement of the Senator and said in a quiet voice, "I have a cadaver, a specimen in deep freeze that represents an organism known in folklore, and to members of my Order, but until this morning unknown to science. He may be of interest to you gentlemen. In life, he went by the name of Billy Hatfield."

"What kind of organism?" asked Weynman.

"A lycanthrope," said the Cardinal. Weynman and Dr. Lannon exchanged a look.

"A werewolf?" asked Weynman, cocking an eyebrow. He turned from the Cardinal to the Senator, "Senator, I assume you didn't call this meeting to waste our time."

"Mr. Weynman. Armand, I was just as skeptical as you are, but the Cardinal has provided incontrovertible evidence of what he is claiming," said Senator Freedman.

"Are we talking about a creature that looks human and then physically changes into a wolf?" asked Dr. Lannon.

"Yes," said Cardinal Frye. "But let me explain more fully. My Order has existed since roughly the eleventh century, but gained official recognition by the Mother Church from the Holy See in the twelfth century. Since those days, we have hunted monsters in a holy crusade to protect the world from the forces of evil. Among the things we have fought are what you might call werewolves. They are rare in these times, but they *do* exist, and we kill them where we find them because their disease is communicable through sexual contact, bodily fluids, injury by their teeth or claws, and so on. I realize this seems incredible, but consider for a moment that tales of these beings, or beings of a similar sort, exist in almost every culture. They remain unknown to science primarily because *we* cover up the truth in an effort to protect the world. And we are, not to be immodest, a very efficient group."

Weynman broke in, "Let's say all that's true. Okay. So, werewolves exist. And we don't know it because there are not many of them around and when they draw attention you sanitize the area and spin the story. It's far-fetched, but okay. For the sake of argument and the purposes of this conversation, I'll momentarily buy it. At any rate, I'll continue to assume a man as serious and busy as Senator Freedman here didn't put me in a room with you for fun and games or because he really likes the oatmeal here. Fine. You want to offer us a specimen? You're a senior member of this secret Catholic Order that's covered things up for nine hundred years. Why would you give us a body instead of throwing it down the furnace or whatever your SOP is?"

The Cardinal nodded and smiled with untrammeled politeness, adjusted his sleeve for a moment, then answered.

"I'll be honest, Mr. Weynman, and I will try to be as direct as you have been. My Order once recruited from European knights and sellswords, and the rougher breeds of the rustic priesthood the world over. In these times, the Church has made many compromises. I will not speak ill of Mother Church, but I have been a more than somewhat vocal opponent of many of the newer policies. In particular, I have been strongly against the unofficial code of silence around sexual crime in the priesthood. And by that, I mean I have classified certain predatory priests who came to my attention as monsters and had them *handled* as we handle such beasts. This has made me politically unpopular in the College of Cardinals and elsewhere in the political labyrinth that is the Vatican. It has hurt funding, and it has hurt recruitment.

"We are a small Order with a long reach, but the loss of hunters in our dangerous work means we must always be training replacements. New soldiers to take up the Cause. Many doors once opened to the *Gladius Dei* are now closed.

"In the interest of fighting our Holy Crusade, new ideas must be considered regarding our vows of secrecy. I will lay aside tradition in this instance. In making this deal, I have requests."

Doctor Lannon and Mr. Weynman looked at each other, then at Senator Freedman who nodded his encouragement to them. This was real.

"Requests? For instance?" asked Weynman.

"For instance, I would like the government's cooperation in helping me recruit soldiers. I'm thinking of men in the military prisons who may be open to Catholic conversion and capable of surviving our training and living up to our vows. People whose identities could be erased and rewritten. I would like cooperation in learning more about our enemies on a scientific, biological level in ways that might help us fight them; new weapons could be developed. Something that might cure lycanthropy altogether would be a godsend, so to speak. We simply don't have the scientific resources that the U.S. government or a contracting agency like yours do, Mr. Weynman."

"Does your boss know about this deal you're trying to make?"

"You mean the High Marshall of the *Gladius Dei*, or the Pope?"

"Either. Both," said Weynman.

"No," said Cardinal Frye.

"You're going rogue."

Cardinal Frye's face darkened, and he very slowly and clearly said, "I believe during the last conference, one of my fellow Cardinals called me 'a stubborn goat of an Irishman, hell-bent on having his way at any cost.' No one in the room troubled to disagree. I would put it differently; I will bleed to keep my Order alive. To keep my people from the tender mercies of their enemies, I would do much."

Weynman considered this for a moment. Doctor Lannon chimed in.

"We have a lab in Oregon. Site Bravo. It's remote. I do the bulk of my genetic research there. It can be set up to take delivery of your specimen very quickly," said Dr. Lannon.

"Senator, you've agreed to cooperate with their recruiting goals?" asked Weynman.

"Armand, I will do everything I can to help support the Cardinal and his ambitions for the *Gladius Dei.* What's more, as you know I'm on several committees concerned with veterans, military spending, weapons development, and applied sciences in government. I can be a powerful friend to ProGen Global when some of what you develop comes to market in exchange for your help in this matter."

"What's in it for you?" asked Weynman.

Senator Freedman flashed his movie star smile.

"What I'm always after in the morning mirror, Armand: a clean conscience."

Weynman snorted, but said nothing.

"Can your hunters get us a live specimen?" asked Dr. Lannon, shifting in his seat.

The Cardinal considered for a moment, then said, "We are hunting two women now that were infected during the Hatfield incident. Another man is a person of interest; his wife is one of the infected, but we are not certain yet if he contracted the disease. He was a Marine, served in Desert Storm in the early 90s and then became a detective for Monterey County Sheriff's Office in California. The three of them have disappeared. If I find them, you can have them . . . with the understanding that our people will be attached during transportation and at your laboratory until these three specimens are put down, which my people will do."

"Agreed," said Weynman.

"Agreed," said Dr. Lannon.

The Senator stood and raised his orange juice. "Gentlemen, I do so *love* bringing good people together."

CHAPTER 7:
ON MEMORY AND THE FOREST

Morning
Thursday, 15 June, 2017
Big Sur, California

After Frank had returned to Lela covered in blood (some of it his own) on the night she was infected, the night Lorne Hutchins had killed Father Giovanni and Nob's crows had killed Lorne Hutchins, Lela had looked at Frank with something he had never seen before in her eyes: disdain. For having left her bleeding there on the floor of *Good Eats*, maybe, but also for having gone off to fight and die and leave her to deal with the aftermath of losing him. From that moment on, things between them were not the same.

He mused on this as he packed up his few belongings. The cabin he had occupied was old, abandoned, quasi-legal, but serviceable enough after he had fixed it up here and there. He knew of other

places. First, though, he wanted to see if Lela had written to him. That meant town. He swept through the cabin again, making sure he had left nothing of himself behind. When he was sure, he shouldered his rucksack and moved off into the trees.

Of course, that first Full Moon after Lela and Aria were infected had been bad. On mutual agreement, he had strapped them down in the basement of the house, which he had converted into a holding cell. He had fitted out two old lion cages for the purpose, shored them up where he could, reinforced the steel, and sunk heavy pylons into the concrete floor down to the foundation to keep them in place. He had fixed both of them with straitjackets and manacles as they scowled sullenly. Lela would not look at him through this process. The moon's approach seemed to make them both desperately irritable and distracted. That night, the noises had been terrible, and in the morning, he learned how close he had come to death as he listened to them growling and snarling and howling from upstairs; the jackets were shredded, the manacles bent nearly out of shape and almost snapped. The doors to their cages had been bowed in enough to compromise the bars. It had been a miracle they hadn't broken loose, and if they had they would probably have come upstairs and eaten him in that mindless, animal state.

It had scared Lela more than it had Frank. The thought of what might have happened drove her even farther away from him. The curse was not going to be managed like some illness or domestic problem they could negotiate with. Lela and Aria were growing closer. Frank noticed their whispered conversations, increasingly, would drop into cold silence when he entered the room. And so they had lived for nearly a year; two werewolf women and a man trying to keep them (and himself) alive, and to prevent further infection.

Frank made good time from the cabin to Chew's Ridge lookout, where the trail met Tassajara Rd. His truck was hidden in the brush down the trail there, and he hopped inside to drive to the Post Office in Carmel where he maintained a P.O. Box. He hoped Lela had sent him a postcard or a line, or anything...anything, really would have made him feel like he still had a wife, like maybe she could come back. Maybe it could, someday, be like it was.

Even as he drove, he knew it was a risk to drive in his vehicle; it was a risk to go to a place where he could be spotted, followed, or picked up. *Someone* knew that he knew about werewolves rather intimately. Would the same people that sent Father Giovanni abide him? Or take him to get to Lela and Aria? Or use him as bait? It stood to reason.

Nevertheless, he pointed the old truck back toward civilization. For foolish love and mad hope he did this, more than for any other reason. He would come to regret it.

It was an hour to town over the winding roads, but eventually he found his way to the mouth of Carmel

Valley in what locals called The Barnyard; a little complex of shops and restaurants, businesses and (it so happened) a Post Office. He parked, and sat in the truck for a long time watching the parking lot for people watching the parking lot. After a half hour, when he was satisfied that nobody was staking the place out, he ran a comb through his hair ("You need a haircut," he heard Lela say in his memory) and walked into the Post Office and over to his box. He turned the key and found two things waiting there for him. One was a letter with no return address in a white envelope. The other was a postcard from Prescott, Arizona. "Miss you," it said. And that was all.

He closed the box and shoved both items into his pocket, watching carefully for anyone watching him. There was no one in the place. It was quiet.

When he was back in the truck, Frank drove a mile or so down Carmel Valley Road with his eyes in the rearview mirror. Then he took a few random turns into the valley, and parked under a tree where he couldn't easily be seen from the road but where he could hear anyone approach long before they saw him. He turned off the truck and sat in the silence for a long time. He drew out the letter (and, grudgingly, his reading glasses), and opened the envelope. Inside was a letter written in a familiar hand and a train ticket out of Salinas up to San Francisco. Frank set the ticket aside and began to read:

Dear Frank,

Your name came across my desk at work as a person of interest. I am concerned. I will meet you in San Francisco at the Fairmont no later than 17 June. Take the train as they're watching for you on the road. Come alone. Tell no one. <u>Do not be followed.</u>

Your Brother,
Bill
P.S. Get a burner and call (703) 275-0383, and none of your shit about refusing to use cell phones.

Why would the FBI get a request for information about Frank? Surely the *Gladius Dei* didn't have its fingers that deep into the U.S. government. Did it? Frank tugged at the beginnings of his beard in thought, then jerked his head up. He whipped his glasses off as an SUV rounded the corner. He reached down for the pistol in the center console, but when the SUV passed it was a young mother yelling at a couple of squalling kids in the backseat.

He heard Lela in his head: "Getting a little jumpy, tiger?"

"More than somewhat," he answered. He pulled out the unsigned postcard written in Lela's handwriting and sighed. "Miss you," it said.

"I miss you, too, baby," he said aloud, then started up his truck.

CHAPTER 8:
A FAILURE TO COMMUNICATE

After moonrise
Thursday, 15 June, 2017
Highway 40, Arizona, near the New Mexico border.

The red lights flashed behind them as they flew down the desert highway that evening. Aria swore with feeling, then began to slow down and pulled off to the side of the road.

"Just relax," said Lela quietly, opening the glove box for the fake registration and insurance, which, she realized, didn't match the plates they'd boosted after the roadhouse incident.

A stocky Arizona State trooper with dark hair and eyes walked up to the driver's side window and tapped on the window with his Maglite.

Aria rolled down the window and said, "Nice night, isn't it?"

"Ma'am, I stopped you for your speed," he said. Lela had spent enough time around cops, being married to one and all, to see this one was a Tackleberry type. There wouldn't be any warning, and if there were something wrong with the registration and the plates, he wouldn't chalk it up to an honest mistake; he'd push it as far as he could.

"What was my speed?" asked Aria.

"I clocked you at 90 in a 75."

"That doesn't sound right. When did you last calibrate your radar gun?" asked Lela.

"As soon as I came on shift, ma'am," he said, eyeing Lela with irritation. "License, registration, and insurance, please."

"Sure," said Aria, handing them over.

"Any reason you were speeding?" he asked.

"I'm not sure I was speeding, officer," said Aria.

"You were speeding, ma'am. I'll be right back." He backed off from the car as the darkness descended around them.

"Ideas?" asked Aria.

"Well, just cooperate. Take the ticket. What we can't do is get arrested. We *cannot* be in jail come Full Moon," said Lela, her voice fast and anxious.

"Right," Aria said. They waited in nervous silence.

A second police vehicle and then another arrived behind them in short order, although it was tough to make out exactly where they were with the lights of the State trooper's cruiser blinding them. When the trooper came back, he came with two others who approached the car from either side.

"Ma'am, can I have you step out of the car?" he said to Aria.

"Sure," she said, slowly unbuckling and opening the car door. "Can I ask what this is about?"

"Sure. I'll explain all this to you in just a moment but first I need you to put your hands on the vehicle. I'm going to pat you down for your safety and mine. Do you understand? If you prefer, I can have a female officer do it."

"I'm sure there's no reason for this," Aria said.

"Ma'am, please put your hands on the vehicle and spread your legs."

She set her jaw, but turned and put her palms on the vehicle, spreading her legs.

"Go ahead then."

He patted her down, then took her right arm and pulled it behind her back. The instant Aria felt the cuffs, she spun, spun faster than he could track even if he'd been tensed up and ready for a fight, and she slammed her fist into his jaw so hard she heard his teeth crack and his eyes rolled back in his head. She was across the road by the time he'd hit the pavement, over a shallow ditch and down a wash before one of the troopers could even start yelling commands.

Things happened fast; one of the troopers drew a horrified Lela out of the car and handcuffed her on the ground. Another checked his fallen friend and began to advise dispatch of the situation. They picked Lela up and put her in the back of a Cruiser, then one of them ran off into the desert after Aria. Lela watched all this with mounting panic. She began to pull against the cuffs as quietly as she could.

It was dark, and the desert was treacherous with snake holes and cacti that rose up out of the

dark so fast they were hard to avoid, but Aria had advantages. She had slipped her skin and ran as a wolf; the darkness was no darkness to her, and she could easily outrun a clumsy two-legged pursuer. It wasn't yet Full Moon, but she had learned the trick of shifting at will, although it was easier at night and under moments of stress or strong emotion, and much easier the larger and brighter the Moon was in the sky.

She was easily a half-mile ahead of him when she crested a low rise. She could see his flashlight bobbing frantically up and down as he ran after her. She watched as he stopped and looked for sign of her passage, left, right, back, forth, then started down another trail.

Aria had lost him. Aria wanted to go back for Lela, wanted *blood*. No. She shook off the wolf voice. She did not want to kill these men for doing their jobs.

Blood and bone and meat and fat under her jaws.

She shook her head again, trying to clear it, even as she began circling back down toward the bobbing flashlight in the dark.

Lela sat in the police cruiser thinking it through, worrying her cuffs and trying to slip out of them. The dark-haired cop that Aria had punched was still unconscious. The other trooper, a sandy-haired man of about forty, had dragged him out of the road, leaned him against a cruiser and knelt beside him. She could shift, snap this car open like a plastic toy, and eat these men one by one. She could make a night of it. Hunting them in the desert. She'd even let them keep their guns. But no. They all had body cameras. Dash cameras. Radios. Backup coming. Even if she and Aria escaped, at this point they'd be wanted by the law, and the church hunters would undoubtedly get wind of them and come looking. She had to get out of this as an ordinary woman. That was going to be harder now that Aria had broken a man's jaw. She glanced anxiously out the cruiser window and hoped that the man in the desert would give up and come back before Aria decided to shift, double back on him and...

A scream rose from the dark. Somewhere in the distance a flashlight fell to the ground and sent a still shaft of light across the sand. The sandy-haired trooper stood, drawing his pistol. The screams got more high-pitched, then suddenly stopped.

"Meyers? Meyers?!" the trooper called. He ran to his cruiser, threw open the door and took out the carbine rifle from its stand in the center. The trooper racked a round and started talking into his radio. Lela was impressed with the calm of his voice, although the color had drained from his face.

A howl of triumph rose into the night, and the trooper went rigid.

"What the hell is that?" he asked under his breath, then glanced at his unconscious friend, then at Lela in the back of the Cruiser.

"Let me go," she said quietly, with curious calm. "And it won't hurt you."

"What? What are you talking about? Is that some kind of coyote? What's going on? I can't just —"

She levelled her gaze at him and said, "Sir. If you let me go, she won't come back and kill you. Let me go now."

There was a noise across the road, a soft scrape of claws on the hardpan of the wash beyond. The trooper looked at Lela.

"Please," she said.

He levelled his rifle at the darkness across the road and flicked on the flashlight on the underside of the barrel. Two eyes like flames stared back at him, and slowly the eight-foot she-wolf rose inch by inch out of the ditch with blood dripping from her fangs and claws.

He tensed to fire and then the Cruiser exploded under him, and a second she-wolf roared out of the police car, shattering the glass, bowing the steel, and landing, bloody and snarling on top of him.

In the distance there were sirens.

Lela's jaws closed around his throat and ripped it open, swallowing the bloody meat in one gulp. Shots rang out and she felt two sharp stings across her back. She turned to see that the dark-haired cop had awakened, stood, fired, and would have fired again. But Aria had risen before him like a nightmare and swept the weapon aside with one swipe of her paw.

Urine ran down his leg, and he tried to move backward, but she caught him in her arms and clamped down, threw down his body under hers and bit into his skull, which caved in like an overripe cantaloupe.

The sirens were closer now.

Lela moved fast to rip open the gas tanks of all three cruisers and hurled both men into the backseat of one of them. She then shifted, melting from beast to naked woman, covered in gore.

Lights cascading crazily from the ridge a mile away and the sound of supercharged engines roaring toward them now accompanied the sirens.

Lela stood stiffly and picked up the rifle the sandy-haired trooper had dropped. Aria, still in wolf form, sped off into the desert when she realized what Lela was about to do. Lela ran toward the wash, steadied herself, and fired the rifle in a burst of staccato gunshots.

The pooling gas caught beneath the first Cruiser. Lela blinked, surprised it had worked. The cruiser went up with a *whumf* that nearly knocked her down. The heat of it was incredible on her face and skin.

The fire enveloped the second vehicle, then the third, until they were all ablaze. Lela crept as close as she dared and threw the rifle into the roaring flames. She turned, and ran for the comfort and safety of the darkness. Her body shifted with watery grace as she leaped the ditch and bounded after Aria.

Three cars rolled up and men boiled out, screaming into their radios.

CHAPTER 9:

A SERIOUS HOUSE

Hart Mountain National Antelope Refuge
Oregon, USA

The Facility is called Site Bravo, but few people know it exists. It does not appear on any map, nor does it suggest itself to satellite imagery because from above it appears to be just an abandoned logging camp at the base of a ridge. Most of the facility is underground or cuts back deeply into the earth. No one is allowed in or out by day, and everyone must use hidden tunnels that crisscross the hills to enter or leave. There is also a secret, underground freight train that can bring in supplies, equipment, and personnel from a secondary site.

All told, the facility is a state-of-the-art, world class campus dedicated to some of the most technical and precise research and development in the history of Applied Science. It boasts ten levels and around 720,000 square feet (as much square footage as the palace at Versailles, as the Director of the Site, Doctor Lannon, is fond of quipping).

The primary purpose of Site Bravo is illegal genetic research conducted on behalf of (but in complete deniability for) the United States government. Security is—as might be expected—tight. Two full company-sized elements of highly trained combat veterans-turned-contractor guard the facility, with a third emplaced at various choke points and near entrances.

Inside, every room is monitored by camera and microphone (except the Director's office). The site is impervious to electronic intrusion thanks to black box technology, and every section can be partitioned or drained of air entirely, ventilation and all. The CEO of ProGen Global, Armand Weynman, makes routine inspections and calls it, (quoting Philip Larkin), "a serious house on serious earth."

Of course, in the poem, the "serious house" is a church. For Weynman and for Doctor Lannon, perhaps Site Bravo is a church as well. If so, then the prayers offered here come in test tubes that house microorganisms capable of wiping out the human race in days and serums that could drive the strongest, most stalwart man to spill his darkest secrets at dosages near hundredths of a drop. This is the place where Billy Hatfield's corpse, the body of a dead werewolf, would soon arrive.

Tests were to begin immediately.

CHAPTER 10:

FRANK TAKES THE TRAIN

Afternoon
Friday, 16 June, 2017
Salinas, California

Frank bought a burner phone from the liquor store down the street from the train station in Salinas and dialed the number on the letter. It rang twice, then Bill picked up.

"Hey, brother," said Bill.

"Hey yourself," said Frank.

"You're getting on the train?"

"Soon."

"But you're in the station?"

"Yeah."

"Go into the men's," said Bill.

Frank rose. The station was empty except for a young couple holding hands on a bench near the back, both of them with wet, reddened eyes. He walked into the men's room.

"Here."

"The third toilet stall, taped to the lid of the tank."

Frank stepped into the stall and lifted the lid of the tank. A packet encased in plastic was taped to the top of the tank. Frank ripped it off and replaced the tank lid. Inside were a passport, California Driver's License, and credit card under the name "Matthew Rainier."

"Don't travel under your own name," said Bill. "Call me when you get to San Francisco." He clicked off.

Frank hadn't noticed the ticket his brother had sent him read "Matthew Rainier." It was the sort of detail a detective should have noticed. He was slipping. Or he was tired.

He tried to remember when he'd last slept well, but gave up. His brother was certainly pulling strings for him. It was sort of impressive because no matter their estrangement, both of them had learned their father's lessons well: blood *is* (cliché as it is to say it) thicker than water.

When the train arrived, Frank boarded along with the girl from the weepy couple and a few others that straggled in. He looked around for any possible threats, but no one tripped his alarms. He found a seat on a second tier of a passenger car and watched the clockwork of the station until the train gave a jerk and tugged slowly, then with more and more speed, away from the station.

They passed through the industrial end of Salinas and were into the farm fields, then another little town, then into the hills. The train rocked and swayed and pressed on, ever north.

Frank was near dozing when they made their first stop to take on more passengers in Watsonville, but he dared not sleep. He watched the platform, surveyed the embarking passengers, but he saw no one suspicious.

When the train pulled forward again and began to build up speed, Frank allowed himself the thought that things might be okay. That he had gotten away from whoever might be looking for him. Sleep was tempting then. The train's slow rock lulled him. He fought sleep for a few minutes, then rose in defiance and went to the dining car toward the front for coffee.

As the dining car opened, he saw them. And they saw him. Three of them, dressed down in dark clothing that was neither bulky nor tight, and that would not restrict movement. They were undoubtedly carrying guns.

Two of them were big men, burly and clean-shaven with the air of meat-eaters. They were the sorts of men who climb mountains because the mountains are there. The third was shorter, a bit older, thin and wiry, with intelligent eyes. They were walking together slowly and systematically back through the car, scrutinizing every face and moving on. They'd glanced up when he walked in, and now he had their full attention.

He didn't need coffee anymore to stay awake. Frank turned and fled the car. Had this been a setup? Were they watching always? How big was this organization? He thought of Lela's postcard. "Miss You."

He moved quickly but did not run through the next car, and the next. He wondered what he'd do when he ran out of train. There were too many civilians here to start shooting, and he really didn't want to kill anyone if he could avoid it.

He lingered in the coupling between cars and considered the situation. The options were few and bloody and would likely make things worse. The car door opened, and the wiry man with the sharp eyes stepped into the coupling, hands where Frank could see them and without the two linebackers.

"No need for all that," he said, evenly.

"Who are you?" asked Frank.

"My name is Gregory," he said. "I'm here to talk. I know you're not infected, and I'm not going to ask you to inform on your wife."

"How did you find me?"

"We can find anyone," he shrugged.

"Just talk?" asked Frank. He was sure his face was as skeptical as his tone.

"Just talk."

"So, talk," said Frank.

"What happened to Father Giovanni Santa Ana? Were you there when he died?"

"Yes, I was there," said Frank. "We were after the one who had infected Billy. We chased him into the woods out in Big Sur. He killed Father Giovanni there."

"How did you survive that attack?"

"Luck."

The car door opened, and two passengers stepped through the coupling, chatting together. The men waited until they were gone, then Gregory said, "Who is Nob Haraldson to you?"

"Owns a bookstore. Also in Big Sur. Or did. He disappeared."

"Do you know what happened to him?"

"Not really," said Frank.

"Are you sure?" asked Gregory.

"I think we're done here," said Frank.

"No, Mr. Crow. We are not finished. I have a great sense of when I'm being lied to. We need the truth."

"I can't help you," said Frank.

Gregory sighed, "Please. I'm trying to help you."

"Just leave me alone, okay? You and your Church."

"It's not that simple. I was hoping I could close this file before it gets out of hand. Where is Nob Haraldson?"

"I don't know, and if I knew I would not tell you."

"But he's alive?"

"I don't know," said Frank. "After a fashion, I guess."

"What does that mean?"

"Nothing, forget it."

The signs were very slight, but Gregory was tensing. His pupils were slowly beginning to constrict. His fingers tapped and then stopped tapping when he caught himself. He was getting ready for something adrenaline-inducing.

"Mr. Crow, if you won't cooperate with us, my hands are tied."

"Mine aren't." Frank put all his strength behind a knockout blow on Gregory's chin, fast and straight and hard.

Gregory's chin wasn't there when Frank's fist arrived. Instead, Gregory's sharp, bony knee found Frank's crotch, once, twice, and Frank collapsed in a heap on the floor. Frank came back up with a wild uppercut that didn't connect. Gregory was fast, but there was nowhere to go. Gregory's head snapped back but he didn't go down. Hobbling, breathing raggedly, and struggling through the pain, Frank snapped out a jab that rocked against Gregory's cheekbone with a satisfying wet crunch. Gregory kicked low for Frank's knee and Frank went down again.

Then the door opened and the two linebackers came in. Frank looked up at them and tried to rise. But a meaty fist came down on him, and the world was pain, then it was darkness. His last thought, maybe it was a whisper, was of Lela.

Miss you.

CHAPTER 11

THE CONVOY

The man who brought Billy Hatfield's remains to Site Bravo was named Cassius Danalov, Crusader Sergeant of the *Gladius Dei*. His journey as escort was curious. Even a member of a secret society could, on occasion, be surprised by the cloak and dagger of it all.

Hatfield's body was in deep freeze in San Francisco. Part of the *Gladius Dei* cleanup team that had sanitized Big Sur of all traces of the supernatural had taken possession immediately after his death on orders from Father Giovanni.

Danalov had been in command of that team, and had arranged for a boat to pick them up in Big Sur to pilot them all the way to the mouth of the San Francisco Bay.

A freezer truck had met them at the dock and drove them to a storage freezer deep in the belly of the city's underground, where many an old and curious thing remained in the shadows of the Order's grim history. That was in 2016.

There the werewolf's corpse had stayed, deep beneath the streets of San Francisco. It was unusual not to have disposed of the body immediately, but orders had come down from very high up in the Order that any confirmed lycanthrope was to be put in deep freeze. Why, none could say, but speculation was rampant.

No one gossips as feverishly as members of a secret society, Danalov often mused.

Now, a year later, he received a call at his home from an assistant to one of the High Justices, informing him that he was to take Hatfield's corpse out of deep freeze in San Francisco and bring it by freezer truck to a location to be disclosed when he was in country. It was a bloody nuisance, couldn't someone else manage this drudgery? He was, after all, a hunter, not a delivery boy. Nevertheless, orders were orders.

As he thought it through, he understood. There were unusual risks in moving this body and risks in where they were moving it. They wanted a shooter with credentials to be involved at every step. Danalov was a legend in the Order, and that legend had grown since his old friend and rival Giovanni Santa Ana had fallen in the Hatfield affair down in Big Sur.

The order they gave him when they had secured the package in the freezer truck surprised him as he did not think he could be surprised anymore.

"What's this? Take him there?" he had said in his thick Russian accent. "They can't be serious."

The Captain of the safe house had shrugged, "Orders."

"Las Vegas?" Danalov asked.

"Yeah, this address in Vegas."

"Why on Earth?"

"If I knew, I'd have a higher pay grade than Captain, pal."

Danalov and his cadre ran a convoy from San Francisco to Las Vegas. He had put Lorca and Stewart up front in a sedan to run interference, scout, and signal trouble early. Stewart had the sharpest eyes in the dark, although his specialty was communication and technology. Lorca, their medic, was a strong driver in moments of danger. As a bonus, they wouldn't drive each other crazy across the miles; the two were as close as brothers and had come up together.

Angela Daniels, the Intel officer on the team, rode in the truck with Danalov. Daniels was ex-Army Intel. She understood that world as well as anyone. She had joined the *Gladius Dei* for reasons of her own. Danalov knew that most were recruited because they'd had an encounter with the supernatural. Vengeance was a frequent motive. If that was also true for Daniels, she kept it to herself. Whatever the reason, she was an exemplary officer and a woman Danalov trusted fully. Even so, it was always a good bet she knew more than she was saying, but this mission had her more tight-lipped than usual. All Danalov had, as commander, was an address, a route, and a promise that further orders would be forthcoming at the objective.

Danalov was in the command slot for the team, although his specialty was as a shooter. Instead, his assigned shooters were Cooke and Markovski in the lightly but invisibly armored pickup truck bringing up the rear.

Those two had a tendency to go over-the-top when the shooting started. Cooke favored a drum-fed automatic shotgun filled in a special combat load of silver-coated ammo with three shells of buckshot for every silver slug. He could spit enough hot death in the air to turn a platoon of enemies into Swiss cheese in under ten seconds.

Markovski was more subtle. A keen woodsman and quiet afoot, he was also very good with a blade or a silenced pistol. He was precision. Focus. Elegant efficiency. But if it got hairy and there was an earnest firefight, Markovski favored twin AK-47s and copious suppressive fire. If things got bad, these two would unleash the Wrath of God.

It was a comfort to Danalov, who preferred to thread a middle path between expansive brutality and minimal violence to bring down a threat. That temperance and ice water cool in his temperament had probably suggested him for Sergeant and command of his own team.

The team was the standard unit for the *Gladius Dei*, and only a handful of hunters had special dispensation to hunt alone. But they also had the authority to call in multiple teams to assist almost at will. Father Giovanni had been such a one, and Danalov hoped one day to earn the same privilege. His star was certainly rising after the way he had cleared a small vampire colony in Corsica last spring, although the nightmares of that bloody business still haunted him.

The team, per standard operating procedure, included a Supply/Logistics/Armorer specialist, this time in the person of a man named Jakes. Specialists like this were sometimes in the field and sometimes operating remotely to prepare accommodations, transportation, meals, and to secure and prep equipment. Jakes, in this case, was already in Vegas, and would meet them at the objective.

The trip to Vegas was long, but largely uneventful except for one peculiar incident and one somewhat illuminating conversation.

"You ever talk to Joseph Marini?" Angela asked.

Her voice startled Danalov as she had been silently looking out at the desert. It was about two hours before dawn, and they had not broken the dull noise of tires rolling on pavement in some time.

"Who?" asked Danalov.

"Joseph Marini? He's G.D. Inquisitor. Scholar spec. They stationed him at the new safe house when the Hatfield thing went down."

"Yes, we've met a few times. Twice maybe. But we never really talked. Why?"

"I was talking to him not long ago. About Hatfield. The beast who infected him was one of the most prolific serial killers in history, although almost nobody knows it."

Danalov glanced at Angela, then back to the road, "Oh, yes?"

"Yeah. Name of Lorne Hutchins. About as bad as it gets; he's the one they think did for Father Giovanni. Hutchins had been infected as a kid in Nebraska in the 19th century. Hatfield wrote a book about the murders. Apparently Hutchins took it personally and instead of just killing him, he infected him. At least, this is according to the reports Giovanni left."

"Did Hatfield guess the truth?"

"No. Not that his subject was still alive, and certainly not that he was carrying the Diana Strain."

"I've never understood why the Order calls it the Diana Strain," said Danalov. "Some Roman Catholic nod to a pagan past, maybe?"

"After a fashion. She was goddess of the moon for the Romans. The lycanthropes of this strain change for the three nights of the month when the moon is fullest. There are other kinds of beast-changers. This name identifies one," she said.

"Where did Hutchins get it?"

Angela shook her head.

"Chicken and egg problem."

"Hard to say. The old lore says it's some kind of animal spirit possession, but the science of it is sketchy. There's probably some spiritual component, but if it's repeatable, then it's subject to the rules of science."

"So, that's why they saved Hatfield's body?" Danalov asked. "They want to get the science on these things?"

Angela considered this for a moment. "Yes. That's where we're headed."

Danalov nodded. "Thanks for heads up."

They pulled into a gas station and the convoy fueled up just as the first pale light of dawn was stretching across the desert. Cooke and Markovski pulled security. Stewart fueled each vehicle while the rest went inside to pit stop, grab coffee, and stretch their legs. Danalov noticed the television above the counter as two faces flashed across the screen. "WANTED" read the heading. Then, there was footage of three blackened husks barely recognizable as vehicles in the middle of an Arizona highway, sending curls of smoke up into the rising morning.

Danalov knew those faces. He gestured to Angela as she stepped out of the restroom and pointed toward the screen. She blinked and came to his side.

"Isn't that—"

"Yeah," she said.

"Well, well," said Danalov.

"Three dead cops, it says."

"Vengeance is mine, sayeth the Lord. I will repay."

"I'll call it in," said Angela, pulling out a cell phone.

"Probably our people already know," said Danalov.

"Yes. I want to know if this changes things."

She stepped out of the gas station and nearly dropped her phone, hung it up, and stared. Both of the shooters were silent, instead of engaged in their usual infantryman's banter. They were staring, too.

The power lines and the canopy of the gas station, every vehicle, every signpost, every rooftop was black with still, silent crows staring, unblinking at the freezer truck.

That truck—with Billy Hatfield's body inside it—was the one surface where *not one* crow had deigned or dared to set a single clawed foot, nor brush one black silken wing.

Danalov stepped out. As one, they rose, cawing and screeching in a cacophony of wings and gravel-throated calls, and as one they rolled in a spiral higher and higher in the bright morning sky.

They rolled grimly on, sure of an ambush from some dark spirit. Instead, they arrived unchallenged in Las Vegas two hours later in full daylight. The address belonged to a somewhat sectioned-off warehouse on the outskirts of North Las Vegas in a half-empty industrial park. A guard took a look at whatever credentials Lorca, in the car ahead, produced from her wallet and let them through.

A man in overalls and a hard-hat came out from a trailer beside the warehouse and rolled up a huge steel door, waving the convoy inside. The warehouse was immense—a giant's clockwork of supplies, machinery, medical equipment, construction equipment, building supplies, food and provisions, and much more stretching high into the rafters on enormous steel shelves. It had a ramp wide enough for several 18-wheelers to travel side by side that lead down into an underground level.

"What is this?" asked Danalov.

"It's the objective. We're here. Time for new orders," Daniels said.

She stepped down from the cab and met the man in the overalls. He handed her a shrink-wrapped envelope with a wax seal on it and told her to direct the convoy to the lower level.

"The train will be arriving soon," he said.

"Train?" she asked.

"Yes," he said. "I was told you'd be taking our train."

And so they had. The packet of new orders directed Danalov to remain with the body of Billy Hatfield and ensure it was destroyed to the last cell when all experiments were concluded at Site Bravo. And furthermore, he and his team were to ensure any new infected were put down when their usefulness to science was at an end. No live infected subject was to survive.

Not for the first time, Cassius Danalov felt a chill down his back as he read these new orders, and trembled at what he might have to do in the name of God.

CHAPTER 12:
KNOWING AND NOT KNOWING

Noon
Friday, 16 June, 2017
Desert cave outside of Lupton, Arizona

At midday, Lela and Aria awoke, naked and curled together for warmth, on the stone floor of a cave. Lela had been dreaming of the baby she and Frank wanted and never had. She felt awash with sadness as the dream fell away.

Both of them wore the blood of the dead policemen they had killed. Aria stretched, her joints popping and echoing into the black, and she staggered toward the mouth of the cave, blinking at the light of day. Lela lay there staring at the shadows on the cave ceiling for a long time before she rose, her belly knotted at the memory of what they had done.

They had lain down some fifty feet back into the cave, away from the light of morning as it broke. Now that it was brighter, Lela could make out the drawings of beasts and hunters and human handprints in hues of red and black on the walls. This had once been a cave for Navajo (or Hopi perhaps) long ago. Now they were gone, but these drawings remained. Something long and lithe and familiar grinned at her from the painted walls. A coyote, she told herself. Just Old Coyote playing his tricks.

"You could have run. Left me. They didn't need to die," said Lela, softly, almost whispering.

"You could have let the cop shoot me with that rifle of his," said Aria roughly, not turning from the cave's mouth. She was staring out at the desert floor. Distantly, she could see the dark line of the highway from which they had come. It was, as all things in the desert, farther away than it appeared. They must have made fifteen miles to the foothills to find this cave. There was a helicopter thudding dully in the distance, like a fly on some afternoon windowpane. It circled near the thin line of smoke that must have been where the last of the car fire still smoldered.

"That's different," said Lela, rising to join her at the cave's mouth. "He had already seen you. You'd already killed one and nearly killed the other. We were already in it by the time I . . . when I did what I did."

"Is it so different? If I escaped and you went to jail, I'd have to either break you out or leave you to try to do it yourself.

"That's not the point, Aria. We didn't have to—"

"And if they took you to jail, sooner or later they'd figure out what you are, and you'd probably be dead. Or in some government lab. Because that's what happens to people with anomalous biological peccadillos, Lela. Or, maybe you'd be dead *and* in a lab. Either way, what happened *happened*, so we could survive."

"Really? You couldn't just let him cuff you up? They had very little to go on. It wouldn't have been much to talk our way out of."

"I guess we'll never know." She set her jaw and said, "I wasn't going to be cuffed."

Lela took a moment to breathe, then spoke.

"Well, now we're naked, in the middle of the desert. No car, no money, no ID, and the cops are looking for us. They'll trace back the vehicle we were in, start looking at gas station footage, and they'll have our pictures soon, if they don't already. Now we're fugitives, Aria. And undoubtedly on the churchmen's radar. They'll come looking. What now?"

"I don't know," said Aria. "I guess we travel by night, steal some clothes somewhere, steal a car, steal some cash, and keep going. We'll lam it if we need to. Don't be so negative."

"Keep going? Keep going where, exactly? The idea was to trace back the disease to its source. Billy got it from Lorne. Who did Lorne get it from? And where? When? We at least had Billy's book about Lorne as a guide, but that's charcoal now." Lela hadn't meant for her voice to keep rising, but it did. She tried to keep from sounding shrill, even as the cave played back their words to them in diminishing echoes.

"Hence Arizona," snapped Aria, "We're looking for Lorne's diner, right? That's what we said we'd find. The one he had in the 20s. We said it might have some clues as to where he got the disease, or whatever."

"Yes, okay, but now we have no car and only a general idea of the area where he—"

A crow landed quietly on a stone at the mouth of the cave and gave a loud caw, looking at both of them intently, from one to the other, directly in the eyes.

They looked at each other, then back at the bird.

"Nob??" asked Aria. Nob had been their friend briefly, when the Big Sur murders brought them all together. He had been an occult bookstore owner, a seven foot tall Norwegian and a Gothi of the Old Norse religion. He had somehow become a shifter by magics neither Lela, nor Aria, nor Frank could understand. He was the one who had saved Frank from the werewolf Lorne Hutchins in the forest of Big Sur by becoming a cloud of crows and picking Lorne's bones clean in a matter of seconds. What had become of him since, none of them knew. Every time one of them met a crow, there was always the question. Was this from Nob?

The crow hopped forward, cocked its head, and rasped a *caw* that echoed deep into the cave behind them.

Caw! Caw. Caw...

It hopped again, flitted lightly into the air, and then circled low and tight, before descending again. Then it moved off down toward the desert floor. It looped back calling to them.

Aria looked at Lela, who shrugged.

"You think?" asked Lela.

"Well, I've done madder things," said Aria.

"Yes. Yes, you have."

So, they set off after the crow they hoped was Nob, or some part of Nob.

It led them overland, mainly in low draws and along screened game trails through the foothills. They traveled almost never in the open and almost never in even distant sight of the highway. When they had to move in precarious view of civilization, they moved low and fast, and took cover where they could.

The old backroads and disused highways of Route 66 were miles from the newer, more modern blacktop freeways. So, bit-by-bit they dropped away from even the sound of a car and eventually found themselves coming up a low-lipped ridge at around sundown.

They cast their eyes on an old highway nearly covered with brown dust and an old, abandoned boxcar diner in the middle of a scattered gravel parking lot. A rusty shingle hung, squeaking as it swung in the wind, over the black gap where a door should have been. Inside it was very dark.

The crow landed on the shingle and croaked dryly. In the half-light, they walked gingerly over the hot gravel of the parking lot into the boxcar diner that Lorne Hutchins had once called *Good Eats*.

The door wasn't the only thing missing. Every pane of glass had been busted out. Lela and Aria stepped carefully around the glass where they could. A car yawned sleepily past on some distant byroad. Though it was out of sight, they both paused and stiffened for a moment, peering into the gloom.

Many of the stools still stood, as did the counter, although some had fallen, and all were rusting. The surface of the counter had warped and peeled. Everywhere was dust, and here and there rat feces or the same from some larger desert creature. In one of the ripped-up booths was a long rattlesnake skin rocking ever so slightly in the draft. It did not look like anyone had been here in a long time, although there was some graffiti on this wall or that bit of floor, but it looked very old and was hardly readable anymore.

"How many people did he kill here, do you think?" Aria asked.

"I don't know," said Lela. "And I don't want to know."

"That's weird to me, that you don't want to know," Aria said.

"Why?"

"Because you killed people last night and burned their corpses."

Lela looked back at Aria, "That was different. We did it to survive."

"Maybe Lorne thought that's what he was doing, too."

"Maybe, but it's not the same, whatever he thought."

"I'm not so sure it isn't," Aria pressed. "If we thought murder was so horrible—"

Lela cut her off, "I don't want to talk about this here. Or now."

"Fine," said Aria. The wind kicked up and a plume of dust rose and settled by the shadowed doorway. "We should find some clothes."

They stepped further in, moving toward the back counter and the kitchen beyond.

"Doubt we'll find any here," said Lela. The kitchen door hung at odd angles; one of its hinges was off. She pushed the door open with a creak and looked into the kitchen where Lorne had prepared his victims before he cooked and served them to his customers. The stove was ripped out long ago, and the fixtures had gone the same way. The floor was unevenly broken, with some holes opening out to torso-sized openings in the floor that gaped down into sullen darkness. It was still and somehow deeply eerie for the stillness.

They walked through carefully, noting the distinct stench of old grease, dust, and the dry, distant aftermath of meat gone bad.

"There's nothing here for us," said Aria, opening the back door with a squealing protest from the hinges. Behind were two outbuildings, and the-crow-that-might-be-Nob flapped down impatiently to light on the one that looked like a residence. The other was significantly smaller and looked like a toolshed.

They walked over, careful of their feet, and stepped over the fallen-in pinewood door. They found a room near empty but for a mattressless metal bed, an old pot-bellied stove, and a collapsed shelf. In among the debris of the shelf was a sun-bleached, curled old book, a very large jar of teeth, and the moldy remains of a green ledger. Aria picked up the ledger and opened it. It made a soft cracking sound and split in two in her hands.

There, written in a faded but precise hand, was a list of expenses and payouts for the year 1938. Aria threw it to the floor and spat a curse.

"There's nothing here!"

"Now what?" asked Lela. It was approaching full dark. "I don't want to sleep anywhere near this place."

The crow swept in and landed on the pot-bellied stove, squawking. They turned to leave, but it began to squawk even louder, more insistently. Lela turned, "Well, what is it? There's nothing here."

It pecked at the stove twice.

Lela stepped forward and opened the stove. She pulled away in fear, pedaled backwards, nearly stumbled, and retched on the floor.

Aria drew out the leather scroll that sat on a pile of ash and black skulls, dry and cracked. She knew instinctively—and as surely as Lela did—that this scroll was neither made of cow leather nor pig skin, but rather that Lorne had written on the flesh of men, or women. Or, given the suppleness of the leather after all these years, perhaps children.

The scroll began like this:

All my hate begins with him. All my hate and all my hunger. All my hate and all my hunger, I thought, belonged to me. They do not. They do not belong to me. They belong to the First Among

Wolves, The One Who Will Eat the World, Grimnir's Bane. I am His vessel. I am His chalice. I am His. His creature. Nine times His wolf, though a pale shadow of His might and majesty, a darkness to echo His Darkness. O Great Fenris, grant me your favors. Send me your hunger and your rage that I may loose them like so many hungry hunters upon the world.

In your dream you bring me before your feast. I sit at Your table. I know Hunger. I know need. And I know that the bottomless hunger of Your Great Maw will swallow the Sun at Ragnarok, O King of Death, Lord of Wolves, and Eater of Gods!

You bid me eat of the flesh of women and men, no longer my kind, and I obey. I eat, and grow strong, but ever hungrier, ever emptier. You hollow me out with eating. I am your husk, your standard-bearer and your herald, howling Death to the Stars. Let Mani, God of the Moon, beware the wolves that will run him down to darkness! Let him beware the Sons of Fenris Wolf!

It began in Hutchins, for me, but stretches back across the land, and across the years. It was the one called Gaspard who gave me the Wolf's Hunger and the Eyes of Fenris. Gaspard was the first old man I ever killed. Who gave the Wolf to him? Only Mighty Fenris knows.

O Fenris, let me go west and make a Great Eating, let me make a table for Your glory, let me prepare the Way for Ragnarok, when the moon will shine with blood and the sun will rise black, and wolves will rise to devour the world of Men! I am nine times Your Wolf, O Great Fenris. Call on me to do Your will.

CHAPTER 13:

TELL US

Evening
Saturday, 17 June, 2017
Monterey, California

Frank swam up to consciousness with a terrible headache, and knew immediately that he would regret it. He could see nothing, hear little, and his breathing was hot and close. He realized he was wearing a black cloth bag over his face, but was otherwise naked in a very cold room.

He was seated upright in a metal folding chair, his hands cuffed behind him, his legs shackled beneath him and a chain threaded through the chair between the handcuffs and leg shackles. He had been there long enough that it was already very painful, and almost impossible to move. He did not try.

Instead, he listened carefully.

There was no real noise. He heard no traffic, no breathing, just a dull mechanical white hum that might have been distant machinery.

"Hello, Frank," said a voice. A man's. Maybe Gregory? That asshole from the train.

Then Frank was blinded as they lifted off the hood. He found himself facing a row of intensely bright LEDs. He blinked, then squinted, but said nothing.

"I said, 'Hello, Frank.'"

"So you did," said Frank.

"Where's Nob Haraldson, Frank?"

"No idea."

"Why is your wife in Arizona?"

"I didn't know she was."

"When did she leave?"

"I don't remember."

"Where were you going, Frank? And why were you carrying fake ID?"

"I don't remember that either," said Frank.

"Frank, let me explain something to you," said Gregory. "I am not a monster. I hunt and kill monsters for the good and protection of innocent people. Your wife and her *friend* killed three cops and burned their bodies on an Arizona highway. They need to be stopped, and they will be. The question is, do you want to help save lives, or do you want to stay silent while people die because you won't accept what your wife has become?"

Frank's face was impassive. Blank. He wasn't prepared to believe anything this man was saying. Even if it were true that Lela had killed cops, Frank wasn't prepared to help these people hunt her down and kill her.

Gregory continued, "Now, I realize that's a big question, so I'll give you some time with it. Just remember, the longer they're out there, the more likely it is that they will infect someone who will go on to do more killing, or they will do more killing themselves. It's up to you to decide if you want that on your conscience, because it will be, at least in part, your fault. You can help us. You should help us. But if not, well, there's an answer for that, too."

Gregory's face was calm, his delivery conciliatory.

"You can have my answer now, if you want it," said Frank.

"Sure."

"Go fuck yourself."

"Well, Frank, I think you'll change your mind if you think things through. Let me try to help you."

He heard retreating footsteps, and suddenly a blast of cold air rolled over him as an air conditioner clicked on behind him out of sight. A door opened and closed again. He began to shiver.

So, he put his mind elsewhere, as he had been trained to do long ago at Parris Island. He thought of his wife and their first date in Ann Arbor.

They had met at a bookstore, of course. She was working her way through Library School at the University of Michigan. She would end with a Masters in Library

Sciences, although she later insisted in her thesis that much of the "science" was really an art. He was a rookie cop with Chicago PD, visiting family in Michigan.

They both happened to be in the History section: he for a book on the layout and architecture of Chicago from earliest days to the present, she for a book on the recent discovery of Ötzi, the Copper Age man found in the ice of some ancient glacier. The body had been remarkably well preserved, and they got into an incisive discussion of forensics.

It led to a cup of coffee across the street when Lela took her fifteen-minute break. Her eyes were beautiful, dark and lovely, and he liked her laugh. She had interesting things to say about things he had never thought about: the ways the Internet would revolutionize the collection and storage of information, the future of telecommunications, the eventual rise of Artificial Intelligence, the possibility of a Second Renaissance, and her favorite films (they both agreed on *Casablanca*).

Frank listened mostly, and they'd covered a lot of ground by the time she had to go back to work. He asked her to dinner that evening. She told him she had plans, would he like to come along? He had said he would.

"Frank?" asked Gregory.

When he came back to himself, Frank was shivering badly, his flesh was cold, numb, and growing very pale, and his muscles had cramped almost beyond use. The air conditioner sputtered and went quiet, the river of frigid air trickled down to a draft, and Frank shook violently under it. Gregory stepped out of the blinding light and put a wool Army surplus blanket over Frank's shoulders.

"Where's Nob, Frank?" His tone was gentle. Friendly.

Frank grunted, "D-don't kn-n-ow."

"Frank, why was Lela in Arizona?"

"F-f-fuck you."

"Okay, Frank. I'd like to help you, but this isn't going to cut it. I can bring you some hot soup, some clothes, get you out of the cuffs and find you a warm bed. I can do these things, or I can leave you here until you start to feel helpful. I'm in the business of saving lives, Frank, and I will grind the grist the mill calls for in order to make that happen. I sympathize with you, but the girl you married is a killer now, and we need to stop her."

He pulled the blanket off of Frank, and made a gesture. Someone behind them cranked up the air conditioner again, and it became a gale of freezing air.

"G-g-Gregory?"

"Yes, Frank."

"Y-you'll be d-dead long before sh-she is."

Gregory stepped quietly back behind the lights and out the door without a word.

The shop was called *Belkin and Brock's New and Used Bookstore*. It was in downtown Ann Arbor, tucked into a side street. The late autumn leaves had turned and early frosts were coming regularly now. Frank was wearing a white t-shirt, dark jeans, motorcycle boots and a brown leather jacket. He slung his black Jansport backpack over his shoulder and walked in.

The place was idyllic that afternoon. The shafts of light came in at that quintessentially autumnal angle, streaming in and catching the dust in the air the way photographers at their best only sometimes manage to capture. It was quiet, more than half empty of customers, but full of warm light on the varnished wood of the shelves that shined like richly diffused gold.

He walked the stacks, turning in at the far end of the History section. Rookie that he was, he had learned how to navigate Chicago well enough as a kid, and field training had sharpened him, but he realized he knew little of the history of how and when the neighborhoods were built. He thought he might brush up, but even as he laid his hand to a book that looked like it might serve, he saw her.

She had dark hair and eyes, tan skin, and wore an emerald sweater against the chill outside. She also wore a nametag in friendly green letters: "Lela."

He smiled at her, and she smiled back, and he was walking forward to greet her before he knew what he meant to say. She had a book in her hand, and his eyes flicked over it. *Ötzi: The Ice Man.*

"You, uh, like books about cavemen?"

She smiled. "I think archaeology is fascinating."

"Oh, yeah. Well, yeah," he said. "It's like a puzzle, isn't it?"

"I like puzzles. How about you?"

"Only if I can solve them," he said.

She laughed a bit, and he found he liked the sound of it.

"What's your record with puzzle solving? Over 500?"

"So far so good, I guess. Haven't figured out cold fusion or anything, but I do okay," he said. She smiled at him in the golden light of that long ago bookshop.

God, she was *pretty*. And *bright*. And... Frank smiled in spite of himself and said, "What they can do with forensics now is amazing, don't you think?"

"You're babbling, Frank. Just babbling," Gregory was saying from some distance. Then he was back in the cold, and something sharp and painful had just happened to his face. He tasted copper—a dirty penny in his mouth. The sounds were sharper again, and his body was practically convulsing. He had the blanket over his shoulders again. He smelled hot soup under his nose.

"Frank, why do you do this to yourself?" asked Gregory. "Let me help you." He offered the soup, steaming and salty to the smell, and *warm* as Frank had dreamed of warmth, but here and real and inches from his mouth. He leaned forward to sip, then stopped. A thought surfaced like a bubble from the bottom of a frozen lake (his mind was a frozen lake): *What if it was drugged? Scopolamine? Pentothal? Something worse?*

He pulled back as far as his restraints allowed and turned his head away.

"How many people would you condemn for love, Frank?" asked Gregory softly.

Frank turned back to look at him, then rasped, dry-throated through chattering teeth, "How m-many you got?"

CHAPTER 14:

BILLY'S BONES

Evening
Saturday, 17 June, 2017
Hart Mountain National Antelope Refuge
Oregon, USA

"Gentlemen. Ladies." He stood poised under the lights of the Conference Room and began in a clear voice. It was a two-hundred-seat auditorium in the Administrative Complex of Site Bravo. The myriad speakers resounded his voice almost musically. The auditorium was full. All personnel had been called in to hear from Chief Executive Armand Weynman and the Site Director, Dr. Lannon. Only security had been left in their usual place; every researcher, technician and engineer sat in the darkened room to listen, and their quiet chatter dissipated when Weynman cleared his throat and began to speak:

"We are not the first generation of scientists to change the world," Weynman was saying, "but the changes we make will be the most significant since the night Man first harnessed fire Thus far the United States and other governments have only brushed across what we now possess: an actual specimen of human-order intelligence, indeed, of human origin, altered into a genetic condition that surpasses humanity in every conceivable way.

"First, I think, a history lesson would lend some context to what we are about to accomplish. The United States Government has known about skin-changers since a curious and disturbing set of circumstances in Vietnam in January, 1972. Research ended abruptly and rather violently just as our forces were pulling out of Saigon in April, 1975. That abrupt end during the Fall of Saigon came to be known in CIA and other black ops circles as 'the Incident,' although few had the clearance or the inclination to tell the story as I will tell you now."

The crowd shifted slightly in the dim of the room. There were a few polite coughs. A huge screen beside Weynman lit up. It showed a grainy image of a jungle complex on a high ridge set about with a number of Quonset huts and concrete buildings. In the foreground were a number of American G.I.s with war paint on their faces and weapons in their hands.

"It seems that in January of 1972, an American Special Forces group designated MACV-SOG came upon *something* in the hinterlands deep behind North Vietnamese lines. A Soviet research facility was using American

GIs to experiment with some kind of animal/human hybridization a la *The Island of Doctor Moreau.*

"The SOG element infiltrated the site, took case files, microfilm, specimen samples, and then sanitized the area. Their reports make for interesting reading. Their commander on the ground, Captain David Mitchell, said they discovered American POWs in cells whose minds had been broken by whatever had been done to them.

At this, the slide changed on the screen. There was a pair of men with vacant eyes lying in the mud of a bamboo-barred cell. Their bodies were emaciated yet oddly misshapen. One man's elbows were reversed as a dog's back legs are. His skull was bulging, and his lower jaw horrifically distended like the jaws of a wolf. The other man in the photograph sagged in obvious pain, his muscles so huge, rigid, and tight that they appeared to have snapped some of his skeletal structure. His image conveyed paralysis, but he was not yet quite dead.

There were gasps from the crowd at this horrific image. Weynman waited for them to settle.

"And in the tunnels below, they found two (and here I quote) 'Abominations.'

"These abominations were upright like men, but one looked for all the world like a tiger and the other like a wolfman out of a Universal picture, only taller and stronger. Unfortunately for us, no photographs of these specimens have survived. The SOG team killed both 'Abominations' (with some difficulty, I might add. Mitchell lost three of his best). They would have brought the specimen cadavers back to Saigon but encountered an ARVN company during exfiltration, and the specimens were lost. When the team returned with what Intel and case files and microfilm they had, American CIA assets took over research and Project Perdition was born.

"Over the next few years, the CIA tried to learn the properties of these skin-changers. Their applications for war were obvious, but how else could they be useful? Mitchell's report indicated the 'Abominations' could heal at a phenomenal rate. Imagine healing from grievous wounds in mere seconds or minutes. The medical implications of such an ability are revolutionary on every level. But no such innovations could succeed with a specimen. We needed a body for research.

"Operations were conducted to capture other specimens, but all met with failure. Covert ops found almost nothing. The Soviets played it tight."

The screen now showed a grainy image of what was left of a Soviet agent chained to a metal bedframe beside a car battery.

"Even under *extreme duress*, high level members of the *politburo* in the country had no knowledge that their government was working on weaponizing human/animal hybrids.

"That's how it stayed until 2003, when a JSOC (that's Joint Special Operations Command, for those of you science types not up on American military acronyms)." Weynman raised his brows and smiled, and a low and welcomed chuckle sounded throughout the room. Weynman continued.

"Then, a JSOC element and a patrol of Blackwater contractors encountered another Changer in the caves of Afghanistan. They managed to trap it—, although again, not without cost. They lost ten men in those caves, but they brought out a live specimen. The problem, of course, is traveling with something like that in the Hindu Kush. Even for such men, it was daunting and dangerous, and they had problems they did not guess at: this Changer had a little family up in those mountains.

"They lost three men on exfil to a safe landing zone, but we got real drone footage of these things." He clicked a button and the screen beside him flared with green night vision light.

The drone footage showed a team of men engaging three large wolf-changers in close combat as a Blackhawk helicopter was touching down behind them on a plateau high in the mountains. The men were firing, emptying their magazines into the Changers who would react to the damage, sometimes falling to the ground. But they would rise again and continue on, even as the men reloaded or, having expended all ammo, changed over to a secondary weapon and continued firing.

Then one of the Changers grabbed one of the men in his jaws and shook him once with terrible strength. The man went limp. The crowd gasped in horror and amazement. Sensing their excitement, Weynmen paused the video with that gruesome image frozen on screen.

"They put the dead Changer on a Blackhawk and pulled back to a Forward Operating Base. But, as the Bard wrote, 'the course of love never did run smooth.'

That night the FOB was attacked by Mujahedeen, and as Fate would have it, the creature got a mortar sent in, special delivery, right on top of it. What they could scrape off the walls, they sent up the chain.

"What followed was a lot of the left hand talking to the right hand at the highest levels of government and even more figuring out what was to be done. The decision was never made to re-establish Research and Development into this particular biotech avenue. It was felt by the Powers that Be that without a live specimen it would be too risky and expensive to proceed. Remember, Donald Rumsfeld was not a man to ask for money in those days."

At this there was another, livelier titter of laughter around the room.

"However, something new has happened, as all of you know, and we are a part of it. Part of history! ProGen Global, already a leader in cutting-edge biotechnological innovation, was awarded a contract to look into this Shapechanger phenomenon, and we are moving forward with an actual deceased specimen."

There was thunderous applause then, and people stood and cheered for a long time. Nodding, smiling, statesmanlike, Weynman gestured for quiet, and the crowd sat and hushed.

"We have immediately retained the services and leadership of one of the most respected and ingenious geneticists of his generation, Doctor Robert Lannon!"

Lannon stood to a brief round of applause and sat down again.

"Site Bravo has been chosen to be the womb that gives birth to a new future. A future where no one would dare make war on the United States of America. A future where American men and women survive and thrive beyond what anyone ever believed possible. A future where the world is at peace because no one dares to make war. We are entering, not the American Century, but the American Millennium!"

The clapping grew louder as Weynman's voice raised high above it. "Colleagues, scientists, midwives of the future! It is my honor to speak before you today and to usher in a new age of peace and prosperity for our country and the world!"

How they cheered then.

CHAPTER 15:

THE HOLE IN THE WORLD

True night.
Saturday, 17 June, 2017
The desert outside of Chambers, Arizona

The women slipped their skins and went as wolves under the rising moon. They fled the abandoned boxcar diner that had been *Good Eats*. They fled equally the rantings and gibberings to Fenris the Great Wolf that had been carved on the skins of children by their dark wolfen father Lorne Hutchins. They were following the crow-that-was-Nob as he glided on black wings across the desert, toward the high country. Leading them on toward salvationary horrors.

They came upon two old trails with ancient ruts in them that must surely have been a century old. There was an ancient, low-slung and gnarled tree there at the crossroads. The crow lit on the tree and rasped a caw.

The wolves stopped at the crossroads and sniffed, then went rigid in the same instant. There was an old, foul stench coming from the nearby hills.

They followed the trail leading to the hills warily, each of them pausing to sniff, then bristle, then check her backtrail. The trail led past a fallen sign, too sun-bleached to make out clearly, except for the word "mineshaft." They passed it by, and the rocks narrowed then narrowed again. They moved upward over a slope and back downward into a bottleneck where the trail died. Where it ended, a short line of railroad ties began, and glowering there at the edge of the shadows slouched a very old mine car, long since rusted in place. The railroad ties stretched back into a long, dark tunnel. The mine.

Lela and Aria stopped and growled. It smelled like an evil place, full of drafts and drops and mold, and rot, and old death, and fear; and yet the crow called down to them. They slipped into the darkness on silent paws.

The tracks led down into the hills, with rotting boards nailed over entrances to various shafts

left and right. It was pitch black within a minute of walking, nearly impossible even for wolves to see by. For all that, they both made out a hulking, rotting shape before them, subtly outlined in the last of the moon-beams and starlight.

Aria growled low in her throat, but whatever it was did not move. She sniffed, then circled it. It did not move. Lela brushed against it, and let out a bark of what could have been nervous laughter.

She slipped back into her woman's skin and said, "It's a car. An old car from the twenties or thirties."

She felt around in the dark for the handle and pulled it, but it would not budge, then after a minute of concerted pushing, it gave a rusty screech and opened with protest. The echo rolled down into the shafts of the mine ominously.

Inside the husk of the car, Lela's fingers told her the leather was cracked, the upholstery rotted. The metal had gone to rust. She felt around carefully, wondering whether or not she was subject to tetanus anymore.

She discovered with a small suitcase on the teetering floorboard. Fumbling with the clip until it clicked open, Lela slipped her hand inside and found what felt something like folded clothes. She felt a cotton shirt, then another, a pair of rough spun trousers, a pair of dungarees, a rolled pair of long, coarse socks, and a box of disintegrated cigarettes with a box of matches inside.

She carefully lit one of the matches, and a little island of orange light flared into existence around her, surrounded by seawater-thick. Aria shifted to her skin and stepped gingerly through the dust into the little circle of light. The ancient match was already burning down.

The naked women divvied up the clothes and dressed as the light guttered, then struck another match and made a makeshift torch out of what clothes were left. Something glittered off to their left, and Aria walked over to pull up a kerosene lantern. They inspected it, and hearing the dregs of kerosene inside, lit the lantern.

The light was brighter coming from the lantern, and Lela gasped as she looked around. There were old cars rotting on both sides of the mine's walls, lined up neatly one before the other. Several dozen in this corridor alone. The dusty chrome glittered back at them.

"Lorne," breathed Aria.

"His cache. Bodies went one place, their effects another…" Lela felt a chill run up her spine.

"Why would Nob bring us here?" asked Aria, fear rising in her throat.

"I'm sure he has his reasons. There's something here we need to find. Come on."

"One of us should carry the light, and one of us should go on four legs. Better eyes, better ears, better nose," said Aria, slipping again into the wolf.

"This is getting easier," thought Aria. "Either because of practice, or because of the Moon waxing. I can feel it." At that moment she wanted to go out from this dark place, this house of Death, and howl at that pale half-circle with her full throat and soul. But she didn't. She couldn't. They went deeper inside.

Lela and Aria turned a corner and the line of cars continued, getting older and older, more and more rusted away, but far in the back there was a yawning shaft probably thirty feet wide. Lela cast down a stone, and they waited a very long time before the report of impact reached them.

"This is where he threw most of their things," said Lela, knowing it was true as she said it.

The crow-that-was-Nob swept by them on silent wings and landed on the lip of the far side of the shaft. The shadows seemed to swirl around him, then he rose, cloaked in feathers and dark wings. His eyes were made of shadow, his flesh the color of ash.

"This is a place very close to the World of the Spirits. A door to the World Beyond the World," he told them, his voice distant, as if he were calling from the far side of a cold shore.

"Why did you bring us here?"

"You are searching for the source. The origin. A way forward to your lives. The way out is through…if there is a way out."

"The way out is through what?"

Nob spread his wings and dove into the darkness of the shaft, cawing dryly as the echoes rolled through the mine and died away.

"Follow," his voice rose from the darkness.

Aria padded away and returned with a coil of rope anchored on one of the railroad ties behind them...

"Let's go," said Aria, throwing down the rope.

"Great," said Lela, staring into the abyss. "Just perfect."

CHAPTER 16:
THE DEVIL, YOU SAY

Evening
Saturday, 16 June, 2017
Flanders Mansion, Carmel-by-the-Sea

As the librarian and researcher in residence, Joseph had taken delivery of the *Cauldron's* inventory, and busied himself for several days shelving and organizing, making space in the basement to house the shop's considerable collection of occult books and paraphernalia. If he told the truth, he enjoyed this sort of work more than any other aspect of being *Gladius Dei*.

There was something satisfying about imposing order on chaos, about taking things buried in boxes and trunks and giving them coherence and focus, about categorization and (in the end) being able to *use* a library to find answers that were hidden among their various, scattered pieces. The wholeness of the thing was pleasing to Joseph.

When he finished, the basement of the Flanders Mansion may as well have been the *Cauldron*, but with a considerably more systematic order imposed on it. Nob had kept things in a roughly associated cloud; Aztec god mythology and Inca shamanism on the shelf with contemporary ethnographies on Candomble practitioners in Paraguay and practical guides to Santeria. Joseph had a more precise system specific to period, root belief systems, and language families. Shelves covered every wall, and in the open space of the basement several rows of compact shelving stacks had sprouted, neatly ordered and indexed with an old-fashioned card catalog in one corner.

Joseph found it marvelous that Nob had managed to collect a number of rare and ancient books of a kind only the most wealthy, serious, and educated collectors would trade in or know of. Volumes like the first printing of *Malleus Maleficarum: The Witch's Hammer*, written in 1487 and considered to be the definitive work on witchcraft in its day and for centuries afterward. Or a signed copy of *The Book of Werewolves* by Sabine Baring-Gould (this was of particular interest at present). Even a genuine (nearly complete) *Gutenberg Bible*. That one struck Joseph in particular. One of the rarest and most expensive books in the world, and it was just sitting in this little shop in Big Sur.

He had put in track lighting and a number of overstuffed chairs throughout the makeshift library, and a desk for the librarian (himself at present, but he had no illusions they would let him stay forever—there was always another job). He had converted an upstairs bedroom to a reading room, but most of his reading was done downstairs.

Joseph was trying to find some clue as to Nob's whereabouts or activities, or his general involvement in the Hatfield Affair that had killed Father Giovanni Santa Ana. So far, he had learned little. Nob did not mark his books, kept them in good condition, and his desk had been a disordered nightmare of teetering piles.

There was no discernable order that might correlate to Nob's doings or goings, but late into the night, after another fruitless sweep of the catalog for some clue, some pattern, Joseph sat down at the wide oak desk in the corner of the basement library and took out a piece of paper. The desk (so unlike Nob's habit) was absolutely free of clutter, without as much as a penholder or a notepad on its surface. Joseph thought for a moment and began a list of things he knew about Nob:

- Norwegian national/American Visa
- World traveler
- Serious collector of occult books and artifacts
- Spartan existence
- Several million in three international bank accounts

Joseph reflected on the disappointment of investigating Nob's house in Big Sur in hopes of discovering some clue as to where he had gone. The team had entered together, making a careful sweep in case of trouble, but all they found was a simple house with almost nothing in it.

The kitchen had a steel pot, a cast iron pan, a wooden spoon, one fork, knife, spoon, bowl, plate, can opener, bottle opener, and a stein. Only one of each item. In the cupboards sat three cans of soup, a can of beans, a box of noodles, a bag of rice, salt, pepper, and a can of tomato sauce. In the refrigerator was a half-empty bottle of mead, two bottles of Spaten, a package of hamburger meat gone over, a package of bratwurst gone over, a bag of old carrots, potatoes, and celery.

In the bedroom, Nob had a large green Army surplus bag with clothes rolled and packed down tightly inside, (six pairs undershorts, three pairs of pants, six undershirts, five button down shirts, six pairs of socks, and two sweaters).

Nob had apparently slept on a black futon, under one thick woolen blanket. There was a small stack of books next to the futon: a contemporary book on the history of the Crusades, a textbook of instruction in Latin from the 1940s, a book on metallurgical innovations in Toledo, Spain during the Renaissance, and a collected volume of Nietzsche's major writings.

The In the living room were w a chair, a lamp, and a desk with writing paper and utensils in it but nothing else of interest. The bathroom had a razor, shaving cream, soap, two towels, two washcloths, and a bottle of shampoo.

Nothing else.

Nothing helpful.

No art on the walls, no drawings, nothing hidden in a vent or a drawer, nothing secreted in a pipe or the tank of the toilet.

Nothing in the desk when they X-rayed it and broke it down to its component parts.

The man lived in a house in the woods of Big Sur like a man ready to leave at any moment. The lease said he'd been there for 15 years—since he'd first come into town, established *the Cauldron* and began doing business.

And nothing was on the walls.

Not a refrigerator magnet on the fridge.

Not a frill.

Well, *one frill.* Joseph considered this, then added to the list:

- Familiar with Norse Runes and their use in warding from spiritual/supernatural intrusion

The windows and door had been marked with the rune called *Thurisaz.* The rune of Protection. Each window graced the charcoal design on the base of its sill. The symbol had been carved into the door. Joseph copied it on a sheet of paper:

The wind picked up outside, and the old house creaked above and around him. For a moment, he thought he saw a shadow flicker on the far side of the basement, but when he looked up there was nothing.

Joseph rose and walked once around the basement, clicking on a small but extraordinarily bright flashlight he had produced from his pocket. He pulled a book on Elder and Younger Futhark Runes from a shelf, looked it over for a moment, and carried it back to his desk.

According to the book, *Thurisaz* was variously translated as "the Thorn" or as "Giant" or as "Thor holding back the Giants to defend the worlds." Was this a clue? Was Nob protecting his home because he believed he was under threat? How much did this man really *know* about the things that live in the shadows?

Or was he just another New Ager with something to sell who bought into some of the Old Religion? And, given the fact Nob was a seven foot tall Norwegian, perhaps "Giant" was an appropriate rune.

A floorboard creaked above, and Joseph looked up. The winds were high tonight, and the trees outside were whispering and groaning, the leaves whooshing in the breeze with one voice. The old house settled on its foundations in protest.

Joseph wrote:

- Familiar with Norwegian form of Old Religion. From childhood?

The Order had investigated Nob's origins, visited his village in Norway, spoken to Nob's mother, but had found nothing conclusive. Were there secrets in Norway yet to be uncovered that might lead them to Nob?

Then Joseph wrote "Further Research:

- Nob's family and village history in more depth
- Werewolf Traditions in the Old Religion

This reminded him of something. The Vikings had a tradition of Berserkers, *Berskr*, meaning "Bear-Shirts." They were a small contingent of shock troops sent in usually as the vanguard of a raid or attack to frighten and demoralize the enemy.

They were so fearsome that it was said they were possessed by the spirits of bears or wolves when they wore their skins, and that this sent them into a kind of killing frenzy in which they did not know friend from foe, behaved as beasts not men. They could shrug off catastrophic wounds while in battle. Was there some tradition or folklore localized around Nob's village? Something he might have absorbed, studied, or tried to emulate?

- Norway. Legendary *Berskr* in or around Heggem, Norway/Reinsfjellet Mountains?

There was a sudden flash, a crash of thunder, and the lights flickered, then failed. Outside, the rain began to fall hard. Joseph clicked on the flashlight and rose. The thunder had startled him, but suddenly he felt he wasn't alone. He drew the crucifix from under his shirt and put it over his heart, then drew a snub-nosed revolver.

"Anyone there?" he asked. He knew several others were at work in the house, or asleep.

No response.

Then a low scratching sound deeper into the basement.

Joseph cocked the revolver and pulled up the flashlight and pistol into a modified weaver position, wondering how many glorified librarians had these kinds of problems.

He moved slowly, methodically, "cutting the pie" inch by inch to see around the corner, then moving up, cutting a new angle, his eyes trained on wherever the light pointed, which (not coincidentally) was where the bullet would go if he squeezed the trigger.

He heard the sound of claws on the hard floor.

His pulse quickened.

Lightning flashed in the half-window, silhouetting the shape of a dark bird perched there and throwing its long shadow across the room as the thunder crashed and rolled through the walls and floors.

"I've got trouble down here!" he called upstairs, hoping they could hear him over the raging storm outside.

He moved methodically, back to the wall, eyes up, toward the stairs. It smelled of a carnivore, musky and sour with old blood. He heard it moving in the shadows, but wherever he aimed his light, there was nothing.

Finally, Joseph made it to the stairway only to see two great, round eyes reflecting the light like a predator, looking back at him from where it was stooped over his desk. He raised the light and revolver. It was large, black, and tall, and in a flutter of shadowy wings it was gone.

The lights flickered back on. The wind howled in the windows. There was something on his desk.

He walked over, wary, and saw beside his list a lone volume, presumably plucked from the stacks here in the basement, although if he had seen it, he had taken no note of it. There was no title on the cover or the spine, but when he opened it, he found the title:

The Saga of Rannulf the Red: Recovered and collected from three fragmented manuscripts and several folk legends of Norway

The book was written by Valdimar Ásmundsson and translated into English from Icelandic by Dr. David Kessler of Oxford University, 1983.

Joseph looked around, holstered his pistol, sat, and began to read.

CHAPTER 17:

THE WILD ONE

Early morning.
Thursday, 18 May, 2017.
Georgia State Prison, outside of Reidsville, Georgia.

Officer Krews of Georgia State Corrections kicked the inmate's bunk at 0415. Jarred, Marlowe McCoy winked one eye open, blinked in the light of Krews' flashlight, and said, "I'm up, sir."

"Get your shit for out-processing, inmate," said Krews.

Marlowe smiled, nodded, and rolled out of bed onto the cold concrete floor. He gathered his few possessions and followed Krews. After he had turned in various sundries belonging to the State, he stood before the property cage to recover his effects.

They included a wallet and chain, a Food Lion shopping card, an expired Driver's License, $60.79 in cash, a pair of jeans, and a very loud Hawaiian shirt with only one button hanging raggedly on.

He dressed alone in the gloom of a half-lit changing room, opened one of the lockers and took a piss inside, then stepped back into the hall. Three screws escorted him to the sallyport, radioed the big doors open, and walked out with him toward the big chain-link fence. It was 05:30, and the first light was glowing in the east.

"Where you goin' now you're free, McCoy?" asked Andrews, one of the older screws on the night shift.

"Guess I'll just find work, stay with my Mama, keep my nose clean, sir."

"You do that, McCoy. Don't wanna see you in here again. Don't you rob nobody else, son, hear?"

"Yessir," said Marlowe, smiling.

"We'll see him in here again," said Krews. "You'll die in prison, McCoy, you piece of shit, if somebody don't gun you down first."

"Reckon we'll see," said Marlowe McCoy, his smile unchanged.

They walked him to the gate and the guard in the tower buzzed it open, then Marlowe McCoy walked out of prison and did not turn for a last look.

From the State Penitentiary it was a five-mile walk to the nearest town. He started down the highway, the clicking of his cowboy boots a metronome clocking the miles. The sunlight had cracked across the gray eastern sky when Marlowe McCoy walked into the City Diner and sat down.

A pretty, blonde waitress with skin the color of cream and who had spent perhaps sixteen summers under the sky came by with a belly full of baby. Her eyes were periwinkle blue, and she had freckles on her nose.

"What can I get you, sir?" There was a smile in her voice. Marlowe McCoy knew he had an effect on women, particularly the wounded and the lost. He was a well-made man, of average height and powerful build. His eyes were smoky and gray with long eyelashes, and his mouth was big and sensuous and sweetly malicious. His hair was dark, and his skin smooth and pale, and when he moved it was with a clean-limbed hunting cat's grace.

He smiled a wolf's smile and said, "I'd like a steak— still mooin'—grits, biscuits with butter, and scrambled eggs, and two bottles of Bud."

She narrowed her eyes at him and crooked an eyebrow, brushing a strand of blond hair from her eyes and putting her pad away, "Beer? At this hour?"

"Sometimes a man wakes up thirsty."

"Are you thirsty?" she said, her pink lips slid into a knowing smile. He smiled back, and the smile stayed long after she walked away.

He ate his meal slowly, with considerable pleasure, and occasionally made eyes at his waitress.

When he'd eaten every bite, drunk his beers, and Shelly (her name was Shelly) came with the check, he said, "When do you get off, sugar?"

"I worked the night shift," she said. "So, I'll be done after this."

"Well, that's just fine," he said. "Where's the one put that baby in you?"

"That son of a bitch is gone," she said with a scowl. "Gone soon as I started to show."

He sized her up for a moment, rolled his head left to look at her, then right, and said with an easy grin, "I bet you're staying with your Mama. That right?"

"That's right," she said.

"I'll get me a room down the way at the motel yonder, if you wanna drive me over."

She nodded coyly, and he paid in cash for the meal. When they got to the hotel, somehow she ended up paying for the room. After a few hours of taking their pleasure, when Shelly was asleep on their rented bed of spent passion, Marlowe McCoy emerged from the room with a metal clothes hanger, two washcloths and a towel, the entire contents of her billfold (minus cab fare home, which he left on the dresser) and the keys to her Chevy pickup.

From there, Marlowe stopped at the last gas station out of town, filled up, and robbed the checkout girl with his finger, then made her pour bleach over the DVR that housed all recordings of the gas station's comings and goings.

That netted him two thousand dollars and the guarantee of life in prison when he was caught.

Fifty or so miles down the highway, Marlowe pulled into the parking lot of a Shoney's restaurant and ate, then he wiped down the interior of the pickup, bent the hanger out of shape and swapped the Chevy for an old Buick.

By nightfall he was across state lines into Alabama, taking back roads and avoiding cities, fairly in the exact opposite direction of his Mama's house in Savannah.

Marlowe McCoy stopped around dawn in Leeds Alabama and slept under the trees in the backwoods. He rose at noon, ditched the Buick in a nearby lake, then boosted a '98 Ford F-150 out of a driveway and stopped at the package shop for two bottles of whiskey and a case of beer. He made two other stops: one to a Waffle House where he ordered three meals to go, and the other at a disreputable pawn shop, where he purchased two pistols (a Taurus compact .44 revolver and a Sig-Sauer 9mm semi-auto) and a shotgun (a Mossberg 12 gauge), a black coat and two woodland camouflage over-shirts, a pair of black Vietnam-era jungle boots, a roll of duct tape, a hacksaw, two holsters, and a tarp. After that, he pointed himself east, and didn't stop until he hit Dallas about twelve hours later.

At 10pm, after a long nap in a dingy motel under an assumed name, McCoy parked in the long, flat gravel lot outside of *Troy's*. It was a cut-and-shoot bar ten miles from the city limits, and Marlowe McCoy had known it for many a long year. He sauntered in with the shotgun under his coat and two pistols holstered, one at his right hip and the other in a cross draw at his side beneath his left arm.

Troy's was a one-story building, low-slung in an adobe style. The parking lot was full, and the honky-tonk music was blaring. The heavy bouncer raised a ham-sized hand to stop him and began to ask for ID as he approached the door, but without checking his gait, Marlowe slammed the big man full in the temple with the butt of the shotgun and the bouncer dropped like three hundred pounds of limp potatoes.

He swept inside, tucking the shotgun under his coat, and made for the bar. And there he saw Cody, tending bar, just as if nothing had changed, and Marlowe McCoy hadn't just spent five years of his life rotting in a Georgia prison because his business partner decided to sing for probation.

Marlowe walked up to the bar. When Cody saw him, the skinny bartender dropped the bottle he was pouring, cleared the bar, and went pounding out toward the back door. Marlowe hopped over the bar and lifted a full, new bottle of Jack Daniels' No. 47, hefted it, then threw it end over end with all his might at the back of Cody's retreating head.

It spun twice and caught Cody right where the skull meets the spine. Marlowe drew out the shotgun and fired it once into the plaster ceiling. The crowd screamed like one animal and crushed itself racing for the door. In seconds, only Cody was crumpled there, groaning and twitching.

Marlowe stepped over him and turned him over, "Hey, Cody."

Cody looked up with unsteady eyes, blood trickling from his ears.

"M-Marlowe?"

Marlowe nodded and knelt over his old friend, tucking the recently sawed-off barrel of the shotgun under Cody's chin.

"Where's Isabel?"

"I don't—"

Marlowe racked the shotgun and said, more quietly and slowly, "Where's. Isabel?"

"C-California. San Diego. That's all I know, I swear."

"I guess she left you, too. Hell, she was always a hard one for staying with a man beyond his use," said Marlowe.

"Marlowe, please, I—"

Marlowe lifted his hand before his face to deflect the backsplash, then blew Cody's brains all over the floor and the back wall of *Troy's*. What blood and bone he found on his hand he wiped on Cody's jeans. He stood from his crouch.

"Died begging," said Marlowe with a shake of his head. He kicked over the bar back and smashed a few bottles of liquor that hadn't broken, then dropped a match. Then he walked calmly back to the car with the shotgun tucked under his coat and distant sirens chiming in his ears. He climbed in, and pointed the truck west, toward Isabel, if Cody wasn't smarter than he looked.

Behind him, *Troy's* was an inferno.

Of course, it couldn't last. All Marlowe McCoy's caution on the road moved him well away from the murder of Cody Grange, well away from the structure fire at *Troy's*, and well away from the Texas state line. He went by backroads and car-swaps.

But, in the end, Marlowe McCoy was going somewhere in particular, and with Cody Grange dead and McCoy on the lam (any fool in the Georgia parole office knew that), they contacted Isabel Rodriguez and waited.

Cody's information had been bad, although he did not know it. Isabel had fled San Diego after an unfortunate incident involving the penal system with yet another of her lovers. She had set herself up in Las Vegas. Isabel was working at a topless bar called *Club Sin*.

When Detective Philip Lowell of the Las Vegas Police Department was assigned to contact Isabel to advise her of Cody Grange's death and Marlowe McCoy's likely interest in her whereabouts (she had, after all, been a witness for the prosecution and was, after all, his most likely target that was still above ground), he found she was not at home. So, he went to her place of employment instead.

There was a red carpet, a red velvet rope, and a red sign out front declaring *Club Sin* to the glittering Vegas night when Detective Lowell pulled up in his BMW. He parked in the half-full lot and wandered over to the empty carpet where stood an imposing (if too pretty) pair of bouncers, one black and one white, both bald and barrel-chested. Lowell wondered if they moonlighted at some all-male revue in town when they weren't bouncing at titty bars.

He flashed his LVPD badge. They let him through without a word, but both gave him that ever-popular conspiratorial nod that certain kinds of security guards, bondsmen, and bouncers gave to cops that said (laughably) that they were all in the same business.

The place was sumptuous in the way Las Vegas strip clubs can be: plush if you don't examine carefully, tinted lights glowing strategically in ways that gave everything a red sheen and provided enough shadows to hide any cracks in the mask, any flaw in the illusion. There was a full bar to the right of the double doors stacked with top shelf liquor and bottled beer but no drafts. To the left was a stage, and all about that in the round were pleather couches, while farther on there was a VIP room glowing red in the neon haze. Detective Lowell smirked that management had invested in a fog machine, to great effect.

The bartender was another strapping lad. He looked like a corn-fed Midwesterner—blue-eyed and blonde with a baby face and broad shoulders. On stage there danced and twirled a statuesque brunette with legs up to her ears wearing a red fishnet body suit and a red fedora with a white band. Her assets were prodigious and swayed as she wanted them to in time to the thumping backbeat of an old Rolling Stones song. Her face wore that porn starlet makeup mask of dark, smoky eyes, glittery eyelashes, and lips that burn as red as landing lights at the airport.

Among the crowd of (mostly) men or young, drunken couples who stared, transfixed, at the girl on stage, other women in various stages of clichéd sexual almost-undress moved like prowling lionesses through the throng flirting, touching arms and shoulders, asking who would like a dance, inviting them to pay a bit more for the pleasures of the VIP Room, and otherwise trying to make the most of the opportunities this particular shift would afford them.

And, here and there, were women in actual clothes (however sexy or suggestive, still they were legitimately, legally dressed) carrying drinks back and forth from the bar to various couches or to the counter around the stage. One of these passed Detective Lowell, who said (above the exaggerated bass and driving backbeat) "Looking for Isabel Rodriguez."

The waitress said, "Who?"

"Isabel Rodriguez," he said again, more loudly.

"You mean Cinnamon?" she asked, pointing toward the red doorway of the VIP lounge.

"Sure. Thanks."

He walked into the VIP Lounge to find the sort of thing one finds. Champagne in every bucket, a beautiful girl pressed against every man who probably otherwise could not have held the interest of such a girl. Cash on tables, and nooks and curtains that hinted at a kind of Japanese privacy. Detective Lowell was a ten-year veteran of the LVPD and a Vegas local born and bred. To say he'd seen all the dewy-eyed vixens, cold machinery of violence, and drug-fueled carnage the City of Sin had to offer was to understate his experience.

But when he first slapped eyes on Isabel Rodriguez, he understood fully and immediately why her boyfriends kept taking stupid risks for big money and ending up in prison or dead, and he truly sympathized with them.

She wasn't wearing a wig, unlike many of the girls, and didn't need one. She had long, beautiful chestnut hair with golden highlights that curled at the shoulder into the kind of cascading ringlets that most men can't help wanting to run their hands through.

She had a small waist, and skin that was perfectly taut and tan without artificiality or blemish. Her breasts were generous but proportional, her figure a tight, slender hourglass that was still somehow slinky. Her face was angelic, with full lips and large green eyes. She wore a white silk corset with faux pearl buttons, garters and hose with lace panties and white stiletto thigh-high boots.

Isabel was sitting on the lap of an older man, gray-haired and jowly in a rumpled gray suit that was proba-bly worth more than Lowell's monthly salary before taxes. She was playing with his (silk, definitely silk) tie and gig-gling as if he were the sexiest man she ever hoped to bed. The VIP lounge also had bouncers, and one fire-plug put a hard, thick hand on Lowell's shoulder.

"You need a pass, sir," said the fireplug.

Lowell flashed the badge discreetly, then asked if they could send 'Cinnamon' out to him at the bar when her business was concluded with her current client. Lowell went to the bar and ordered a Coke and waited, his back to the stage. Only once, one of the prowling lionesses approached him. She was a thin, pretty blonde with a star tattoo on her hip who was undoubtedly a sociology major at UNLV. She touched his arm, and he looked up from the work email he'd been reading on his phone, but when his eyes met hers, she could see he was not meat, and she excused herself with a nod, receding into the shadowy red neon fog.

Ironically, Marlowe McCoy never made it to San Diego to learn the truth of Cody's story, but he did stop in Las Vegas to feed some of his appetites for gambling, women, cocaine, and whiskey. He made a stop in at *Club Sin* on the way to California.

Marlowe McCoy tipped the bouncers at the door a hundred each and walked through the double doors like he owned *Club Sin*, or had at least cornered the market on what it had to sell. He wore his black jungle boots, dark blue jeans, a Dead Can Dance t-shirt and leather jacket. His hair was long and black and fell in oily waves something like a young Elvis around 3am. Marlowe McCoy sauntered over to the bar, his pinprick red cocaine eyes rolling from the lionesses to the show onstage, and sat down at the bar next to a man that (less addled, less drunk, less distracted, less lusty, perhaps) he would have immediately taken for a cop.

"Double Jack Daniels Number 49 neat, no back, brother, and keep 'em comin'," said Marlowe. The bartender poured him a double, and Marlowe put a fifty on the bar and swiveled in the chair to watch the stage.

"Not bad, eh?" he said to Lowell, tapping his arm and nodding to the newest girl onstage, a petite young Asian in naughty schoolgirl chic and latex thigh-highs.

Lowell looked up from his phone to the stage, nodded, grunted, and got a look at Marlowe for the first time. Flags went up in his mind at the exact moment that "Cinnamon" swayed up to the bar, tapped Lowell on the shoulder and eyed the other man at the bar. Isabel recognized Marlowe, Marlowe recognized Isabel, and Lowell recognized the improbable turn of events in the same instant.

"I heard you were in California, Is. Nice to see you," said Marlowe.

To her credit, Isabel betrayed none of the fear unfolding like a spider in her throat. Lowell (trying to play as if he hadn't just had an adrenaline spike) was impressed at the cool water in her veins when she said, with perfect equanimity and poise, "Marlowe. I was hoping you'd come see me when they let you out."

Marlowe McCoy just looked at her.

When he said nothing, she said, "Maybe we can pick up where we left off? This town is your kind of place, baby."

"You testified against me, Is. You cheated on me with Cody and worked behind my back to get me thrown in slam for things you *asked me to do*. Five years. How many other men have you ruined since then?"

She began to back away, her face a mask. Her voice was level when she said to the bartender, never taking her eyes from Marlowe, "Daren, call the cops."

Marlowe shook his head, "I actually loved you, Is."

Then Marlowe McCoy reached for the pistol on his hip, and Detective Lowell put his gun to Marlowe's temple.

"Hands up. LVPD," said Lowell. "Don't even *think* about that piece or I'll burn you down."

Marlowe put his hands up slowly, his eyes sliding over slowly to Lowell. Even coked up and drunk, he knew his brains would be on the bar before his hands reached halfway to Lowell's gun. He cracked a wry smile and said, "Of all the fucking luck."

Sunday, 18 June, 2017

It took some time to work out who would prosecute whether it would be the various states where McCoy had committed multiple felonies ranging from grand theft auto to murder, or the federal government. In the end it did not matter.

One dark night, the screws rolled him out of bed and out-processed him from the Cooke County jail and put him in a transport van, shackled hand and foot. A silent driver in dark fatigues and no identifying badge, insignia, or nametag drove north to an industrial complex. He went through a gate, into a dark warehouse and down a long tunnel.

When the van doors opened, two burly men in black battle gear took him out. There was, confusingly, a subway train waiting there beside the van in the semi-dark of what seemed an enormous tunnel or crude station. Two other men covered him, one with some kind of air gun fitted for tranqs, and the other with an MP-5 submachine gun. They didn't look like cops.

"What the hell is this place?" he asked. They did not answer.

The men searched him carefully, stripped him naked using scissors to strip off his thin orange jumpsuit and wash-grayed underwear on the cold concrete floor. They did a cavity check, had him open his mouth, and then laid him out and strapped him down tightly onto a gurney.

"I guess you boys aren't much for conversation, but—mph!"

One of them snatched his mouth with rough hands and shoved in a gag, then duct taped his lips shut.

Marlowe started to panic, but then he felt a sharp pain in his neck, and the world got fuzzy. The lights started to dim and dance, tracers streamed across his vision, and he knew no more.

When he awoke, he was still on the gurney but in a white room, and a man in a white biohazard suit was standing over him.

"Good. You're awake. We must talk, Mister McCoy. I am Doctor Lannon, the Site Director here. And you, sir, are Test Subject One."

CHAPTER 18:
THE DARK WORLD

Elsewhere.
Outside of time.

t the end of the rope, Lela and Aria fell, and kept falling. They landed on a mound of skulls that crunched and splintered beneath them. They rode a wave of broken skulls to the floor of the cave and lay winded for a long moment.

"You okay?" Lela finally asked.

"Never...mmmph...better," Aria said, once again in a woman's skin. "Not that I don't like having my fall cushioned by a skull pyramid, but why are we here?"

"This doesn't make sense," said Lela. "He disposed of the bodies at the diner. He didn't bring skulls here. And... this doesn't look like the mine anymore. Look down there."

There in the distance they could make out a faint light coming from a tunnel that looked as if it was lined and supported with large, ancient bones, most of them too big to be the bones of men.

"Did. Did Nob just send us down the rabbit hole? *Seriously, Nob?*" Aria's voice bounced and echoed down the long corridors of darkness, across a million runnels of bleached bones in black shadow. The enormity of her echo quieted her outrage and replaced it with fear.

Lela just glared at her until the echoes died away, then hissed "Be. Quiet."

They slipped and stumbled away from the skull avalanche their fall had brought down in a wave of bone chips and broken smiles. They moved toward the thin, flat light. The corridor seemed to narrow. The architecture of bone grew ever more intricate, but sometimes a space would open in the walls for a passage, or a grating of knitted femurs something like a cell or a cage.

Cold air like the breath of some sinister demon frozen in Cocytus blasted through some of these holes, moaning and jangling fingerbone windchimes, as the walls got closer, and closer, and closer. Lela and Aria were now hunched, crawling toward the light. They reached a door small enough for a child to enter. It was cracked open just enough to let pale rays of gloomy light spill out into the catacombs.

Aria was ahead of Lela. She pushed the door open and stepped out to meet whatever waited there.

It was a high, fire-charred hill under the biggest, brightest moon they had ever seen. In every direction, as far as they could see (and under that moon, they could see much) was a labyrinth made of smooth black basalt.

Lela and Aria turned, together, like children playing "Ring-Around-the-Rosy," a full 360 degrees. They saw a hundred openings into the maze, like the toothless mouths of oblivion, and all began at the base of the hill. From what they could make out, the tunnels, archways, corridors, and long cobblestone pathways went crazily up, down, hither, thither, and yon in ways that not only defied navigation, but also occasionally what seemed physically possible (there was, in the distance, a stairway that twisted like a double-helix a full 720 degrees, turning back on itself like a madman's dream, running over and under a tower in the air, suspended in the night without walls).

Great statues of beasts, gargoyles and wolves made of stone and iron and bronze stood before each of the openings to the labyrinth, and behind them was a door without a structure around it, small enough for a child, closing with a snap and fading into nothingness.

Lela looked at the space where the door had been and set her jaw, trying to slow the hammering terror in her heart.

"What is this place?" asked Aria.

"A dark place," said Lela.

"Why would Nob bring us here?"

"Because this is where the answers are," said Nob from behind them.

They both started and turned to see him towering above them, a wraith dressed in shadows and black feathers with hollow eyes that wept darkness.

"Nob? A-are you a ghost?" asked Aria.

Nob turned his head as a bird might, sharply, "I am a servant of Crow."

"And...why are we here?" asked Lela.

"You set off to find out where it began. How it is you came to be Cursed, and what it meant to slip your skin and become a wolf under the moon. This is the place where all secrets come. This is the place where all darkness hides in deeper darkness. This is where you may draw the Leviathan from the Deep and know the Names of the Unborn, and this is where your dark father waits for you, and your bright father as well. I have brought you to what you seek, if you would truly seek it."

"I don't know what most of that means," said Aria. "I just want things to go back to how they were before I met Billy. Before...before all this."

"Back? Go back? You can only go forward, Aria Wolfsdottir. You can only go forward to meet your Death, or run, if you can, and let Death find you out just the same for all your efforts. There is no back. There is birth and a grave."

"Which way do we go, then?" asked Lela, looking down from the hill.

"I cannot guide you to your fate. I do not know your path. I can only bring you through the door. It is not given to me to do more. I am not Virgil to bring you through the Inferno. I am a crow above the battlefield."

Nob crooked a clawed finger at them both and said, in a dry rasp, "Choose."

He pulsed then, shadows coiling into new shapes, and a hundred crows flapped screeching into the sky and disappeared.

They looked at each other, then at the labyrinth around them.

"There's a way out of here," said Lela.

"Maybe," said Aria.

"There is," Lela said. "We just need to think about this. Maybe each of the guardians down below is a clue. We can think about what we're after and see if any of them can offer us some kind of hint."

"You're thinking about this rationally, but I don't think this is a rational world," said Aria, starting down the hill. Lela followed, looking concerned.

"So, what are you thinking?" asked Lela.

"I think we just choose at random. Like he said, Death will find us, or it won't."

They walked up to one of the openings, a jagged piece of work with a leering azure jackal laid across the path. Aria looked left, then right, then at the jackal, and moved to the smooth opening with a jade owl atop it, looking down with a curious, pensive expression.

"So, maybe not entirely at random…" said Aria. She stepped into the labyrinth, and Lela followed.

CHAPTER 19:

ON THE SORROWS OF FRANK CROW

"**F**rank?" The voice was distant, but it wouldn't go away. "Frank? Hey, Frank?"

"Mmpf?"

"Wake up."

He opened one eye. He was reclining. Warmer than he had been, if not warm. Strapped down.

Blanket over him.

A cot? No. A table. Something sturdy in case he thrashed. He tried to focus and found himself looking at the one called Gregory.

The room was bare, without windows. Fluorescent lights. A sterile room with high green tiles up to the ceiling. Thin, grated vents.

An operating room? It chilled his blood, suddenly.

"Little bit brisk earlier," said Frank, trying to wiggle each finger and toe to discover if they were still there. They seemed to be, but he couldn't help worrying about phantom limbs. Frostbite. Hopefully they hadn't made him a eunuch.

"Frank, let me help you get out of this situation," said Gregory. "I need to tell my bosses something. Well, a few things. The first thing is that you're cooperating with us to help us stop any threats to human life. The second thing is that you're not going to do something silly like talk about us or anything you've seen or think you've seen. And the third thing, and this is optional, but I really hope you'll consider it, is that you'll join us in trying to find Lela and bring her in alive."

"Alive?" asked Frank. "Sure. Pull the other one."

"No, I mean it. We want her alive."

"Is that usual for people in your line?" asked Frank, playing it much cooler than the dull ache in his gut would suggest.

"No," said Gregory. "Very unusual. But orders are orders. They were very clear that she and Aria should come in alive and as unharmed as possible. I know you want that, too."

"I don't want them to come in at all if it means being in your power. Yours or anyone's."

"Well, Frank, the facts of life are these: we are an organization that kills monsters and protects human beings. Your wife has become a monster, and so has Aria. They have already killed people, and given time, they will kill more. That's a statistical certainty. We are in the business of making sure monsters don't hurt civilians, and we take that responsibility very seriously.

"You are a man who can help us end bloodshed, or you are a man who will have blood on his hands because he chose to protect monsters. Now, I want to help you, and I want you to help me, but if we can't come to some arrangement, I will find your wife and her friend, and I will not hesitate to put a bullet in her head and burn her to ashes, orders or no orders. Or you can help me. She lives. You live. We all live and figure out next steps then."

"But you've got me strapped down because you already know what I'm going to say," said Frank.

"I assume there will be some profanity. You'll bluster. You'll threaten. You'll rage. And afterward, you'll see my way is the only way."

"Go fuck yourself."

"I'll leave you with your thoughts, then, Mr. Crow."

Frank's thoughts took him to his wife's face, the way it had become a wolf's face the first full moon after she'd been infected. That beautiful face had become something monstrous. Empty of love.

Animal.

Furious.

And hungry. Ravenously hungry.

Frank had never said so, or thought so, but others he knew had called him a hard man. A man who made it through four years in the Marine Corps. A man who had done nearly twenty years as a cop. A man who was familiar with, even comfortable with a certain degree of violence and tragedy as a matter of professional course and personal understanding.

But his wife's face that first night of the change, when he saw her down in the basement convulsing, heard her bones breaking, sinews snapping and realigning, saw her spine curl and crumple and lengthen like a serpent roiling under the skin (skin he had loved, kissed, and touched…now monstrous) had nearly broken him. For the first time in his adult life, he had gone upstairs and stared at his .45 and seriously considered killing them both.

He had thought then of his first real date with Lela. His violence had always bothered her, and she had seen it early, but she had not fled.

They had gone to a nice seafood place in Ann Arbor called the Gandy Dancer that Friday night after they'd first met. It was no mean feat that he'd been able to get away from work on a Friday night, but he'd managed it.

Frank figured he would have a beer with dinner, and maybe they'd go someplace afterward for a drink. Because he would be drinking, he had opted not to bring a weapon. Besides, Ann Arbor was a long way from his beat in Chicago.

Their conversation had been pleasant. She'd never dated a cop, and so had all the usual questions. Had he used his weapon in the line of duty? He had. Was he ever afraid? Sometimes. Did he want to do it for life? He did. Would he take a desk job with some rank, or did he want to be on the street? Under no circumstances did he want to report to a desk as a default mode.

The drift of her questions had the whiff of, if not disapproval, then at least concern about loving a man who might not come home one day. He could sympathize. Frank had dated a few girls since he got out of the Marine Corps, and more than a few while he was in, but never anyone like Lela.

She was smart in ways Frank had never known anyone to be smart. She had ideas and questions and opinions and insights to things that made him feel like lights were switching on in his brain, illuminating rooms he had not guessed at in himself. They talked through dinner, then talked through drinks in a back booth at an intimate bar downtown.

But then, (of course) something happened. Someone loud and very angry came into the bar and yanked a girl off her stool, called her names. He wasn't drunk; he was high. High on something that had him amped.

The amped fellow, Frank would later learn, was named Joseph M-for-Martin Tucker. He was twenty-five, and he was high on PCP, and he was *very* unhappy with the girl at the bar, whose name was Angel St. John. Angel, apparently, resembled a girl named Staci (states away, and wisely so) who had left him. Joseph M. Tucker was well and truly convinced Angel *wasn't* Angel, but really Staci, and he decided to choke the lying out of her.

The bartender and several bystanders tried to intervene. One guy broke a heavy oak chair over Joseph Tucker's broad back, but he just kept right on choking the life out of Angel St. John. Men tried to pull him off of her, but all they managed to do was make him mad, and maybe drag them both around the floor, but no good came of it. He wouldn't let her go. She was nearly unconscious when Frank got up, pointed to the payphone outside the restrooms, and told Lela to call the police.

"What are you going to do?"

"Just call 911, and tell them to get here."

Frank walked up, "Hey, partner. I said '*Hey, partner!*'"

Joe looked up, somewhat uncomprehending.

"Let her go," said Frank, moving in a bit closer.

Instead, Joseph Tucker, high on PCP and out of his mind, clenched every muscle, bared down, and gritted his teeth until the veins popped in his neck. Frank took that for a no, and Angel was turning purple, her eyes fairly popping out of their sockets as she gasped and clawed for air.

So, Frank swept in and swiveled his elbow into Joseph M. Tucker's face as hard as he could, with all the might and weight he had to throw. It was a start. After about three of those, when Frank couldn't feel his arm anymore and his shoulder was screaming, an unconscious Joseph Tucker let Angel St. John go and fell into the arms of the men who had been trying to pry him from the gasping woman's neck. They dragged him out of the bar, leaving a trail of thick red blood like a line of smudged paint on the barroom floor.

The barman was trying to restore order. Two women who had been with her were tending to Angel. Her eyes had gone glassy, but she was breathing (raggedly—she was near to a crushed larynx, it turned out). Three of the men who had dragged Joseph Tucker outside were laying into him with boots, dragging him to the curb to crush his skull.

Frank stepped out with a full throated command voice imparted by osmosis at Parris Island and bird-dogged them back into the bar with a voice like the Wrath of God and a blood-spattered suit. It hadn't come to blows, but Frank was evidently terrifying. He knew just how terrifying when he looked up and saw the horror on Lela's face as she stood in the doorway of the bar in total incomprehension of his capacity for violence of action.

And that first night of her Change, the night the Curse took hold, when he could hear the monsters growling and scratching in the basement of their home, Frank had wondered if that violence of action inside him would be the end of her, of both of them, after all.

He decided against it. He put the weapon away. No. There were limits. This was his limit.

He would do no harm (could do no harm) to the woman he had loved since that night in Ann Arbor. In that moment, she had looked at him with a face that said, with dawning horror, that *he* was a monster. She had stayed anyway.

CHAPTER 20:
STORM CROWS AND NIGHT WOLVES

Danalov had never been squeamish, but Site Bravo began to worry him very early on. The train began bringing test subjects. Drugged. Strapped down. The holding cells and the lab rooms started to fill up with convicts whose identities had been erased.

These subjects were mostly from military prisons, but some were just bad eggs whose cases had "slipped through." Some had "died in custody." There was someone powerful pulling strings to feed these scientists their "volunteer" guinea pigs. It didn't sit right with Danalov.

His life was about protecting humans from the inhuman, the innocent from the profane, or, barring that, the potentially saved from the certainly damned. The *Gladius Dei* didn't hold with killing humans unless and until it was absolutely unavoidable. Danalov sat in a chair in the rounded hall of the Security Control Center and watched this beehive, this clockwork of men and machines and frightening experiments through a dozen monitors, and the more it buzzed the more he began to wonder if this was what "necessary" looked like.

They had put Danalov and his team up in fairly comfortable accommodations; it felt less like a barracks and more like a series of interconnected suites at some executive-level hotel. Every access point was biometric. The automated scanners checked retinal and facial recognition data as well as voice recognition and fingerprinting, but it all happened so smoothly that Danalov and his people could get where they needed to go with barely a pause.

Nevertheless, Danalov and his team were observers, and their movements were restricted. Some doors would not open for them. Some camera feeds were blacked out, and he *really* didn't like that.

They were here as part of an agreement someone high up in the *Gladius Dei* had made with whoever had put this party together. Someone powerful, monied, and political, Danalov knew, but who? And they were to make sure anyone infected with the Diana Strain was put down and that the Curse did not spread beyond the labs. If they couldn't go everywhere, see everything, ask any question at any time, then their mission was a show.

Sitting in the high-backed leather chair, watching the monitors and musing on this dangerous, impossible, precarious mission he'd been given and the lives he'd been put in charge of, Danalov shook his head in disgust. He cursed in Russian then stood and began to pace in the illuminated blue light of the monitors. He thought again of home.

Cassius Danalov had been born in a village near Pokrov in 1985. After his parents died in a car crash, he'd had been raised and educated in Moscow by his father's father. Danalov's grandfather was named Pyotr Vulkovich Danalov, and he was a Professor of Russian Literature at the University.

Danalov grew up. After he'd done a hitch in the Russian Army from 2002-2004, he had been recruited by the *Gladius Dei*. His recruitment had everything to do with a particular night in the summer of 2003 when his platoon had encountered something strange on patrol in the frigid darkness of Siberia during a training op.

Danalov and two of his mates had survived. The rest were taken by something. A creature made of maniacal, sweating darkness with eyes of smoldering witch fire. A monster that left only bloodless corpses in its wake. The three of them had survived by crossing a river, starting a high, hot fire, and one of the men he was with sang prayers until dawn.

The inquest was officially sealed, and it took the administration less than a year to decide to drum them out of service for ...well, no one could say exactly what. Nevertheless, it was highly embarrassing to have a platoon-sized element inextricably massacred during a training operation in a remote area of the mother country

"And what isn't remote in Russia?" Danalov wondered.

It was more embarrassing that the story they had to tell was so full of superstition and drivel. One of the privates, Sergei Petrov, swore it was Baba Yaga, the old witch of Russia herself. Danalov was less certain then, but he didn't especially want to know, either. He wanted to put it behind him, and yet he found himself drowning his dreams in vodka night after night in his late grandfather's sprawling house in Moscow.

That was when the knock came.

A Russian priest named Lobichenko from Church of St. Louis of the French came to the door one morning while Danalov was nursing a mid-sized hangover, but he brought a man who was not a Russian, although he spoke the language passingly well. He introduced himself as Father Giovanni Santa Ana, an Italian from the Church of Rome, and a representative of a Holy Order called the *Gladius Dei*.

Danalov waved them into the parlor, which he had to admit was in a state of considerable disarray. Grandfather Danalov would not have approved, fastidious man that he was.

Mounds of cigarette butts threatened to overflow the ashtrays. A dozen open books sat on their faces here and there about the room. A riot of empty vodka bottles littered the floor, and the cats (seven at that time) had used the curtains for scratching posts and the rugs for toilets.

When they sat down, Lobichenko excused himself to use the restroom, but looking back this was a pretext. Father Giovanni had been direct.

"You are not mad," he had said. "I can see that what happened to you and your comrades is destroying you.

I can help. My Order can help you fight monsters. The ones out there, and the ones inside."

Danalov was incredulous. "How could you know? These matters are sealed. I am forbidden to—"

"It suffices that I know, my friend. I see and believe you were set upon by an evil being bent on harm, and hate, and feeding on the blood of the living. I understand one of your group sang songs of prayer until first light. This undoubtedly saved your life. Such creatures are repelled by acts of true faith and devotion to Our Lord."

"And this is how you fight them? Singing prayers?" asked Danalov.

"Some take that approach. I prefer flames, bullets, and white phosphorous grenades myself, but we all pray in our own way."

"And you want me to join you? I'm not Catholic. I don't even know if I believe in a God, much less your God."

"Many of the people who encounter the supernatural are not believers at the time of the encounter," said Father Giovanni, nodding. "But if you think it through, then the only choice that doesn't drive you mad is that there is a Goodness stronger than the Evil you met. A Great Goodness, whose Power can destroy the darkness. If we believe this, the rest follows. If not, you'll collapse in on yourself by vodka and rot and despair. This is a chance at a life of purpose and a death with honor. Fighting for the *Gladius Dei*, the "Sword of God," is a chance to rewrite the story that plays over and over in your darkest dreams, Cassius. Think about it, eh?"

Danalov nodded dully, and when the other priest came back from the restroom he made mild conversation for a few minutes, offered them tea or coffee (which they declined), and showed them out when it was polite.

It had not been a decision he entered into lightly.

It began when, slowly, Danalov started to empty the ashtrays and throw the bottles away. He had the rugs steam-cleaned, scrubbed the floors, changed out the cat box, put the books back on their shelves, and replaced the curtains. He aired the place out, did laundry, bathed, shaved, brushed his teeth, and poured the last of the vodka down the drain. He started running again, and working out down at the boxing gym on the corner, and, in about a month, he made his way to the Church of St. Louis of the French, found Father Lobichenko who had visited his home, and asked him to send word to Father Giovanni that he was ready to begin.

They had sent a car around to fetch him a week later with a fresh-faced young man for a driver. Danalov had half-expected Father Giovanni, but the young man said he was in South America somewhere. They had taken Danalov by an empty, but very fast private plane to Heathrow. Then by car with smoke-dark tinted windows to a place the Order called "The School." It was the third chapterhouse in order of rank and importance to the Order, after the Library in Barcelona and the Mother House in the Vatican.

The London schoolhouse was to be his home for a year while he trained in the basic skills, arts, Sciences, religious instruction, and lore of the *Gladius Dei*. His instructors were veterans of the war with Darkness, and they were harder and crueler than had been his sergeants in the Russian Army. He trained in armed combat using sword, knife, club, and improvised or makeshift weapons.

Danalov trained in firearms, shotgun, rifle, pistol, sharpening the skills his Army time had already given him. He trained in striking and ground-level arts: Brazilian Jiu-Jitsu, Krav Maga, Boxing, and military combatives. They taught him covert tradecraft: how to encode messages, how to know you're being followed, how to elicit information, how to bug a phone, how to lose a tail, how to pick a lock. They took him to Scotland for training in survival, evasion, resistance, and escape—also known as POW school. Then, after a year at the schoolhouse, it was time to pick a specialty.

There were two paths, for a start. The path of the Crusader, and the path of the Exorcist. The Crusaders were direct action elements comprised of cells that specialized in different areas of the Hunt. There were shooters who acted as infantry, door-kickers, body-snatchers, snipers, and assassins. Then there were the Comms/Tech specialists who ensured the team was in communication with the higher command and with each other, and who could operate as a hacker or general technical specialist for the group in the area of technology.

Each team also had a Medic, who was usually an ER doctor. There was the Intel officer, who operated as cat burglar, pickpocket, sneak thief, and the information clearinghouse for the group regarding any and every detail that might be relevant to a mission, region, or obstacle. Intel officers could be a more subtle kind of assassin, and often developed assets and informants in strategically important positions for the *Gladius Dei.*

Finally, someone could take the support specialization and ensure the team always had weapons, ammo, transportation, and whatever other equipment they needed to get a job done without ever leading back to the Church, either by electronic or paper trail. A good Support Officer was a ghost in the system who got everything and anything quickly and who could dispose of things as big as tractor-trailers or as delicate as bodies when a job was over, as if they had turned to smoke.

The Exorcists were diplomats, scholars, archivists, reliquarians, librarians, and (sometimes, very occasionally) visionaries gifted with Sight. This last, the matter of Sight, was rare and highly controversial, but no one could argue with the results.

Danalov had chosen to be a shooter. He had the aptitude, had excelled at combat training, and was temperamentally suited to the role. He had no compunctions about killing in the name of a just cause, and he enjoyed concussive forces in a quiet way: focus and concentration and a healthy boom could solve many problems, in his view.

After he chose his specialization and graduated from "the School," Danalov had taken his vows and become a priest of the Roman Catholic Church. Even so, his relationship to the religion was what he called, often with a wry smile, *complicated.* Father Giovanni had been right as far as it went. Belief in God was a candle in the darkness now that he knew of what stalked the night, but he didn't believe that the Pope was the infallible Vicar of Christ on Earth. He had trouble with the idea of the Virgin Mary as divinely conceived herself. He also wasn't entirely convinced that every book they had thrown out at Nicaea was apocryphal, nor that every one they had included was complete and unadorned.

He had doubts, but he kept them to himself. They were irrelevant to the job of stopping monsters from killing men, corrupting women, and devouring children.

Now he watched on the blue monitors of the Site Bravo control room as they injected a screaming man who was strapped to a table with a green solution. He began to foam and the mouth, his jaw distended, and his screams took on something inhuman and he writhed and twitched on the table, his muscles bulging into distended shapes, his yellowing eyes rolling madly in his head as his lengthening jaws champed together. The man's body grew in mass before the eyes of the scientists, but the restraints held. Danalov watched, horrorstruck, and asked himself again if this was in any way right.

Why had the *Gladius Dei* agreed to provide Billy Hatfield's body and allow for these experiments? Why had it trusted these scientists with secrets it had held for over five hundred years? Danalov had no answer. He lit a cigarette and watched the violet smoke curl into the darkness.

Shooter school had been a very heightened six months of combat training. The focus was on speed of foot and mind, smoothness of hand and action, controlled violence, and extreme levels of physical and mental conditioning. The campus had been a compound outside of Bozeman, Montana toward Saddle Peak in the mountains. It was a hard place, and they began every day well before dawn running up the mountain to do combat drills at high elevation in freezing conditions. The cadre of seasoned shooters rotated out from the field every six months to teach recruits.

They invariably tried to simulate injury and panic during those frigid mornings, in order to teach the Novices how to fight beyond fear or pain, or the animal brain of panic. The drills varied, but generally involved some kind of physical matchup on bad ground in cold and darkness. Sometimes groups would square off against groups, and sometimes a team would try to take a Novice from behind at an invisible sign from the Instructors. After those drills, they came down for breakfast in the mess tent, then it was range time.

They got acquainted and comfortable with nearly every weapon on the market in the last fifty years on that long, flat expanse of dirt. Afterward was lunch, then calisthenics and weight training, then the Kill House drills practicing dynamic entry, clearing and sweeping in teams (and alone, God forbid) until well after dark. They got a final meal, washed, and were in bed by ten where they slept like men dead.

There were, occasionally, female shooters. The physical rigors of the program tended to wash them out, but sometimes it would happen that a woman would rise to prominence as a great shooter. They were housed in a separate tent on the far end of the compound and afforded a different bathroom, but otherwise, the *Gladius Dei* was too short on personnel to deny anyone who wanted to serve and could hack the work a place. They would take anyone who could do the job, whatever sexual politics might be at play in the larger Church.

Danalov had excelled at shooter school, but had broken no records.

All of them, *all of them*, were held by one Father Giovanni de Santa Ana. He had the record for longest stalk, longest shot on point, fastest entry with three or more aggressors, and fastest solo sweep with no aggressors missed or surviving. In any other category worth bothering about, Father Giovanni was the first, last, and only name to beat. It awed Danalov that Father Giovanni had been his recruiter, and so, it was of moment when Father Giovanni turned up one day to provide a block of instruction on what it was like "out there."

"The world," he had told the recruits, "is a place of sorrow and illusion. The only way to respond, as a Hunter, is to disbelieve. Even when you're sure the monster you've shot is alone, assume it is not alone, and assume you have missed. Whatever your caution, double it, and when there is clarity, when there is *no doubt*, assume it is a trap, double back and wait to see. The *Gladius Dei* are too few, our enemies are too many, and the world is too full of darkness. "

"The moment you think you have won is the moment you have lost. I know each of you is ready, is *eager* to stride forth and vanquish the enemies of God. But the truth is, you're best served by striking from the shadows and returning to them for another strike. For this is not a battle nor a war but a campaign that will last millennia between the Light and the Darkness. And while the Light will always be greater, the Darkness is persistent, plentiful, and full of hate."

Danalov had taken much from that lecture. Now he stared at the blue monitors and wondered what Father Giovanni would have made of these experiments, this facility, and what they were working toward here. Billy Hatfield had been Giovanni's kill (as so many had). Now Hatfield's infection was bringing more infection from beyond the grave.

On the monitor, the misshapen creature was recognizable no longer as a man nor as a werewolf. It was some kind of unstable, shifting hybrid of both, screamed and howled in mute fury on the blue monitor.

It shivered and continued to convulse, its chest expanding, shoulders rolling into denser and denser slabs of meat and muscle, hair and bone. He widened, deepened, thickened, and finally he popped two of the straps that held him down at the buckle and ripped his way free of the steel table with startling ferocity.

Danalov cursed in Russian and entered a code into the monitor to lock down the lab and the wing where the creature was. An alarm blared as steel reinforced walls rolled down all over the Site Bravo, emergency lighting engaged, and an automated voice boomed. It directed staff to shelter in place and remain calm, shelter in place and remain calm, shelter in place and remain—on the monitors, the werewolf hybrid was ripping a scientist's throat out with his teeth while others lay dead or screamed and clawed fruitlessly at the locked doors.

Danalov spoke into his radio, "Security team One, this is Security Control, we have a breach in Laboratory 103. Initiating protocol alpha. Please advise when you are in range. Security team Two, you're the reserve unit, standby."

Cooke's voice came over the channel, "Roger Control, team One moving to Lab 103, eta two minutes."

Lorca's voice came over immediately afterward, "Roger Control, team Two is the reserve element. Standing by."

Danalov watched team One's progress over the cameras as they hustled downstairs and across the long hallway to the lab. They were in full battle gear with weapons at the ready. He raised and lowered the barriers with a few keystrokes as they passed.

There were six of them on team One, Cooke and Markovski, his two *Gladius Dei* shooters, and four Pro-Gen contractors out of Blackwater, one a former Delta Force Operator, one from the SEAL teams, and the other two good old-fashioned Infantry. Lorca and Daniels were on team Two along with a handful of ProGen contractors cut from the same cloth. They were all good, but Danalov had insisted *Gladius Dei* personnel had the command, not the ProGen guys. Lannon hadn't been happy about it, but in the name of working together, he had grudgingly acquiesced.

Now Danalov sat with ice in his veins, watching Lab 103 as it became an abattoir. The hybrid creature had grown to twelve feet in height, maybe it was eight feet wide at the shoulder, with bone-growths like bloody yellow blades poking through at the elbows. It had killed all five scientists inside and was feeding on them feverishly. It had two rows of crisscrossed, mismatched fangs that nevertheless seemed very effective at ripping flesh and crushing bone.

Doctor Lannon came pounding into the Control room just as the Security team got to the door of Lab 103.

"Which lab?" he asked breathlessly.

Danalov pointed to the monitor, "103."

"Subject Four," said Lannon. "What happened?"

"One moment, sir," said Danalov. "Security team One, this is Security Control, be advised all personnel in Lab 103 are gone. One subject, infected and in Transformation. I am initiating protocol alpha. Maintain a perimeter."

"Roger."

Danalov watched as team One fanned out, weapons trained on the door, and waited.

Lannon was in his ear, "What *happened*, Sergeant Danalov?"

"The subject ripped his way free of the restraints and killed your staff, Doctor," said Danalov. "I'll put this in a report, but first we need to deal with him."

He tapped the monitor where the creature was muzzle-deep in a blonde scientist's chest cavity (disconnected entirely from the lower trunk of the body, spinal cord hanging limp on crushed vertebrae).

He keyed instructions into the computer, and watched. Very quickly the air was being sucked from the room and sent down an incineration shaft where it would be sterilized of any lingering microbes. The creature began to gag, then started to claw its throat savagely as its eyes bulged and its tongue lolled. It ran, stumbled, ran again toward the door, and rammed it full force, denting the steel. It slammed into the door twice more, then stumbled, fell, and went still before the ruined titanium doorway that had bowed considerably, but had not broken enough to admit air.

Danalov and Lannon watched that little blue monitor in silence, staring at the horror and desolation of Laboratory 103.

Five minutes went by.

Then ten.

Nothing moved. The hybrid's last stirring of breath had been 20 minutes ago.

Only the klaxons blared, and the calm automated voice spoke in measured tones, "Shelter in place and remain calm, shelter in place and remain calm, shelter in place and—" Danalov decided enough time had passed.

"Team One, this is Control. You are authorized to breach the door and sanitize the area."

"Roger. Breaching."

Cooke gestured at a ProGen contractor. The man went to the door quickly, placed a small circle on the door, stood back and within a few seconds it popped inward like a balloon, all but disintegrating as it exploded. In less than a second, the team was in the room. Cooke put two silver slugs in the creature's head and two in its massive chest, then held it as the rest of the team swept the room, more out of professionalism and standard operating procedure than out of any hope for survivors or additional infected. A ProGen man checked the hybrid's vitals and nodded to Cooke

"Room is clear, Control," came Cooke's voice. "Seven dead, plus the Test Subject. Big mess here."

"Roger," said Danalov. "Hold in place, and stand by for further."

Lannon broke in, "We'll get a cleanup crew in there, take samples. You notice it didn't shift back to human the way Hatfield did when it died? And that strength? We knew these things were strong, but those straps could hold a rampaging gorilla! Stress tests indicated nothing short of an elephant could break out. We're really onto something here." He was breathless, all but panting.

Danalov eyed him coldly. "What do you want done with your colleagues, doctor?"

He caught Danalov's eye and said, "They knew what they were signing up for, Sergeant Danalov."

"Oh, yes?" said Danalov. "Well, that makes it all right then."

"It's not a question of all right or not all right. It's a question of scientific discovery unparalleled since the discovery of DNA. We stand on the precipice of—"

"Doctor." Danalov stood, his eyes as cold as his voice. You have no idea what you are meddling with, and if you're *very lucky*, you never will. Now, if you'll excuse me, I have to debrief my men and write a report."

CHAPTER 21:

DECISIONS AND REVISIONS

Joseph arrived at the warehouse where they'd been keeping Frank Crow late that stormy night. He hurried, rain-soaked, through the door when the sentry, Anatole, buzzed him in. Joseph shuffled quickly down the stairway to a break room. There, he saw Gregory staring through the window at the warehouse floor where Frank Crow sat bound and blindfolded fifty feet away, on the other side of the breakroom window.

There was a book in Gregory's hands and a big bowl of candied peanuts on the table beside him along with a near-empty bottle of ginger ale and a half-smoked cigar. His clothes were rumpled, and his face was wreathed in the shadow of the day's stubble.

Gregory nodded. "Good evening, Joseph, my friend. I was not expecting you."

"Gregory, yes, hello. We need to talk."

"So I gather." He spread his hands on the table and edged out a chair with his foot. Joseph sat.

"First, is Frank Crow going to come in and work with us?"

Gregory shook his head. "No.'

"Love," said Joseph wryly.

"It might be that he loves his wife that much. Maybe. Or he's just a very stubborn man," said Gregory. "Your version is more romantic. What's going on?"

"I don't think we need Frank, and I think we can let him go. I had a visitation of sorts at the chapter house. I read a very curious text, and now I think I know where they're going and why."

"A visitation? What do you mean?" asked Gregory.

"A spirit? A creature? *Something* came to me. It was in the library with me, down in the basement. I saw it over by my desk as I was trying to get out alive, then it was gone. And there was a book on my desk that wasn't there before. Whatever it was, it wanted me to know these things."

"And what did you learn?"

"We have called it the Diana Strain, but really it shouldn't be called that. We know it comes out of Norway around the 800s, A.D. I think we know the first bearer of this particular kind of Curse. Not all shapeshifting generally, mind you, or even all forms of lycanthropy, but *this* specific kind of lycanthropy. This specific line of the communicable physical and spiritual disease, which we call the Diana Strain can be traced back to a

Berserker named Rannulf the Red, who served the King of Norway at the time."

"Okay," said Gregory, glancing at Frank, who sat still and quiet. "So, this tells us where Aria Davis and Lela Crow are headed?"

"I think they're looking for the source. They want a cure. Rannulf the Red is the source, but there are links in the chain. They want origins. Guidance. Maybe to find others like themselves."

"So, they'll start with Lorne Hutchins. He is the last werewolf they knew of in the chain," said Gregory, leaning forward, then standing. "And then work backward."

"His old diner in Arizona isn't far from where they killed those state troopers," said Joseph. "This bears me out, I think."

"They're trying to get a clue as to who infected Hutchins?" asked Gregory. "So, next stop?"

"Hutchins, Nebraska, Lorne's hometown, the site of the first murders he committed in his career. So says Billy Hatfield's book *The Hutchins Murders*," said Joseph.

"Joseph, you're a genius."

"No. Someone or some*thing* wanted us to know this."

Gregory frowned at that, and his brow wrinkled as it did when he was trying to puzzle out an adversary.

"Generally it is unwise to trust spirits," said Gregory.

"I know. And the Church teaches as much. But do we ignore this clue? I think it's all we have to go on, unless you can break Frank and get him to talk, or win him to our side."

They both looked at Frank for a moment.

"So, we go. And bring Frank?" asked Gregory.

Joseph paused, considering.

"No, I think we let him go," said Joseph at last. "He's innocent of their curse. He shouldn't be made to betray his wife."

"That's not going to fly with the bosses. You know they don't like us to make enemies and then turn them loose."

"Do we work for them, or for the Lord?" asked Joseph.

"If you asked them, it's one and the same," said Gregory.

They looked at each other for a moment, neither wanting to say what he thought.

"I don't think we should just give him up. He's too valuable," said Gregory, scratching his chin.

"He's a man caught up in something. We've seen this before. What's his crime? Protecting his wife?"

"She's a monster. They're both monsters. Murderers. And they'll kill again until we stop them. You know that."

"Yes, but they are as tragic as he is. I understand doing what must be done, but where we can be circumspect, let's cut no closer to the bone than we must," said Joseph.

"I don't disagree, but—"

A chime broke in on them, and Gregory lifted his cell phone to his ear, "Yes? What? Yes, yes, of course, Your Excellency. Tonight? Yes. We will. I appreciate that. Of course, but wouldn't it be better if we maintained control of — No, I understand. Of course. No. I only mean to say that this is highly unusual, your Excellency and I — Yes. Yes. As you say. I understand. We will be there. Goodbye, Your Excellency."

His face reddened and he shoved the phone back in his pocket, then threw a handful of peanuts in his mouth and chewed angrily.

"What was that?" asked Joseph.

"Cardinal Frye has taken a special interest in the case. Our earlier conversation about releasing him is moot. The Marshall wants us to hand Frank off to some third party outfit called ProGen. No explanation as to why, but they're going to take him into custody and ship him God knows where."

"I'm not a field man, per se, but isn't this unusual?" asked Joseph.

"Which part? Direct phone calls from a Marshall to a lowly Crusader like me or handing off a normal human being to a mysterious group not obviously associated with the Church?"

"Either. Or both."

"Unheard of. Twice," said Gregory, plucking, lighting up, and puffing on his half-smoked cigar.

"When is the handoff?"

"Tonight. Near the old trestle bridge off Highway One."

"Are we...are we really doing this?" asked Joseph.

"Orders are orders," said Gregory.

"Yes, but—"

"You can call him back and explain about your compunctions, I guess," said Gregory, although his face was a mask of buttoned-down fury. The bosses were asking him to do things that the *Gladius Dei* simply did not do.

They both looked at Frank, shadowed and shackled in the chair, then at one another, and they did not say what was in their mouths to say, nor give voice to the doubts that had begun to flower in their deepest secret hearts.

"Orders," said Joseph after a time.

"Orders," said Gregory with a nod.

"I'll come along, shall I?"

"May as well," Gregory said.

CHAPTER 22:

THE WRAITHS OF FENRIS

The Dark Labyrinth
Outside of time.

The labyrinth was impossible, at least. The moment Lela and Aria entered, they lost the way they had come. Lela had been careful to keep her right side pointed to the right wall, but almost immediately the wall curved in around itself, circled a ruined wolf's head the size of a city bus, and ran in a crazy zigzag for a mile or more (distance was nearly impossible to measure, but she counted 6,000 steps and figured that was as good as a mile).

The walls were higher than they had seemed from the hill, and the moonlight slanted in perhaps only halfway down the slick, moss-covered walls roped over with the thin, dark tendrils of small, creeping vines. The ground itself was a hodgepodge of broken up cobbles, dirt, slate, and moldering red brick. It smelled of damp, mildew, and mushrooms, of earthy vegetation rotting in the dark.

Each turn looked like another for a time, then they were at a dead end.

Aria looked at Lela and said, "I feel like we're missing something here."

"What's that?" Lela turned her back on the high wall that had risen before them, trying to figure out where the wall would lead if they followed it around to the right.

"This place is a puzzle, right?"

"Yes."

"Okay. So. There's always a key. A way of looking at a puzzle that makes it easier to solve, right?" Aria asked.

"Yeah. It doesn't seem like the rules of physics apply. We've been following the right wall on our right, but it's not helping me map where we've been. I'm— are you disoriented?"

"Yeah."

"Me, too. There's something about this place that makes it—"

A deep, terrible howl of hunger and rage rose in the distance, grew louder and louder in their ears, and then slowly died away.

Aria's eyes widened. "What was that?" she whispered.

Lela had gone pale. "Something. The minotaur in the labyrinth, or whatever would be in a place like this..."

The howl rose again, closer than before, and other howls joined it. A hunting cry.

"Oh shit," said Aria, fear in the back of her throat.

"I've got something for them," said Lela, scowling.

She took off the clothes she had been wearing, folded them neatly and made a bag of them, then she called the Wolf, and began to slip her skin. Lela's body shivered, and began to grow longer, heavier, with muscles, hair, jaws, eyes, and then she stood before Aria, ten feet of wolf-woman, and threw back her head to howl in defiance.

"That's one way to handle it," Aria muttered under her breath as she stripped. "Pick the fight. Okay. Great. I'd just as soon have avoided the whole thing and slipped out the back door before they knew we were even here. But whatever. I guess we're doing this now. Don't even know what we're fighting or how many there are but let's just go ahead and—" So, naked in the moon-haunted shadows of the Labyrinth's high walls, Aria too began the Change.

The entire landscape, the entire *world* around them was different with the Wolf's eyes and ears and nose. The path was clear, as obvious as a river or a golden string; a ribbon of clean air pointed them back to the high hill, and fouler air that led them deeper into the Labyrinth.

The scents of other predators, their dens and the charnel stink of their hulking forms was as clear as a roadmap under the summer sun. The *things* (they weren't wolves, they weren't of the World, but they wore the garments of wolfishness around something like *Hunger Itself*) were coming with terrible speed, bearing down on them. Lela could distinctly make out at least five.

Lela and Aria bent double and went on all fours, racing around the corner to find a better place to make their stand. They raced down long corridors, through dark tunnels, through rises and drop-offs, leaped over pits of oblivion, and all the while with their Wolf's ears, Lela and Aria could hear the champing of monstrous jaws. They could hear great, powerful legs churning up the earth and stone behind them.

Finally, the wolf-women came to a stone bridge that ran over a dark, slow river perhaps a hundred feet across. The river was narrow; Lela and Aria had to go single file to cross, but as they approached the middle, *they* appeared on either end of the bridge. Two of them. Wraiths.

They were larger than the wolf-women, about twenty feet from nose to tail, but they were skeletal, emaciated, with holes of rot in their matted, bloody pelts. They reeked of death and blood. Their eyes burned with a baleful and luminous green fire. Their jaws were monstrous and cruel, with heavy-gauge black needles for teeth that dripped a sickly-green venom that sizzled as it pattered unevenly on the ground, and at each drop, noxious threads of smoke rose from the blackening stone.

Lela and Aria stood back to back in the center of the stone bridge and growled as one, low in their throats, ears flat, fangs bared, claws spread wide in a mirrored gesture that was reflected above and below by the moon-light on the slow black river below.

"Come with us," one of them said in a high, sharp voice, redolent with malice.

"Yes, come with us willingly," said the other, his voice bubbling, lower, deeper, unctuous and wet like the bottom of a putrid bog.

Aria barked, "Go to hell."

Lela howled again, defiant and furious and promising of death.

"Hell?" one of them laughed, a terrible sound. "This is Hell, little wolf. But you will go to the City of Bones, before Great Fenris, Eater-of-Worlds, and *wish* for the tender embrace of the Labyrinth before the end."

Lela had a split second to ask herself what she was doing, who or what she thought she was and what strange turns of fortune had brought her, a librarian from Middle America, to this. Then she was in the air, leaping for the wolf-wraith's throat. Aria was not as reflective; it was only fury that swept her like flames on a parched hillside. She slammed, roaring into the wolf-wraith that waited on the other side of the bridge. Lela expected flesh, but instead she found a choking vapor of black smoke. She passed through it and then pain exploded in her bowels. The *thing* had its claws deep in her belly. It leaned in and snapped its great jaws closed like a wolf-trap on top of her skull as she screamed in pain and fury, scratching at it in panic, but it was like trying to grapple the wind.

The thing was everywhere and nowhere, biting, scratching, ripping, breaking, and she was on the floor, mouth full of her own blood, coughing, breathless, sightless, ribs broken, entrails spilling out on the filthy cobblestones of the stone bridge. Aria, too, was down when Lela looked across the bridge. The wolf-wraith on the other side of the stone bridge sank its teeth into Aria's shoulder as Lela watched, and Aria's flesh immediately turned black and began to pulse with venom. Aria cried out, screamed wrenchingly, whimpered, and then went limp and silent.

Challenging them was a mistake, Lela thought, as if from a great distance. When she looked up at the green, glowing eyes of the wolf-wraith she had tried to kill, it looked down at her with mad amusement. It was growing dark. Blurry. Had it bitten her? Was she poisoned as Aria was? It was hard to think. Hard to move.

Lela's last thought before the world went black was of Frank. His face in the morning, beside her with the rising sun hitting the stubble of his chin, lighting it in reds and golds.

Love you. Pain. Then darkness.

CHAPTER 23:

ON HUNGER

W hat happened in Lab 103 was most unfortunate," said Dr. Lannon. "I'm the first to admit that.
We underestimated the power these creatures
might possess, but now let's discuss what we've learned."

The other scientists in the meeting nodded assent,
but Armand Weynman sat silent and motionless at the
head of the long conference table. Danalov stood unobtrusively in the shadows by the door.

Dr. Lannon continued. "Of our original ten subjects,
three have survived. Test Subjects One, Seven, and Nine.
Two males and a female. Subject One, a Mr. Marlowe
McCoy, (convicted murderer, arsonist, armed robber,
the list goes on) was given the unaltered strain more or
less directly from the original specimen. His reactions
have been typical of what our associates with the *Gladius
Dei* have indicated we could expect. This is as follows:
a creature that appears human, is highly, lethally allergic

to silver, heals at an accelerated rate far beyond anything documented in scientific history to date, has an incredibly high metabolism, something like an actual wolf or an Olympic athlete in training.

"It ages extremely slowly because of the regenerative powers it possesses on a cellular level. It is also tied to the moon and must shift into a 'wolfman' form, if you will, on the three nights a month when the moon is fullest. It also appears to be able to shift at other times and even possibly voluntarily when high levels of arousal, fear, or aggression are present. They tend to be stronger and faster even in human form, are more attuned to their environments, and they appear to have some kind of powerful pheromone that strongly attracts sexual partners.

"Incidentally, after a colleague-cum-test-subject's little *indiscretion* with Subject One, we have learned that in addition to being transmittable through bites and scratches, this is also a sexually transmitted disease. Dr. Greer was, apparently and rather unfortunately, had intercourse with Subject One under the influence of the pheromone. As a result, she is now part of the experiment. This is why we have instituted a new policy regarding any member of staff never being alone with any test subject going forward."

Weynman broke in, "The *Gladius Dei* informed you of this in advance, and you did not take precautions, Dr. Lannon?"

"Sir, I am willing to take responsibility for the mistake, but the information it has given us is a net gain for our research. It is personally unfortunate that Dr.

Greer has become what she's become, but I prefer to consider it a serendipitous mistake for the furtherance of scientific knowledge."

"How long was she infected before you knew?"

"We knew immediately. Security caught the entire exchange, reported it, and she was immediately escorted to a holding cell to await tests."

"It sounds like you set her up," said Weynman.

"That would be unethical, sir," said Dr. Lannon coolly.

There was a long, uncomfortable silence in the room. A few scientists shifted in their seats. Someone coughed.

"To continue," said Dr. Lannon, "Subject Seven. Sarah Platt, a military prisoner convicted of espionage for a foreign government, was given the second iteration of a genetically altered compound serum. This was a prototype serum designed to lower hormone levels that excite aggression in order to render her a more docile specimen more easily controlled, and less tied to the moon. The military applications of this are obvious, of course. A single operator working behind enemy lines under our orders could infect an entire army of what we are calling 'war dogs,' all of them under our control. What we have learned, however, is that without aggression, there is a strong tendency toward depression thus far.

"Subject Seven has survived longer than her fellows, but she is currently on an IV drip for fluids and is being fed through a tube. She stopped eating and drinking a few days ago, and is withering at a very rapid rate. She will probably be dead within the week, although we are hopeful for a better outcome. The relationship between aggression and the Moon appears to be intrinsic to the nature of the infection. There is more work to be done on this front. We will continue to develop it."

Danalov could hold his peace no more. He cleared his throat from the rear of the room.

"Pardon me, sir. I beg your pardon. I realize this is a meeting for men of science, and that I am only here to represent my Order's interests and clean up when your experiments are over, but did I hear you say you're considering infecting enemy *countries* with this curse?"

Armand Weynman turned in his seat and said, "Mr. Danalov, my understanding was you were to sit here in a security capacity, and to advise us if we had questions for you. This is not a moment for Q & A about our methods or plans. If you would please wait *outside* the door, I'm sure we'll call you if we need you."

"Mr. Weynman, before I communicate with my superiors about what I have heard here, perhaps you would like this opportunity to clarify, so nothing confusing happens between your organization and mine."

"If your bosses have questions for me, I'll happily entertain them. You, however, are a sergeant here on a security detail, and I am not going to halt this meeting to discuss ways and means with you. Is that clear enough for you, Sergeant Danalov?"

"It is, sir." Danalov turned on his heel and left the room. Cooke and a ProGen contractor waited in full battle gear outside the door.

"What's up, Sarge?" asked Cooke.

He leaned in and said, quietly, "Pull all of our people into Security Control in 30. Keep it down."

Cooke nodded, and Danalov went to make a phone call.

He picked up the phone in the Security Control Room to call High Justice O'Gallagher, the man who had given him the mission to begin with.

"O'Gallagher. Go ahead."

"Sir. It's Danalov. We have a problem."

"Go ahead," said the High Justice.

After he explained what he had heard in the meeting, there was a long silence.

"I'll talk to Marshall Frye. This order came down from him, but I don't know if he got it from higher. I'll call you back. Sit tight, and do whatever you have to do to ensure the Curse does not go off-site."

"Yes, sir."

When they hung up, Danalov wondered what was about to happen. He smelled the approach of violence, but for the first time there was a danger that he would have to kill ordinary human beings and maybe a lot of them, instead of monsters.

CHAPTER 24:

THE HANDOFF

Before dawn.
Friday, 23 June, 2017.
Outside of Marina, California

Gregory and Joseph put Frank in the back of a van and drove to the old and defunct train trestle that sagged over the Salinas River. Gregory wanted to be early to size up the area before their counterparts arrived. Rain made the night darker than usual. The world seemed only to be sodium streetlights in the distance and the little strip of road that rolled under the headlights as the rain pounded the windshield.

There was almost no one on the road at that hour, and when they pulled up, a black van with tinted windows was already waiting on the muddy shoulder in front of the trestle. Gregory looked at Joseph.

"I guess they're already here. Earlier than we are," said Joseph.

"Whatever happens, follow my lead and if anything weird happens, get behind cover," Gregory said.

"Right. Do I need to say I officially don't like this?"

"Your official dislike is noted," said Gregory. "I'll file it next to mine in the book of *Things the Bosses Don't Worry About*."

"So long as we are clear," said Joseph.

Gregory nodded then opened his door to step out. Joseph followed suit and stepped out into the falling rain as the mist rose from the slow-churning dark of the Salinas River. Two tall, thin men in dark clothes with black baseball caps and dark jackets were also getting out, driver and passenger both, from the black van beside them. They were running without lights. Even the black van's interior was impenetrable, for no lights had gone on when they opened their doors.

Inwardly, Gregory cursed. He had wanted to walk this ground before he met with unknowns, and if he had his druthers, there would have been a tactical team waiting in reserve and a sniper on overwatch to make sure things were on the level. A dose of healthy paranoia kept you alive when you killed monsters for a living. After all, most promotions beyond sergeant in the *Gladius Dei* were almost invariably the result of someone's death.

Many promotions were field promotions when you fought things that didn't have to obey the laws of nature. He had, however, been ordered to go alone. To tell no one. To make it happen tonight and then head to the Chapter House for debrief and reassignment to a new cell. It smelled to High Heaven of a cover-up. He had decided to bring Joseph as insurance because he knew what was going on, he was near to hand, and he was, at least, another *G.D.*, even if he was a scholar from the Exorcist Division.

The first dark man had a scarf around his nose and mouth, a ball cap on his head, and heavy lamb chop sideburns visible between the two. He approached Gregory. The second man stayed back five feet and at a 45-degree angle.

Gregory decided they trusted him as much as he trusted them.

"You've got a package for us, sir?" asked the man.

"Yeah, maybe. Where are you taking him?" asked Gregory.

"It's classified, sir. Need to know only. Better you don't know."

It was a boilerplate response, but Gregory hoped the question downgraded him in their minds. Old salts don't ask questions at the delicate moment because they know there's no point. If these men underestimated Gregory, it might provide an edge.

"Right, right, sorry," he said.

Joseph had taken up a position slightly behind and to the left of Gregory. He had angles on the safety officer and the talker, but that meant they had angles on him, too. Was the librarian faster? These two looked like meat-eaters to Gregory.

"Let's have him, then," said the talker.

"Sure. Just, uh, can I see some ID or something?" said Gregory.

The talker just eyed him icily. "I am here on the same orders you are, sir. There's no need to make this more complicated than it needs to be. Let's just exchange the package and be on our way."

"Yeah, sure. Just a second."

Gregory and Joseph moved to the back of their van and opened it. Frank was shackled and crouching on the bench of the van with a black hood over his head.

"This isn't right," said Joseph quietly as they reached for Frank's arms to stand him up.

"What's going on?" asked Frank, his voice strangely calm.

"Some orders came down. You're going to a third party. Not sure why," said Joseph in a whisper.

Gregory eyed Joseph and said, "Be quiet."

Joseph met his eyes, "This isn't us. This isn't what we do."

"We can hand him off or kill him, or go in and explain insubordination to the Bosses."

"I vote for let him go," said Frank.

"Shut up, Frank," said Gregory.

"Fine. Fine. Let's hand him off," said Joseph. Gregory turned and walked back toward the waiting men in black. Joseph slipped something small out of his pocket, pulled up the black hood and popped it into Frank's mouth.

"Swallow that now, before I walk you over."

Frank did with a small grunt of pain, then opened his mouth to catch a little rain and swallowed gratefully. Then they walked over together, Joseph's hands on Frank's back as he took short, halting steps toward the waiting men and the black van.

The talker took the hood off of Frank and held up his phone in a black case, snapped a picture with flash right in Frank's face that more or less blinded everyone, but Frank apparently was ready for that.

He slammed his forehead into the tall man's nose and heaved straight backward with a driving mule kick to Joseph's solar plexus.

Then Frank dove sidewise, horizontal and parallel with the ground, in a rolling arc straight for Gregory's knee. Gregory just had time to step back slightly so his knee didn't quite snap, but he fell and grunted in pain, feeling his kneecap wrench under Frank in the muddy gravel.

Frank was already up again in an almost comical lolloping gallop.

The second ProGen man was after him with long strides, clean-limbed and limber like a hunting cat after a crippled elk. Just when it looked like he would overtake his quarry, Frank spun, dropped into a roll behind the ProGen man as he slipped to a halt in the mud.

Frank threw the shackles around the man's neck then heaved back with all his weight. There was a struggle, then a wet snap, and the man began gurgling under his crushed windpipe. Frank was up and running again.

Gregory drew his pistol and drew a bead on Frank as best he might in the dark, and fired.

Frank screamed, cursed, then there was a splash. Gregory pounded after him, came to the edge of the trestle and turned on his flashlight, sweeping the river and its banks. Frank was halfway across, short stroking for all he was worth and sputtering.

Gregory was impressed he'd made it that far with arm and leg shackles. He shook his head. He couldn't say Frank didn't have balls. Maybe shit-for-brains, but the man had balls.

He pounded across the bridge and waited for Frank, who made it to about ten feet from the edge of the far bank, heaving, panting, coughing, sputtering, and shivering.

Frank stood haltingly, his muscles trembling at the effort. He checked the bullet hole in his thigh then tried to run. Gregory slipped out of the shadows and kicked his bleeding leg.

Frank fell, screaming in pain. He heaved a river rock that connected with Gregory's right eye. For a moment Gregory was dizzy, falling, on his back disoriented, then Frank was on him, squeezing his neck.

Gregory struck Frank hard in the temple with his elbow, then across the jaw, then in the side of the neck. Then, when Frank's grip had gone just a bit softer, he swept an arm over Frank's hands, broke the choke, and rolled him onto his back.

Gregory couldn't see out of his right eye. He felt searing pain all down his face, and warm blood dribbled from a large cut on his face. His cheekbone was swelling, and his eyelid was already swollen shut. He coughed, sputtered, and tried to keep Frank at bay.

But Frank wouldn't stay down. He rolled away and found another rock. He lifted it, and it exploded in his hand with a deafening crack.

Joseph stood on the bank with a revolver in his hand and said, "The next one ends you, Frank."

Frank stood there, shivering, and left his hands in the air.

"You think I'm afraid to die?" asked Frank.

"I think you want another opportunity to escape. This isn't it, though. To kill Gregory will be your death. Now let's go..."

When they stumbled back to the black van, the Pro-Gen man that Gregory called "the talker" had already packed up his dead comrade in the black van. The talker was in a white fury. His nose was a reddened pancake. His passenger and partner was dead.

He hastily searched a panting Frank, bound up the bullet wound with a very quick field dressing, put his own manacles on Frank's wrists, and returned Gregory's muddied and blooded restraints.

"See you around, Frank, you stubborn asshole," said Gregory.

"Go fuck yourself, Gregory," said Frank. "You see me again, it'll be the end of you. You think you're saving the world? You're just another kind of monster. You think you're serving God? God doesn't need you to fight his battles. You're—"

The talker pushed a Taser into Frank's chest and squeezed the trigger. Frank convulsed as the voltage rattled through him, then sat back on the bench, coughing and groaning, barely conscious.

Then, without a word, the man in black closed the doors, started the van's engine, and roared off into the night.

"That went well," said Gregory, eyeing his swollen eye in the rear view mirror as they climbed into the van.

"You're going to need stitches," said Joseph, handing Gregory a handkerchief from his pocket.

"Yeah. All part of the job," he said, putting pressure on his gushing cheekbone, now swollen to three times its normal size. "You know, like handing off civilians to mysterious men in black in the middle of the night."

"That civilian just killed a man—a highly trained man, I think," said Joseph. "And he nearly killed you. Whoever, whatever Frank Crow is, the words 'innocent' and 'civilian' don't bring him to mind."

"But he's not a monster," replied Gregory. "Or, anyway, he's not any more monstrous than we are. That man won't bend over for anybody. And I think maybe you're right...he loves his wife something fierce. I think those men in black better kill him soon, or they're in for a hard time."

CHAPTER 25:

THE CITY OF BONES

Elsewhere.
Outside of time.

When Lela and Aria awoke, they were lying together on a large, dark bed adorned with heavy purple velvet curtains. Their wounds were dressed with well-wrapped muslin, and they were not otherwise dressed at all.

There was pain, but not like what they had known when they drifted down into unconsciousness. Not that blinding, animal-panic pain. This was more like a throbbing ache.

Lela felt Aria roll into her and lay her head on Lela's breast, and the girl began to weep in dry, convulsive sobs. Lela held her and let her cry for as long as she needed. Aria seemed to fall into a light sleep, and Lela rose, gently easing Aria off her and tucking her under the silk sheets.

The room was sumptuously appointed in something approximating the Victorian Gothic style. It was round and its bed was an elegant four-poster with wrought iron wolf's paws for legs.

High-hung, vivid and disturbing tapestries draped the walls. They depicted scenes of medieval carnage between wolves and men, and men who were coming to be wolves, and women letting wolves enter them with lascivious expressions and too many teeth in their curling mouths.

An open wardrobe on one wall had two dresses in it, one of black satin and one of green taffeta, both rather risqué to be strictly period. Beside them were the appropriate underthings. This was like someone's modern conception of a burlesque Victorian festival or something.

What was happening here?

Lela decided that whatever came next, dressed, even dressed as garishly as this, was better than undressed for the moment. She put on the green taffeta dress, stockings, and boots hurriedly, then looked around the room. No weapons. A fire in an old stone fireplace was burning low.

She went to the window and gasped. They were in a city—a massive, silent city—with great palaces and spires, minarets, castles, longhouses, skyscrapers and ziggurats made wholly and entirely of billions, perhaps trillions of interlaced, mortared linen-and-bleach bones.

They stretched up and up, rising, rising into a baleful, luminous green sky with a sickly moon shining like a dead man's grin over the whole grotesque pile.

"Welcome to the City of Bones," said a smooth baritone voice. She turned and took in a darkly handsome man in a smoke-colored linen three-piece suit. His eyes were coal-black, as were his mane of curling locks, his immaculately trimmed moustache and his sharp, crisp goatee.

"Let me guess," said Lela. "You would like to be allowed to introduce yourself. You're a man of wealth and taste."

The man smiled like a hot spotlight of honey and liquor to the brain. It was enough to twist even a prepared woman's belly into a giddy knot, if only for a moment.

"As a matter of fact, my name is Malcolm Middlesex," he said. "I am your escort here."

"What happened? We were attacked by those... things."

"Ah, yes. That. Well, yes, the Labyrinth has some rather uncouth elements, Mrs. Crow. They are occasionally somewhat overzealous in their appointed rounds, and they bring the souls they find to the City of Bones for Judgment, as they brought you. The King of Bones ordered you brought here until you were fit for the Choosing, and assigned me to see to your needs."

"The King of Bones?"

"Yes. The Lord of this City. The Father of Werewolves. The Wolf Who Will Devour the World."

"Fenris."

"Yes, Mrs. Crow. Precisely."

"All right. And I'm —we're, here for Judgment?"

"Yes."

"When?"

"Soon. I think soon, but let me show you something first, if I might."

She nodded, and he offered his arm. She did not want to take it. Did not trust his warm smile, his easy manner, his cultured way of putting things. He was saying things that did not make sense and that it would frighten her to understand. Worse, understanding him might be like an infection that would grow inside her to house the City of Bones in a place under her skin.

But she did take his arm, did smell his clean sandalwood and English saddle leather scent, did let him open the doors of their chamber and lead her down the spiral staircase down into darkness. They reached a door with a stone demon grinning, shadowy and thrown into relief by a torch burning in the sconce beside it, leering over that doorway arch with undisguised and malicious pleasure. She let Malcolm open the door for her, gesturing her in smoothly, kindly, and with a delicacy almost spider-like.

Inside a ruddy light seethed, and she knew she should flee, but instead, Lela stood staring, not quite sure for a moment, and then fully comprehending. She was standing in the swirling fog outside the door of her home in Monterey, looking in the window at a blazing fire in the hearth.

She saw Frank carrying a tray of hot chocolates with whipped cream and her handsome young sons, thin and smiling, but already broadening at the shoulder like their father. They were the sons she and Frank never had and then she saw their little daughter dressed in a pink nighty. She would have been named Sarah, and she squirmed into her father's lap as he sat down to pass around the mugs. A Christmas tree sat in one corner.

"Say yes, and it can be real, Lela," said the smooth baritone in her ear, soft as a kiss. "You can go home. You can go to *this* home, and have your husband, your children, your life. And no one need sicken, or die, or suffer...you can have this life for the asking."

She bit her lip. Turned away. Turned back.

"It isn't real," she said.

"It's as real as it needs to be," he said gently. "Reality is overrated, anyway. And besides, this way you don't face Fenris. If you take this deal, he will forego his Judgment. You won't be devoured. You will live in simple peace and happiness. Isn't that better than living like a hunted thing? Like an *animal?*"

She turned to face him, her eyes to the dark pools of his own.

"Who are you really? What is this?"

"This is a beautiful opportunity brought to you by your last hope. If you want to walk through that door, you can live in bliss, in perfect love. You can have here what will forever be denied you in the life you left behind. You can have your Frank, you two can have your children, grandchildren, and forget. Forget all of it. Let it go, and it will recede until it is not even a memory of a memory."

"Forget," she said softly. She turned to look again, and took a step toward the door, then a second. She put her hand on the doorknob and began to turn it.

And then a voice in her head...not a loud voice but a quiet, clear voice said, *So, this is it, then?*

And that was so unusual—because she generally wasn't a woman who heard voices in her head—that she stopped turning the knob and was still.

"Yes," she said aloud.

This isn't real. That's not Frank. Those aren't your kids. You don't have any kids.

"I. I know that," she said. "It doesn't matter."

It might. Who are you giving yourself to? What are you agreeing to, exactly? What do they get out of this? The room you woke up in looks like a cheap two-bit mockup of some teenager's wet dream. The room where Aria is supposedly sleeping...

"What do you mean 'supposedly?' What are you saying?"

You take too much for granted. You're not really where you think you are, are you? Those things from the Labyrinth, those wraiths, they didn't dress your wounds and tuck you into bed, did they? Come on...they tear and rend and eat and never, never stop. And Malcolm Middlesex is a Mephistopheles right out of central casting. You're buying this because the truth is ugly, and this sloppy, slapdash lie is easier to entertain than the nightmare waiting, crouched, behind it...

"Who are you?" she asked, her eyes clouding with tears.

Isn't it obvious? I am the light in darkness.

"No, who—?" But the fog was rising around her, and the house was dimming. Frank and the children came to the window and were looking out at her with strange, hungry expressions.

Malcolm Middlesex walked out of the fog and said, with rising fury, "If you refuse this gift, you will be cast down, cast down into the darkness that eats!"

His handsome face began to crack as his mouth worked furiously, snapping and growling, champing and frothing. His skin began to chip and splinter. Beneath, green, baleful eyes of luminous hate stared out from a skeletal wolf's head.

"You dare not refuse *us*, Lela Wolfsdottir!" The thing that had been Middlesex began to scream.

She turned her eyes to her house, and the family that might have been hers leered back with monstrous fangs and glowing green eyes.

Then she ran, back toward the door and out onto the stairway, up toward Aria. She shifted her skin and raced up the stairs, burst through the door to find, not a bedroom, but a bone-laden killing floor that stank like a charnel house. This was no tower. The moon glowed above them. There was no ceiling, but a long high rounded wall circled her. She was in a Colosseum made of the bones of giant creatures, too large even to be whales, but rather of some kind of horrific leviathan out of Deep Time.

The floor was suddenly shifting sands, and through the swirling winds, she saw Aria in her Wolf's Skin running toward her, terror in her eyes. Behind her, wolf-wraiths boiled out of the darkness. Another burst from the door from which she'd come, and then a second and a third.

Lela was running for Aria before she decided to do it, and they met halfway, in the center of the Colosseum of Bone. The wolf wraiths ringed them in a circle of hateful toxic waste eyes and white teeth, black flesh over white bone.

"You might have accepted our offer," said one of them in a voice like ground glass in an open wound. "You might have been *like us*."

"Yes," said another. "Now you die."

"Where is Fenris? You are not in command here," said Aria. "Where is he?"

One of them gestured to their right with a clawed finger.

"Look," it hissed. "Look, and be afraid."

They did look, and they were sore afraid.

High up on a black basalt throne, perhaps a mile high and two miles away sat a Great Wolf, the Greatest of All Wolves, the Father of Wolves, the King with eyes like twin moons of blood. Its maw was a black tunnel in the side of a dark mountain with roots as deep as the dark sea, and a crown that humbled the sky. Its fur was a forest inescapable and midnight black, its teeth were like thundering forks of lightning, and its lolling tongue a crimson flag of blood waving over the nations of the Earth.

Don't look at him, said the voice inside Lela's head. *Look down.*

"You've got to be kidding me," she said aloud. There at her feet was a longsword of pure, glittering silver, twinkling as the shifting sands uncovered it.

The wolf-wraiths looked at her, then looked down. They snarled as one beast and began to move forward.

Lela, who knew nothing of swordplay and knew she knew nothing of swordplay, picked up the blade in her great, clawed hand and screamed as the silver seared her skin. But the instant she hefted the blade, the wraiths stopped. The light of the moon winking from the blade of the silver sword seemed to discomfit them.

Lela took a step forward, though her hand was a blistering agony of almost unfathomable pain. Sure enough, the wraiths took a step back as one.

The first wolf wraith made a run at her, and Lela swung the blade. It was light in her hands and when she made contact with the wolf-wraith's shoulder, it split open like an overripe tomato, kindling green fire and dissolving the snarling beast into a greasy black spot on the sand.

The others scattered then, howling and wailing. Lela dropped the silver sword when the last one disappeared into the dim. She grasped her hand as it bled and burned. She wept from the pain.

They'll be back. Take up the sword and run.

Aria moved just as Lela did to grasp the silver sword, and they looked at one another. They were both hearing this voice, they realized. With a nod to Lela, Aria took up the sword, whimpered in pain, and they ran toward the wall of the Colosseum of Bone.

They climbed together up the bone and mortar sides of the colosseum wall, and when they looked out, they saw a hungry black sea pounding on the distant outer walls of the City of Bones. There, kneeling drowsily atop the lip of the wall they had climbed, was an old man with a long beard, clad entirely in white lambswool and albino doeskin. He looked at them with kind eyes and smiled benignly, then gestured.

They heard the voice again.

Follow me.

Lela and Aria looked at each other quizzically, then, without a backward glance for Great Fenris, they followed the old man in white.

CHAPTER 26:

THE GALLOWS TREE INN

The Gallows Tree Inn was something of an institution in Hutchins, Nebraska, and really in the whole county round. It had all started around the year 1910 with a man named Bartholomew Anderson out of Deer Point, Arkansas. His family was old money from the Old south.

Mr. Anderson, in his travels about the country, came to meet and fall in love with the lovely and talented Annabel Murrow while she was away at college. She, a girl of wit and beauty, was born and bred in the little town of Hutchins. Mr. Anderson, whose home had been in the Ozarks, took the flat expanses of Nebraska as nothing less than an ill omen from the Lord on High that this was no place to stop and await the Second Coming of Christ.

Nevertheless, his love for Annabel won out over his better judgment, and although it was not his inclination, he stayed to woo and wed her in Hutchins. Local legend had it that he rented a room for their first night as a couple at a local clapboard boarding house and had purchased train tickets for the following morning back to the bosom of the Ozarks where they might live on his family estate in considerable comfort and luxury.

However, when morning came, Bartholomew Anderson, haggard and with the look of a man who had not enjoyed his marriage bed, nor the embrace of sleep, made an offer on an undeveloped plot near what was not then, but would one day be, the center of town, and closed escrow that very day. The next morning, it was reported by the town gossips and persons of low account that Mr. Anderson looked considerably more cheerful and rested for his decision to invest in and remain about the town of Hutchins, Nebraska, undoubtedly in no small measure due to his wife's particular opinion on the matter.

The story of Annabel and Bartholomew Anderson, as many such stories, does not end happily nor well. Beautiful Annabel was enamored of a certain farmhand whom her husband had lately employed during those early years. And although Bartholomew was a charming and generous man and his wife was a lively and amiable woman, he and Annabel were unable to agree as to what should be done on that particular point.

Mr. Anderson built for them a large and beautiful home on the lot he'd purchased. It boasted twenty bedrooms, two kitchens, two dining rooms, a grand ballroom, a billiard room, two studies, a library, and a music room, making it by far the grandest home in Hutchins and three counties round.

As it happened, their disagreements grew rather more than academic. In time, she bore the marks of it on her face. Her young farmhand took exception to the rough treatment his love experienced at her husband's hands, and the matter came to a head one stormy summer night in July when the lightning storms roamed the flatlands like hungry ghosts.

The tall, square, Midwestern farmhand with hair the color of hay and eyes the color of clear Nebraska sky met the scion of the Ozark Andersons in a duel upon a dawn, and the husband of Annabel Anderson proved the surer shot.

Interestingly, perhaps dismayingly for Bartholomew, the people of Hutchins felt more or less inclined to emotion regarding the outcome of the duel. The young and handsome youth of their own breeding had been sent to an early grave by a relative stranger whose opulence and conspicuous decadence they had noted with some distaste. As such, a mob broke in his doors that very evening as the young farmhand lay cooling on a slab in the funeral parlor not two blocks west. The mob apparently thought it a capital idea to hang Bartholomew Anderson for murder from the rafters of his own mansion.

Since that time the place has been, in its turn, an abandoned mansion. It was rumored to be haunted and built like a boarding house, much in the style of the one Bartholomew had stayed in while he courted young Annabel (her story, alas, is lost as she left Hutchins the night of Bartholomew's hanging, likely in the hope that her own adultery would not be examined by the benevolent mob that widowed her). The house finally became an inn doing a brisk trade in honeymooners, ghost hunters, highway travelers of means, and, in later days, conventioneers looking for reasonable accommodations in Middle America.

This was the fateful place where Gregory, Joseph, and two of their closest brothers-in-arms checked in, three nights after Frank Crow's botched handoff. They came in high hopes of encountering and detaining Lela Crow and Aria Davis.

Gregory and Joseph arrived near dark in a gray sedan. They parked in the half-empty parking lot of the Gallows Tree Inn. Joseph switched off the car, and they sat in quiet for a moment.

The parking lot was ringed with green ash trees, and a tall eastern Cottonwood waved in the rising night breeze beside the three story Inn. Of other people there was no sign. Hutchins folk were probably sitting down to their dinners, or finishing the last of the evening's chores in their barns, sheds, shops and haylofts.

"You're sure about this?" asked Gregory.

"I'm pretty sure," said Joseph. "But it's too late now, anyway. We're here."

"Fair enough."

"You think Sully will join us?" asked Joseph.

"If I ask him, he'll come, and I asked him, so he'll be here."

"How many will he bring?"

"Probably not a full team. Just people he trusts. Two. Maybe three. But they'll be loyal. That's the main thing." said Gregory.

"Okay. Let's go, then."

"Hold up," said Gregory. "I know you're not used to this. I know you're not a field guy, generally. There are some things they don't teach you at the school-house that you probably ought to know. First off, you don't give up your gun. Even if one of those things has me by the throat, if you give up your gun it'll just kill me, then kill you, and that will be that. Second, if you think something's off, it probably is. Don't shrug anything off. It's way better to be overly cautious and be wrong than to assume everything's fine and be wrong. We are here for two wolves, but this is the place Lorne Hutchins started. There may be others here we didn't look for and aren't expecting. Head on a swivel, eyes open, ears open, and always within reach of a teammate. Okay?"

"Yes, okay. Incidentally, can we...can I ask you what you plan to do when we meet these women, or if we encounter Nob?"

Gregory narrowed his eyes, "They have to be stopped."

"Yes, but we're beyond the boundaries of our authority here, Gregory. There has been no official final sanction by the *Gladius Dei*, and the possibility of sanction is remote since at this moment the bosses think you're on a plane to Milan and I'm reading books in the basement at the Carmel chapterhouse."

"I realize we're out of pocket, but these women were mixed up in Father Giovanni's death."

"I think they were victims, and I think they're looking for a cure."

"Hasn't that been tried?" asked Gregory.

"Yes, but—"

"With any success?"

"No, but—"

"So, they killed three state troopers in Arizona looking for their cure. No. I'm sorry. They're done. *Auto-da-fay* or no."

Joseph exhaled slowly, then said, "Listen. I'm going to say something because I want to hear it spoken aloud, and I want you to think about it: something is wrong here. Why would a spirit, or whatever it was, want to clue me in about Rannulf the Red and the source of the Diana Strain? Why would the bosses want Frank to go to a third party and then ship you out after you'd made the handoff? Why would they want us to capture these women alive? I'll bet it's to hand them off the same people who took Frank. That's not our way. Something's wrong here. Something is off with the Order, and these women are involved somehow. We need to know more."

Gregory considered this for a moment, looking out the window at the dim parking lot. An older man with gray hair and white moustache went by on a bicycle out on the nearby road, his blue jacket flapping in the wind.

Gregory watched him go, then said, "Maybe. So, capture and question if possible? That won't be easy. We have no Order resources, no safe houses, no backup. If the law gets involved, we're on our own. We're off the reservation. Neutralizing them is one thing.

Transporting them without exposure, questioning them without interruption, and then disposing of them without a trace is harder with no Order cleanup teams, nothing but us, Sully and whoever he brings."

"I realize it's not ideal," said Joseph. "But I think this is important."

"I'll talk to Sully. We'll figure something out. First we have to find them somewhere in this town."

"Thank you."

Joseph popped the trunk, they each grabbed a bag and went up the steps of the porch, through the front door of the Gallows Tree Inn.

The lobby was warm and comfortably appointed with a fire in the hearth and hardwood floors with thick rugs under rustic furniture. There was a vacant brown leather couch, bookshelves in a corner with a small sign that read "Lending Library," and a maroon armchair by the fire with a sartorially splendid gentleman in it.

This gentleman wore an Irish tweed three-piece suit with a cream colored shirt and dark green tie. He looked to be in his late fifties and was fit and lean with large hands and fingernails kept fastidiously well-trimmed. He had a chain running from his waistcoat button to his pocket, with an engraved silver fob dangling in between. He had a book in his hand but looked up politely when they entered before going back to his book.

In the far corner was a sweet-faced, plump woman in her early thirties, seated behind a low counter who smiled up at them as they entered.

"Reservation for Smith. Two rooms," Gregory said to her.

"Yes, Mr. Smith," said the woman, and began the process of checking him in. Joseph took note of the well-dressed gentleman and cocked an inquiring eye at Gregory, who nodded very slightly.

They got the keys, plucked up their bags, and walked to the third floor landing. There they found fellow *Gladius Dei* crusader Daniel Sullivan waiting just outside their rooms. He stood leaning against a wall with a feline grin on his face.

"Lads, glad you could make it," he said. "Sure, didn't I drop everything in Boston to meet you and show up first?"

"Hopefully we didn't pull you off anything big," said Gregory.

"They can spare me for a bit. I already gave them what I could for Intel. Joseph, almost didn't recognize you without your face in a book, lad." said Sully.

"How have you been, Sully?" They shook hands. Sully was not a large man. He stood only about five foot six, and he boxed in the featherweight division.

Joseph opened his room and gestured them in. Without a word, the men swept the room quietly, quickly, to ensure it was empty. Then they sat.

"How many others did you bring?"

"One other. Michaelson."

"Nice pull," said Gregory.

"He'll do," said Sully.

"I don't know him," said Joseph. "What's his spec?"

"Supply and logistics. Figured we'd need it if we're going dark," said Sully.

Joseph nodded, "Very sensible."

"So, what's the job?" Sully asked.

"Two changers. Diana Strain. Females. One in her early twenties, the other in her late thirties. They're trying to track the Curse back to the source. The one who infected them came from here," said Joseph.

"And why isn't this sanctioned by the bosses?"

"Maybe it would be, but they reassigned me after we handed off a person of interest, the husband of the older one, to a third party on orders," said Gregory.

It was the right answer, and Sully frowned. "A third party, is it? Who?"

"Nobody I knew," said Gregory.

Sully's frown deepened. "Starting to think we're in deeper waters than just a dark op."

"Welcome to the party, Irishman," said Gregory.

There was a brief pause as Sully seemed to roll the idea around.

"I'll gather what I can for ye," he said.

"Thanks," said Joseph. "Really."

"It's a debt I owe to your man here," said Sully. "An old debt, but it's my life he saved. He asks, and sure Danny Sullivan will be there."

Each rose from his chair at once, and Sully clapped Gregory on the back.

"It does me good to see you, Greg. And Joe, always a pleasure. I'll go see about young Michaelson. Let's meet downstairs in an hour, and we'll get to work."

"Suits me fine," said Gregory.

Joseph nodded, then said, "Did you notice the gent in the three piece suit on the way in?"

"Sure. Done up, isn't he?"

"He wore a silver medallion as his watch fob," said Joseph. "Either of you see that?"

"Aye," said Sully. "What of it?"

Joseph continued. "Did you notice it was a picture of a wolf? Strange coincidence, eh?"

Both of them looked at him for a long moment.

"There are no coincidences in our world," said Gregory, thumbing his pistol and easing it out of the concealed holster on his belt.

"Yeah, but no shape-changer willingly carries silver so cavalierly," said Joseph. "He might be in the know, though."

"Just because it looks silver doesn't mean it is," said Gregory.

"Let's just pop out and see if your man's still down there. A bottle of what you like says he ain't," said Sully.

They slipped out of the room as one, down the hall, pistols drawn and down, hidden behind coat hems and shirtsleeves, but the well-dressed man with the silver medallion was gone.

"Search the place top to bottom," said Gregory.

"Aye. Teams of two. I'll get Michaelson. We'll take the top and work down," said Sully.

Gregory nodded, "We'll take the basement and work up. Meet in the middle. Make loud bang noises with your gun if there's trouble."

CHAPTER 27:

THE MAN IN THE MOON

The City of Bones
Outside of time.

T he man in white led the women along hidden ways,
over roiling pits, and through high places where the
raging black sea below pounded in their ears. Finally,
they came to a small opening in a stone wall high on
the outer walls, at the edge of the Palace of Bones. They
were in a middle place with the Labyrinth on one side
and the Sea of Shadows on the other.

He pulled back a flapping rag of a curtain to reveal
a doorway in the mountain and smiled at them to enter.

Aria smiled back toothily and ducked inside. Lela
simply followed, wary but resigned.

Inside was a smooth edifice carved no more than ten
feet back into the stone with a small cot, a rock-circled

pit and tripod for a cook fire, a bucket of water, and a rather full gray bag at the foot of the cot.

They entered, then turned to look at the man in white. He came in and sat on the cot.

"We will be safe to talk here," he said. His voice was kind, and warm, and yet it carried a quiet strength that both women suddenly and completely trusted without knowing why. As they had suspected, it was the voice they had heard in their heads. They both realized it at the same time and beyond a doubt. They looked at each other, then at him as he continued.

"I imagine you have many questions. It has been the way of things for many seasons that I have been imprisoned here in the City of Bones, but with your coming, perhaps we can help each other. Now, let me see… you are Lela, who dreamed of home and hearth in her temptation. And you are Aria, who dreamed of the frontiers and the wildlands and of freedom in all things in her temptation."

"And what is your name, sir?" asked Lela. "And why did I hear your voice in my head?"

"Because my name is Mani." He took a kettle from the tripod and poured each of them a measure of tea from wooden bowls he produced. Each accepted the tea heartily.

"Mani?" said Aria, half to herself. "I know that name." She sipped the tea. It tasted of jasmine and ginger and honey and lemon.

"I have been the Great Wolf's prisoner for many a long night," said Mani. "For I was brought here by the hand of another and can only leave by another's hand."

"Ours?" asked Lela.

"Perhaps. But first, I think we need to see about your hurts."

Lela and Aria looked at each other quizzically.

"Our hurts?" asked Aria.

"Yes, the wolf-wraiths did you great harm, although your skins do not show it. Drink the tea, and we shall begin."

They drank. The tea sent warmth radiating through them. Aria fairly purred. Lela called out in surprise as her fingers began to glow with a pale, pearly light.

Then her whole body, every inch of skin, shone with a pale gloaming. There was darkness running through her veins, and she saw the same darkness under Aria's skin, circling like a dark snake. Mani put his hands on Aria's shoulder where the wolf-wraiths had envenomed her, and Aria crumbled onto the cot. Her eyes rolled back in her head, and she began to convulse and call out, entranced and shaking like a snake-handler in a Pentecostal church.

Mani drew the darkness from her wound, a living black pus of foul-smelling venom. He threw it into the fire where it curled and writhed and burned away to nothing. Slowly Aria quietened, whimpered, and went still. Lela watched, transfixed, but when Mani approached, she stepped back.

"Is she okay?" Lela growled.

Mani smiled indulgently and said, "You don't want that inside you. Let me help. She will be fine. As will you."

"What would it do, that stuff, if it stays inside?"

"It will make you rot inside, and you'll eventually succumb. Either to death or wraithdom."

"What are those wraiths?"

"Men and women who, walked as wolves in life. Who, when tempted, sold their service to Fenris in exchange for the illusion of their heart's desire."

"But I passed the test. I didn't accept the offer."

"Yes, and that was to your great credit, child. But temptations can be offered again and again. You only need to be weak enough to accept just the once. When we are ready to accept a comforting lie instead of a terrible truth, we are ready to be corrupted."

He stepped closer, and this time, she did not back away. There was terrible pain and darkness. Lela felt as if she were being drawn away as her breath sucked out. She heard her own voice saying things she did not understand. And then there was nothing.

Lela awoke on the old man's cot beside Aria, who blinked awake instantly and perked her head up. A thick mist was pouring in from the cave's mouth, chilling and dampening them. Mani, frail and thin-boned, shivered against the slick darkness of the wall opposite them, his cheeks sunken and sallow, his color sickly.

Lela stood and walked to him, crouched, and with a gentle voice asked, "Are you alright?"

Aria followed, touching his shoulder. "He's freezing cold," she said.

"It is not so easy as it was to call upon charms and to heal with my hands. There was always a cost, but the cost is more these nights." He hacked too long with a wet, wheezing cough deep in his chest.

"What can we do?" asked Lela.

"Can you take me from this place?" asked Mani.

"You know a way out?" asked Aria.

"Yes, but it will be a hard way. And costly. You'll need that." Mani pointed to the silver blade that now leaned against the opposite wall near the entryway of the cave.

Lela shivered and looked down at her blistered hand.

"Why didn't you heal this, too?" she asked.

"Some wounds are too deep for my skill. Your Curse is one such wound. My power is weak here in this fearful Realm."

"What is this place?" asked Lela.

Mani coughed raggedly, then said in a tone of deep exhaustion, "It is enough for you to know it is a prison, and a marshalling place for dark things to assault the world you know. I will say no more now."

They carried him to his cot and covered him with a curiously clean quilted blanket of cream and deep blue. He shut his old eyes then and slept. Aria gestured toward the doorway, Lela nodded, and they slipped out of the entryway of the cave together. They stood on the ledge looking out over the Sea of Shadows, and tried not to turn their heads to regard the Labyrinth on the other side of the cliffs.

"What do you think?" Lela asked.

"We take him when he wakes up, take the hard road, and get out of here fast," said Aria.

"And then?"

"I don't know. Why? What are you thinking?" Aria asked.

"I miss Frank. And maybe this is impossible. Whatever terrible rabbit hole we've come down to find a cure, we took a wrong turn somewhere, because there's no cure. Just...some kind of hell for werewolves like us who choose Damnation. I want to go home..."

"There is no home to go back to," said Aria, gently. "And if you try, you'll probably wake up one morning to learn you had a bad dream, shifted, and maybe killed the people you love most. There's no going back."

"I know. I know. But what's the point of running forever and never belonging anywhere to anyone or anything except the Moon or the Great Wolf?"

"I think a lot of werewolves are suicides because they asked themselves that question, Lela. It's dangerous to start down that path. We're alive. We're here. That's enough."

Lela sighed. Nodded. "Let's go back inside then," she said. "It's cold out here."

CHAPTER 28:

MARLOWE MCCOY TAKES THE MIDNIGHT TRAIN

Dusk.
Friday, 23 June, 2017.
Site Bravo

They had turned him into a werewolf somehow. That much he knew. Then, they had hurt him. Bad. Just to watch him heal up, he reckoned. To time it on their damned stopwatches. To see what he'd do.

To see if they could trigger his shifting (madness under his skin, breaking bones, reversing joints, his bowels in knots, his mind a jumble of red animal murder). They tried many ways to trigger the change: pain and fear and cold and heat and thirst and hunger and lust.

They had poked, prodded, drawn blood, taken spit, stool, urine, semen, skin. The bastards hadn't left him alone, they'd just kept on and on with their tests, no matter how he raged or howled or snapped or tried to break free. And worse, after whatever happened in the lab down the hall, they had doubled his restraints and kept men with guns ready to hand outside the labs all the time, just in case.

They had learned things though... They figured out how to produce some kind of chemical that forced him to shift—some injection at first, then a gas. Even when he fought it, they could make him change with this drug that was somehow a distillation of anger, fear, hunger, and the full moon in the sky. He could barely hold on to a man's thought then, but only wanted to *eat* and rend and rip and fuck.

Marlowe McCoy watched. Marlowe McCoy waited. And then, one night (he knew it was night, he somehow *always* knew when it was night outside), he saw his chance.

Actually, it was a hard chance to miss. He awoke alone in his holding cell, the place they shoved him when they weren't doing some devil-hatched experiment on him, and found the door open. He heard the pumps and knew they had gassed him before he realized he was already shifting. The terrible pain of the Change drowned his Man's mind, and he wanted meat, blood, and cracking bones.

Then he was up, roaring. He ran out the door and down the sterile hallways. Some part of him recognized that the landscape had changed; the hallways were locked down, or dead-ended because of barriers that hadn't been there before when they wheeled him to the labs.

He was, he realized, being corralled toward a particular place in the complex. And yet, he could smell man's sweat and breath and hear muffled talk at the far end of one of the long hallways and into a number of what looked like living quarters.

Distantly, some part of McCoy thought, *they want me to kill someone.*

But it did not matter. He was hungry, and he would eat, and the higher considerations of defiance, or why they had contrived this, whether it was as an experiment or an assassination or some highly improbable oversight, seemed irrelevant. He moved down the hall quietly, on the stalk. He heard a man talking. There was a woman in the man's room, too, he realized, and his mouth watered.

"The bosses say sit tight. That there must be some mistake. That perhaps Weynman and Lannon are confused about the agreement. That they will address it," said the man's voice, a faint accent tinged with the tones of something foreign.

"And what do you think?" asked the woman.

"I think what I thought before. This is out of control. We need to put a stop to it. If the bosses don't like it, that's too bad. This is not what we signed up to do; deliver a curse upon the world for the profit of worldly governments…"

"What are your orders?"

"We need to scrub the site of all genetic material and research, and eliminate the test subjects. I'm willing to spare the scientists, and I don't want to kill civilians. But anyone who tries to stop us should be neutralized by the least force necessary to stop the threat."

"I'll tell the others. For the record, I think this is going to get very messy, and the bosses won't have your back over it. This could be your career."

"Your objection is noted, Angela. Nevertheless, my orders stand."

"Understood, Sergeant."

Daniels moved toward the door, then she was in the hall. The door snapped closed behind her. She stopped in the hallway out of old and well-honed instinct.

She looked left and right, then she looked up to see the werewolf, massively muscled with a cruel smile of white fangs and red eyes burning. It had pressed itself between the ceiling girders above her.

McCoy pounced as Daniels drew her pistol and called out. Her first shot was true and clipped him in the shoulder. Then he was on her, slashing and biting. His claws sliced deep into her hands and arms.

The pistol went flying, and his great animal mouth was on her throat before she could scream again. In defiance, she gouged for his eyes, plucking one out with a wet pop as he howled in pain and rage, then ripped her throat out.

Danalov came boiling out of his room and levelled the M4 carbine rifle he kept ready to hand at all times when he was on mission. But the creature was ready and dove through an adjacent door, smashing it down with his bulk. He fled into a darkened room before Danalov could squeeze off a shot. Danalov was fairly sure it was a vacant room for the present. His team quartered farther up the hall, and for that he was momentarily grateful.

He kept his eye and weapon trained on the door, radioed for backup quietly, and moved to Daniels. He felt for a pulse, but she was gone, eyes open in shock, mouth open in a mute scream of horror, and her throat a red, gaping hole in the center of a spreading pool of bright blood.

He cursed in Russian, then tried to radio again. No answer came. The hair on the back of his neck began to rise. He was alone with the beast, and perhaps it had been contrived to be so.

"Come on, then," he called to it. It was remarkably quiet.

None of the other operators were in their rooms. It looked like a number of barriers were down that led to other hallways. They had funneled it here using the door controls from Central Security Control. He was as sure of this as he had ever been of anything. This was an attempt on his life for making waves. It was undoubtedly Weynman and his people that had planned it this way because they clearly underestimated Danalov and knew nothing of the cruel tutelage of the shooter school of *Gladius Dei*.

No answer came from the dark room where the beast had fled. He took Angela's pistol with his left hand, did a quick press check to make sure there was a round in the chamber, and put it in his waistband. He wore only his fatigues and a t-shirt, as he had been dressing when Daniels came in.

A few minutes of delay on Weynman's part and Danalov could have begun directing the team to sanitize the area of anything related to scientific research and development around the Diana Strain. Now, Cassius Danalov would have given much for a grenade, much more for a teammate. He approached the door very quietly at an oblique angle and waited, listening.

He heard the beast growling in the other room.

"Idi nahui," cursed Danalov under his breath, and switched on the flashlight under the barrel of his M4. He backed slowly up to his quarters, slid through the doorway with his rifle trained on the hall, and backed slowly into the corner, the weapon in his hands pointed and ready for the first scratch on the door.

The way Danalov saw it, there were four possibilities. One, the wolf would come and kill him, and he would make it pay dearly for his hide. Two, it would wander off in search of someone easier, which seemed unlikely. Three, they would let another creature loose, and they'd both come in here and rip him apart. Four, the team would figure out what was happening, take command of the Control center, and come in like the Yankee cavalry to save him.

Of course, these options could come as combinations. Some of those combinations might be grim.

Danalov waited in the quiet.

All was stillness. Adrenaline roared like a firehose in his arteries, heart jackhammering. He was straining to hear any little sound that might betray an approaching beast. Whether it was seconds, minutes, or hours, he could not have said, but he when he did hear a sound, it was that of an approaching tactical team. He saw the lights above flicker back on. Heard the knock on his door and Cooke's voice.

"Sarge? It's Cooke. Don't fuckin' shoot me."

"Where is it?" asked Danalov.

"Not sure. Hasn't left the room according to the feeds. Fuckin' Daniels took its eye out as it was killing her. That's hardcore…"

Danalov stepped into the hall. His team was stacked on the door. Daniels still lay, splayed on the cold concrete floor.

They stacked on the door and assaulted the room, but what they found was no werewolf, just a bit of blood on the walls in the shape of clawed hands, and a spreading puddle of water coming from the bathroom where the toilet had been ripped out and shattered all over the tiles. The thing had clawed its way beyond the smaller pipes, and dropped into the larger drainage system to escape.

Marlowe McCoy had found the sewers of Site Bravo. They stood looking down the bubbling hole, and Danalov shook his head.

"It's war, then," he said. "Get all our people ready, and see to Daniels' body. She can take my cot until the threat is past and we can exfil. No one sleeps until Weynman and Lannon are in custody, the infected are dead, and the research is in ashes."

"Yes, sir," said Cooke.

And so it began.

Marlowe was down the main line of the sewer system when the rumbling began and he realized where he was. He had crawled on his belly through the pipes where he had to, and out to the larger catwalks and service ways and now had emerged under the subway station bathrooms.

He smiled to himself. Somehow he had shifted back down to human form there in the pipes—maybe the duration of the drug was at an end, or his survival instinct had recognized he couldn't fit through the relatively narrow sewer lines as a wolf. In any event, his eye was gone, and his eyelid had sealed over it with yellow pus. But it itched as his broken leg had itched as a boy, and Marlowe wondered if that meant it was healing.

His shoulder, where the woman's silver bullet had grazed him, was assuredly not healing. He supposed it might go septic with raw sewage in it if he didn't attend to it soon. The pain had been terrible and surprising, and it had brought him back to himself a bit; the hunger had subsided and his desire to escape the facility where they kept him as a lab rat (and where he was probably destined for the furnace) had grown. So, instead of killing the Russian, he had fled.

Marlowe rounded a corner and found a utility closet with access to the station. Inside the closet was a small bank of lockers with hardhats, jumpsuits, tool belts, and a number of tools, hip waders and galoshes. He rinsed himself of the clinging sewage as best he could in the sink, particularly scrubbing his raw red shoulder wound and eye with watered-down bleach. He bit down on his screams, donned the workman's uniform and galoshes, a tool belt, and a heavy steel wrench, and climbed the stairs to the train station.

The station was large and empty. But in the distance, he heard gunshots. Marlowe McCoy found a nice electrical compartment for cable housing in the rear of the train where he could wait. After all, the train had to move, sooner or later. He would follow it to the end of the line, and put as many miles between himself and this place as he could.

CHAPTER 29:

THE ALPHA AND THE PACK

The City of Bones
Outside of time.

Lela and Aria drowsed together in the cave, but did not sleep, and when the old man who called himself Mani roused, they were awake. They went to him offered him water.

He took it gratefully, drank, and said, "We had best be gone, if we are going."

They nodded, and he stooped, cracking his old back to stand straight. He then wrapped his deep blue and cream-colored quilt around the silver sword, fastened it with a cord and top and bottom, and put it across Aria's shoulder.

"Carry this," he said with curious weight. She nodded gravely, more because it seemed so important to the old man than in full understanding of his meaning.

"Whatever happens, follow, and do as I say. Even, or especially, if it seems strange to ask," said the old man. "We are going back into the Labyrinth, but not the route you took in. We will go out another door."

They both nodded, not sure why they trusted him so fully, so implicitly, and so deeply, but nor did it occur to either of them to question. His very aura seemed to gentle them, somehow, though neither could have put the feeling of his rightness into words.

He walked them out onto the ledge, down the narrow pathway, and through a small crack in the cliff wall they had barely registered on the way in. Down they went, down a long, dark stairway that seemed to go on and on, curving gradually down through the Palace of Bones, into an open place high above dark water where only the pale glow of Mani's skin and their own strange and newly luminous bodies lit their way, reflecting far below.

They travelled down, down, down, into another tight crack in the stone, and along a hidden draw. They came to a chink in the wall of the Labyrinth, and passed into it beneath the stone bridge. They traveled along a hidden byway beneath the bridge and sheltered beneath eaves and troughs for runoff.

They followed silently and with surprising speed. In the Labyrinth, Mani wasted not a gesture or a second, but passed in silence like the shadow of a bird across the face of the moon.

They came to an archway, passed through it and up, up a long rise from which they could see the high hill in the distance, and passed again beyond it. Once, they hid beneath the statue of a warrior bearing a long-axe, as wolf-wraiths prowled on the other side of a low wall. But they soon went their way, and after a time, Mani gestured them to follow, so they moved along.

Down a stairway, round a long curving street, and under a crumbling set of steps rising to nothing. Then, there was a smooth, round stone. Mani gestured that it must move, and the three of them pushed it, and after a time it gave a groan and moved, inch by inch, to uncover a black pit into which no light could penetrate.

"Down," he whispered, "Aria first with the sword. Lela, hold on to me."

Aria nodded, looked back, looked down, and leaped into nothingness. No sound returned to them of landing or fall. She was simply gone. Mani clutched Lela, and she held him, and they leaped together into the abyss.

The basement of the Gallows Tree Inn had a history of its own, and it kept its secrets. It happened that the old plot purchased in the name of Mr. and Mrs. Bartholomew Anderson for their home way back in 1910 had an even older history than they knew.

It had once been the farmstead of none other than Santiago Vega, a murderer and cutthroat fugitive who had made an enemy of the werewolf Gaspard when he killed the wolf-woman Bethany in a New Orleans murder years before, and who had raised (by cruelty, malice, and privation) young Lorne Hutchins.

The basement was where Vega had kept Lorne, alone and in the dark, for any transgression, real or imagined. Sometimes for hours, and sometimes for weeks. It had been the place Lorne was twisted to evil, shaped by his fear into a fearful shape himself.

When the old wolf, Gaspard, had finally come for revenge, neither Vega nor Gaspard survived but Lorne had.

Lorne, young Lorne, had been marked by Gaspard in the struggle. And the Diana Strain had passed to a boy who would become one of the most prolific serial killers in American (and werewolf) history.

It all began in the basement. And so, just as the mine where Lorne dumped his victims' things was the place where Lela and Aria entered the Realm of Fenris at the mouth of the Labyrinth, this basement was another doorway out, the doorway, as it happened, from which they unceremoniously emerged at exactly the moment that Joseph and Gregory opened the door at the top of the stairs and descended into the dark.

"You see anything?" asked Joseph, shining his flashlight down the ominous-looking stairway.

"No," said Gregory, "but we have to go down there anyway."

"Right," said Joseph, not relishing the idea.

"I'll go first. You cover me. And don't get nervous and shoot me in the back, Librarian."

They brought both weapons to the low ready position, barrels toward the low dark of the bottom stair.

"I got top marks in shooting at the schoolhouse, I'll have you know."

"How many years ago is that?" asked Gregory.

"Your point is well-taken. I will not shoot you."

They began down the rickety, creaking stairs into the basement. It was musty, cobwebbed, and ran the full length of the large house in both directions.

The hairs on Gregory's neck stood on end. "We're not alone," he said, very quietly.

His words were swallowed up by the gloom. It was just as they had taught him: if you get a feeling something is off, it is. If you think you're not alone, you probably aren't. Prepare accordingly.

Now in play were the two of them, one a librarian who handled a weapon once a quarter for mandatory qualification and hadn't seen a practical scenario since his schoolhouse days, and a very large, dark basement on unfamiliar ground with maybe a werewolf in it. Everything told Gregory to back out and wait for the other two operators he had, even if one was specialized in logistics. Sully would be good to have in this situation, Intel or not. Sully was a man to have at your back in a fight, if a fight there was going to be.

"Let's back out. Slowly," said Gregory.

"Okay," said Joseph, a tremor in his voice.

Slowly, very slowly, they backed up the stairs. From within the deep bowels of the basement, there came a guttural growl, and at the same moment, a shadow fell across their backs from the open doorway at the top of the stairs.

The gentleman in the tweed suit with the silver fob dangling from his watch chain stood above them in the half-light.

Gregory spun and advanced on the man, who raised his hands when he saw the gun. Joseph followed, mindful of whatever growled down below. Not sure which way to point his weapon, he erred on the side of the threat below them, trusting Gregory to handle the man in the suit.

"What's your name, mister?" asked Gregory, who halted his advance about five feet from the man, just short of the doorway.

"My name?" The gentleman looked bemused. "I'm called Ethan Wainwright. You don't need that pistol, sir. I'm sure we don't mean each other any harm."

"Back up, and keep your hands high," said Gregory.

Another growl issued from the darkness of the basement, louder and closer. Ethan Wainwright cocked his head slightly, then backed slowly into the little kitchen pantry that accessed the basement.

"What was that?" he asked.

"Joseph, call the others and we'll clear the basement together," said Gregory calmly, stepping into the pantry and closing the basement door as soon as Joseph was clear of it. "Weapon on the door while you do that, please."

"Someone left a dog down there, I suppose?" asked Wainwright. "Sounds like a big, fierce fellow."

Gregory did not take his weapon from Wainwright as they stood in the hall.

"What were you coming down here for?" he asked.

"Oh, I must have taken a wrong turning looking for a restroom on this floor," said Wainwright.

"Is that so? Are you carrying any weapons?" asked Gregory.

"I beg your pardon, sir, but before we go much farther down the path of this somewhat hostile conversation, I wonder if you might do me the honor of your name and apprise me as to whether or not you are associated with some jurisdictionally cogent law enforcement agency with which I am obliged to cooperate."

Gregory blinked. "What?"

"He wants your name and to know if you're a cop," said Joseph, pulling out the burner phone he had picked up and dialing Sully's burner number.

"I'm not a cop, and since I have a gun, I'll ask all the questions, and you'll give me sensible answers," said Gregory.

There were footsteps, heavy footsteps, coming up the rickety stairs on the other side of the basement door. Sully picked up and Joseph spoke their location quickly and softly into the phone, then hung up.

"I wonder if that's our canine friend now," said Ethan. "Although it sounds rather as if she goes on two legs instead of four."

"She?" asked Gregory, "How do you—"

The door exploded outward, popping off of both hinges and flying across the room. Gregory just had time to leap out of the way as it careened end over end toward him.

Lela as wolf-woman with a newly glimmering tattoo of the moon on her shoulder, leaped out of the dark and slammed full force into Gregory, knocking him to the floor where he landed in a dazed heap. Joseph took aim, but the wolf form of Aria with a tattoo of a silver sword glowing on her shoulder boiled out of the dark like a silent nightmare, pounced, and landed on his chest, knocking the gun away and crushing him beneath her.

He cried out as he felt his ribs snap like dry twigs. He lay there gasping and pinned like a butterfly.

Lela as Wolf-Woman growled into Gregory's ear, her voice low and deep with fury and menace, "Why do you smell of Frank? Who are you? Where's Frank?"

"I say," said Wainwright, clearing his throat. "This *is* unseemly."

Lela looked at the old man and wanted to bare her fangs, but something stopped her. His scent was hot, exciting, and strange. She shook her head to clear it. He was, strangely, very strangely, and very suddenly, *intensely* attractive. She felt herself quiver. A look at Aria's face told Lela she was having the same reaction.

"I do believe they have phoned for some backup. Two men, as I understand. Best to be gone, I should think, and rather soon. Join me in an evening stroll, would you, dear ladies? If one or both of these gentlemen has information about this 'Frank' of whom you speak, perhaps they would like to discuss it in greater privacy than the Gallows can offer us just at present..."

CHAPTER 30:

VEGAS, BABY

Evening
Saturday, 24 June, 2017
Site Bravo

When the shooting stopped, matters at Site Bravo were somewhat altered. Of the original security force, twelve ProGen contractors remained of the original fifty. Half of the facility was no longer functional as it had been a battleground. One lab was a total loss.

Doctor Lannon and Armand Weynman had a meeting to discuss their next steps. They decided they needed to request a rather sizeable resupply. So, they put in the order and dispatched the bullet train after a thorough search of its holds.

The train left the station at Site Bravo at 7pm that evening, and in all that time no one had thought to check the electric panels and excess cable housing where, for all those hours, Marlowe McCoy had slept peacefully.

The trip from Monterey to Las Vegas had been un-eventful, mostly because the thin man had drugged Frank at every stop. At some point, they weren't riding with the corpse of the man Frank had killed anymore. But whether they disposed of him through company chan-nels, dumped him at a hospital, or buried him in the desert, Frank had no memory and no clue. Whatever the drugs they were pumping him with, he (mercifully) did not dream.

Frank was just starting to come back to conscious-ness when they pulled into the warehouse and the thin man got out. There was silence for a long time except for the sound of industrial air handlers and the buzz of high-powered sodium lamps high above the van. The hot engine ticked down the minutes irregularly. Slowly, Frank came back to himself. His thoughts were slug-gish, dragging through mud. He was nauseated and his mouth was cottony. His eyes were sore and ached in his head, and his skin felt like it was crawling with spike-legged spiders.

He overheard a nearing conversation: "…killed him at the handoff, just like that. I wanted to put a bullet in him right then, but I guess what's coming for him is worse."

"From what I hear, they need a big resupply. Might be a few hours while the trucks make deliveries and we load the train. We could grab something to eat and come back. Bullet train isn't even due for another half hour."

"How the hell did they build a 400-mile-long bullet train underground, and nobody freaking noticed? That's what gets me." The voices were level with the vehicle now and passing on beyond it toward the door.

"Ah, they probably paid off the right people, told the stupid ones some story about earthquakes or tremors or something, and scared the nosy ones away. You know how shady this company can be when the government gets involved…"

The conversation drifted into noise, faded, and was gone.

Frank tested the restraints for the hundredth time, wiggling each muscle to see if he could loosen or wiggle out of it, but to no avail. He was well and truly stuck. Or was he? Joseph had slipped him something to swallow. Could he retrieve it? Probably not at present, but he would wait for his chance.

Marlowe McCoy rolled out of the cable-housing panel at the rear of the train. He felt the full moon rising outside, and his skin began to prickle with the Change. He began the slaughter in the rear car and worked his way forward, finishing just outside Las Vegas by devouring the conductor from the soles of his feet to the crown of his skull.

Curiously, it did not fill him up to eat so much meat, but rather he felt emptier, lighter, hungrier, and drunk on savagery with each bite. Marlowe McCoy made no effort to learn the train's mechanics as it approached the station, despite the fact that bullet trains travel at 200 miles per hour.

The ensuing collision and subsequent explosions destroyed the station, much of the warehouse, and would have burned Frank Crow alive if the van that would have been his coffin hadn't been parked near the open steel doors at the edge of the warehouse when it was blown backward into the nearly empty parking lot.

The van sustained minor damage, but the gurney where Frank had been strapped down had bounced off the wall at one corner, and his restraint had loosened.

It was enough to work with, and Frank started to work it when Marlowe McCoy came striding out of the flaming warehouse—ten feet of muscle and teeth and blood-matted fur and murder, eyes gleaming madly like twin red suns redolent with ravenous hunger.

The slender man and his companion had just pulled into the lot and drew down on the werewolf that was Marlowe. But they had no silver ammunition. They unloaded their magazines into him, and he screamed in fury, lifted a vehicle with terrifying ease, and hurled it at the truck they had arrived in and were now using for cover.

It landed with a sickening crunch and the sound of breaking glass, then a *whumf* and a concussive blast that pushed the van a foot as both vehicles exploded. The werewolf howled long and with terrible malice.

Unnoticed (by the Grace of God or just blind luck), Frank broke free of the first restraint and began to work the others when the beast cleared the parking lot, loped down the dark desert street, and ravened into the night.

Irving had been playing, and losing, at the Bellagio that evening. His wife, Fran, was at the slots, and for this he was grateful. Fran had been pushing for a Vegas vacation ever since he got his Christmas bonus, and nothing would do but that they flew first class, stayed at Caesar's (where they'd stayed when they got married, lo those many years ago when Irving had hair and Fran was tolerable). Irving considered his hand. A sixteen, Jack and Six of Clubs.

"Hit me," he said. The dealer flipped over a King, and Irving went bust. He sighed as the dealer raked his chips again and rose.

"Thanks."

When he stood, his wife Fran, who had positioned herself to best observe him, read his resignation, his hang-dog defeatism, and prepared with no small amount of pleasure to harangue him all the way back to their room, which she had taken special pains to criticize. Fran's philosophy was her mother's, too. Men shouldn't get to feeling too pleased with themselves and shouldn't be allowed to forget who runs things.

If a man works, it should be to please his wife, and whatever he makes should be placed at her feet. Irving hadn't been a tough nut to crack when he was young, and now he was broken to the saddle. She didn't even have to give him one of her looks to keep him from wandering to the bar to have a drink before he told her he'd lost what she'd allotted him to gamble with for the weekend. After all, if he was out of his allowance, how could he pay for a drink at the bar? She watched him approach, careful to keep her face neutral. But inside she was as much looking forward to chastising him as she had been of the trip itself.

Irving, for his part, was reviewing all the things about this trip that hadn't gone right. It was like a curse. The cab that picked them up outside their house in Miami had been extremely late, traffic to the airport had been incredibly slow. He'd been pulled out of line at security and was patted down while his wife sped to the plane.

But it was too late, and they had to reschedule. This meant they had to wait four hours in the airport. Fran had taken a special delight in blaming him for all of it.

Then, the airline lost their luggage, their room wasn't ready for over two hours after check-in, and when they'd finally made it to a buffet, his acid reflux started acting up, and he couldn't handle much more than a salad and a glass of water.

Now he'd lost most of his money doing what all the smart blackjack books say you should do. Split tens, hit on sixteen, stand on seventeen, and double down on a ten or eleven. Yet every bet had gone against him. Irving was beginning to suspect, after thirty years of marriage, that he was going to die a miserable, lonely asshole, rubbed down to nothing by his wife. And there was nothing he could do about it.

"I guess you lost it all, didn't you, Irv?" said Fran as he approached.

"Yeah, Frannie."

"Well, I hope you don't expect that I'm going to—"

There was a crash, and many people screaming and glass shattering, gunshots, and the terrible sound of an animal howling. They both looked up to see a monster standing on top of the nearby craps table.

It had impaled a dealer on the roulette wheel. A wave of people stampeded by, knocking Fran off her stool, but Irving hunkered behind the banks of slots as people poured by on either side. Fran crawled to him, screaming, her red flower-print Mumu bunching up and catching under her knees, slowing her progress.

Then there came a thump, and the monster was standing on the slots looking down at them with slavering jaws. Security guards called out, but what they said was lost in the general din of panic, and they opened fire, the gunshots a series of staccato pops that vibrated in the air.

It looked like the creature took a few hits, but it reached back almost casually and hurled a slot machine overhand at the guards, two of whom scattered and reloaded, and two of whom could not get out of the way in time. These two flattened like blood-gutted mosquitos under a Sunday newspaper.

The other two guards gave up reloading and fled then, and Irving looked up to see the thing staring down at them. It threw back its head and howled with untamed animal ferocity, and leaped down onto Fran's plump, jiggling frame as she cowered and stumbled on the floor.

"It's probably excited by the red of Fran's Mumu," Irving thought crazily.

It ripped her heart out with its jaws and swallowed it, still beating. Then it leered at Irving, who only stood there, his mouth open, a stain of yellow piss running down his pant leg.

The beast moved forward, savoring its advance on him. In a stride it would be on him, and it would be over. Then, another gunshot, and the thing yipped, jumped, and snarled in pain, then turned.

Frank Crow fired again and again in rapid succession as he emerged from the cover of the slot machine banks. The monster was already in motion, running for the elegant doors, ripping through them to leave twisted metal and shards of glittering glass there on the marble floors. Frank raced after him, breathless.

Then there was a strange silence. The hall was nearly empty but for a few corpses, Irving's wife among them. He rose and looked down at her bloody, prostrate form, numb. He wandered like a man in a fog to the bar across from him where a bartender, a girl in a tuxedo shirt and vest, cowered.

"Scotch?" he heard himself say in a quivering voice.

The girl looked at him in disbelief.

"W-what kind of Scotch?" she asked.

"Uh, what's good? I always wanted to try but my wife — uh, what do you recommend?"

She stood, fingers shaking, and drew out a Scotch whiskey from the row behind her. She put that bottle (a bottle of Johnny Walker Blue, in fact) and a glass in front of him.

"On the house," she said.

Irving poured himself three fingers and sipped, his hands shaking, his lips numb, then nodded, smiled, and belted it. It tasted more delicious than anything he had had to drink in thirty years.

Maybe it was his lucky day, after all.

The beast hurled itself down the Strip lamely, bleeding from the leg where Frank had shot it with the silver ammunition he'd found in the thin man's van. No less than three news helicopters were filming from above, and the sound of sirens was rising to a deafening wail. Frank followed.

Waves of people were screaming and stampeding into the shelter of casinos. Cars jammed in on the street with nowhere to go sat empty, doors ajar, as their drivers had seen the wolf and fled. The wolf that was Marlowe McCoy ducked low in the impacted traffic of the Strip and all but disappeared from Frank's view. The searchlights from the helicopters above helped Frank track it for a time, but then one of them would sweep over him and he would be all but blind. Some of the vehicles had crashed into others, making a sort of twisted maze with something far worse than a minotaur lurking there.

Frank put a fresh magazine in the pistol and pressed forward. Every hair on his arms and neck stood on end and his chest seemed to pound directly into his forehead. He took slow breaths, concentrated and measured, with the long practice of a man who has fought down panic for a living. It was almost impossible to hear between the thundering of the choppers, the distant screams of the crowds fleeing in every direction, the approach of sirens, and beneath those, the usual clanging din of the Las Vegas Strip by night. He would not hear the wolf if it approached, he realized, and if it found a way behind him, he would be dead before he knew what killed him. He dropped to the ground, checking for feet under the cars. He saw no claws, no great paws, no leering animal face to meet him in the shadows. The searchlights roamed over the abandoned cars: the gaudy Casino signs created a strange strobe effect that made it hard to focus on what was moving and what wasn't. He rolled under a vehicle, then out the other side, watching.

Blocks away, the sirens were almost on them now, racing toward the creature's last known location. Frank strained to hear anything but the sirens and the thump of the helicopter, and then he saw a car rock on its tires scant yards away, and heard a low, guttural growl. His blood froze in his veins, and his scalp prickled with the familiar adrenaline spike that preceded violence.

The wolf was hiding in the vehicle beside him. Slowly, very slowly, Frank peeked out to look at the car and saw it was a very large black Cadillac SUV with windows tinted the color of thick smoke. The two front doors were open, the two rear doors were not, and for a moment everything was still. Frank rolled to a shooting position, weapon

toward the vehicle, and waited. If all went well, he figured the police would flush the werewolf, and Frank
would empty his magazine into the beast at point blank
range. He had found two magazines in the slender
man's van, and nearly emptied one already. This was it.
There were ten rounds in the Glock, and two in the
magazine he had nearly spent. If he needed to do a combat reload (which he wouldn't have time for) and the
other ten rounds hadn't been effective, then would those
last two be helpful, even if he could put them on target?

Six cruisers barreled in from both sides of the block-
wide maze of abandoned vehicles, wrecks, and destruc-
tion, establishing a perimeter. The officers took up positions behind their doors, covering various sectors of
the area with carbine rifles. The three press helicopters
had moved off and a police helicopter was hovering above,
low but not too low. Frank saw the SUV shift on its
tires again, subtly. The sharp spikes of static that meant
radio chatter were all but lost under the wind and thunder of the helicopter. Methodically, they passed a search-
light from vehicle to vehicle. The werewolf slipped like
a liquid shadow, like a silent avalanche of dark flesh, from
the passenger door nearest to Frank, hefted the vehicle
under which Frank had been hiding, and launched it at the
low-flying helicopter with a roaring bellow of defiance.

Several things happened at once; it looked down and
saw Frank with a puzzled expression that quickly became
hate. The vehicle flew in a lazy arc and connected with
the blades of the helicopter, snapping them, a ball of fire
consumed the area around the fuel tanks. The helicopter

listed and fell in a meteor of flame toward the doors of Harrah's Casino, and Frank unloaded his entire magazine into the monster that had been Marlowe McCoy.

The explosion of the helicopter into the casino was enormous and the police on that end of the perimeter were already moving to help as they could, but several officers moved in, toward the gunfire, rifles at the ready, tactically by twos, to find the bullet-riddled body of the Beast, quite dead, lying over a bloodied and unconscious Frank Crow.

CHAPTER 31:

DARK INTERVENTIONS,
OR WHY WE KEEP SECRETS

Midnight
Sunday, 25 June, 2017
The tunnels beneath New York City

H e thought of himself as a shadow. Nothing more. Whatever he had been before, now he was nothing. A whisper in the night. A forgotten thing.

But he served. The Masters he served were terrible indeed, and he was, if nothing else, their terrible instrument.

He once had a name but now had no need of one. The Masters called him Keller in this century, and he answered to them by whatever name they gave him.

And Master Alexei had called. So, Keller had answered. Now, he slipped from the deep shadows of the train station into the tunnels and subterranean depths of the subway, all but invisible and unregarded in the deep of the night.

Down he went. Down, and down, into the deep bowels of the city underground: a place where only municipal workers a century in their graves might remember paths and caverns of echoing tile and stone long since forgotten. The trackless darkness was unblemished by hateful light and had not known the sun.

Then a door was before him, nearly invisible even in proper light. It stood so heavy that no ten men could move it. Keller grasped the seam gently and eased it gingerly; it made no sound as it opened on a rough stairway into the Master's lair. Keller halted at the threshold, and opened his mouth to speak.

"Master Alexei?" But a telepathic sending of terrible strength rocked him on his heels.

Enter. Alexei could have found Keller across continents, if he wished. He could have crushed his servant's mind into abject animalism without identity.

"Yes, Master."

Keller crossed the threshold and swung the door closed behind him with a definitive boom. He descended down the stairs into a series of identical rough-hewn corridors that had never appeared on any schematic: the work of long dead blood-slaves who were sacrificed upon the completion of the stonework, Keller knew.

He felt his way toward the Sound, too low for human ears, of the ancient heart slowly beating as it had beaten for ages. In the center of the rough-hewn stone maze, a chamber waited, and in that chamber was a throne of skulls, each bleached and smooth, each perfect and unbroken.

Atop the throne sat a creature whiter still, dressed in blackened rags, with eyes as red and burning as fire-drenched moons. It radiated such terrible power in deep, almost tidal waves that made it difficult to move, to think, to do more than kneel, crawl, grovel.

I have learned a thing that must not be.

"Command me, Master. I will obey."

He tried not to snivel and failed. The presence of the Masters was always thus, and Keller was always ashamed at how small they made him simply by being. He felt himself, all that he was, diminishing and dissolving to utter subservience and occlusion before his will.

The thrice-damned Wolf-Changers of Rannulf's line are unmasked before mortal eyes. It must be addressed. See to it, Keller, and you shall know my favor. Fail, and you will suffer for eternity.

"As you say, Master."

There is a place in the east. Find it. Destroy it. And punish the men who have dared this trespass into the shadow world. If they enslave the accursed Wolf-Changers, it will not be long before they discover us. The secrets of our world must be kept. Go.

"Yes, my Lord."

And he was gone in the dark, faster than mortal instruments could track, as silent as the shadow he was.

CHAPTER 32:

THE WOLF TRAP

Night
Saturday, 24 June, 2017
Outside of Hutchins, Nebraska

There was a stand of trees, almost a little forest, clustered near a stream a mile out of Hutchins. There, Ethan Wainwright bound Joseph and Gregory by hand and foot to a tall, wide oak tree.

They had been unconscious for the ride in Wainwright's old Plymouth, and awoke bound in the half dark of the high, pale moon through the whispering leaves. A night breeze kicked up, and Wainwright struck a match and lit an old kerosene lantern that caught and flared to make his face ghostly and yellow.

Behind him, Lela and Aria stood as women again, staring at the two bound men and wondering at the strange magnetism of the mysterious Mr. Wainwright, wondering why he seemed so attractive, and why his suggestions seemed so very right.

"Good gentlemen, I have many questions, but let's get the first things out of the way. You each bear identification that name you a Mister Joseph Marini and a Mister Gregory Parker, both out of beautiful Carmel-by-the-Sea, in sunny California."

The men said nothing. Gregory wheezed with the pain of breathing around his badly broken ribs, and Joseph looked away.

Ethan lifted Gregory's gun to regard it, then looked back at them.

"What brings you to Hutchins so well equipped for mayhem, gents?"

Again, they responded with silence.

"And why do you smell like Frank?" asked Lela, moving into the light.

This time, when they didn't respond, Lela moved in and kicked Gregory hard in the ribs. He let out a belching wheeze as all the oxygen fled his lungs and he nearly blacked out from the pain.

When the air returned, he groaned. Lela stopped short. She knew the aggression of the Wolf, but she'd never felt so inclined to violence before. She hadn't chosen to attack, rather, she'd *felt* her way to attacking, felt a little nudge. She looked back at Wainwright.

He fixed her with a look, and she felt herself *flatten*. He had power over her, she realized. She looked at Aria and saw the same hunger and adoration in her eyes. Ethan had power over them both. How?

"Stop it," said Joseph. "We don't know what you're talking about."

"She will kill your friend if you don't start talking, Joseph," said Ethan.

And Lela suddenly knew she would if Ethan so much as nodded at her. And she was afraid.

Then the breeze changed, and she smelled them. She looked around, and noticed shadows moving out from shadows. Shadows in the shapes of wolves and wolf-men and wolf-women. They were quiet, but not at pains to be so, and they had hungry, luminous eyes. There were six, and in their bones Lela and Aria understood without words or conscious thought that they were well and truly in the presence of their own kind.

Gregory had begun to recover, and he coughed out, "We would rather die."

"That can be arranged. In fact, because I suspect you are a wolf hunter given your decision to use silver ammunition in your firearms, I am happy to oblige you." Wainwright leaned in and his voice suddenly went from cultured and conversational to lethally cold. "But you will probably beg to die before we are finished with our talk, Mister Parker."

"I'm—" Aria started, her voice uncharacteristically soft and meek. "I'm opposed to torture…"

Ethan looked back at her, arching an eyebrow, and she felt her stomach lurch. She felt like dropping to the leaf litter and baring her throat, but instead she trembled with the effort of standing upright, and gritted her teeth. Bullet-sized beads of sweat began to form under her lip and across her brow. His unflinching regard pressed down on her like a hydraulic press. The wolves gathered closer in.

"I appreciate your principled stand, my dear, but surely you recognize this is an enemy who has tracked you to us, and such an enemy has intelligence that we must needs extract for our very survival. In a sense, the Law of the Jungle necessitates our unfortunate but obligatory brutality. I hope you can reconcile yourself to this inevitable fact." His eyes, unblinking, bored into her skull, as hard and unrelenting as his words had been conciliatory.

"I—uh. Yes. I understand, b-but…"

"Good." He turned back to Joseph and Gregory, "Now, as I was saying, why don't we start simply? What are you doing here?"

Gregory spat blood at Ethan's feet. The wolves closed in, a tight ring of moon-pearled teeth and growling throats in the night, drawing close to the circle of lantern light. They promised death, willing their jaws forward, but held back awaiting Ethan's merest command. After a long moment, Ethan moved forward and put his hands around Gregory's neck and began to squeeze, slowly, with measured, resolute, and seemingly effortless power.

"Now, then," said Ethan, "what are you doing here, Joseph?" Gregory tried to kick and gasp, but no sound came from his throat as he began to redden and thrash.

"Let him go."

"I will. Happily. Just answer the question."

"You can't — please, stop..." Lela said, "Not in cold blood like this." And yet part of her willed him on. Some dark bloodlust was excited by the death in the air. She pushed it back, rejected it utterly.

"We were here looking for them," Joseph said. "For Lela and Aria."

"Ah. How salubrious that you found them," said Ethan, releasing Gregory to gasp and choke air back into his lungs. He stepped back.

"Why were you looking for us?" asked Aria.

Between ragged gasps, Gregory said, "Don't tell them *shit!*"

Ethan kicked Gregory savagely in the knee and the plate of his kneecap snapped like rotted plywood. Gregory screamed; the ring of wolves and teeth drew tighter around them, hackles rising, snarls frozen.

"Stop! Stop! I'll tell you what you want to know. Stop hurting him, please." Joseph's voice was high and hoarse with terror.

"Proceed," said Ethan, coolly detached.

Lela and Aria could feel the heat, the burning desire for the kill rising like perfume from Ethan Wainwright's skin. It was an intoxicating scent, and they felt the Change rising, suggesting itself. It would feel good. Natural. Normal. Right.

"The Order has been doing some strange things ever since—" but he was cut short when a bullet ripped through Ethan Wainwright's shoulder; another shot instantly caught one of the wolf-changers in the head, and the pack scattered in all directions.

Lela and Aria dove headlong into the dirt, and a storm of well-aimed rounds sizzled and buzzed above them like furious hornets. Three more wolves fell in ten seconds as they were racing through the trees, and Wainwright shifted, favoring his right foreleg, crawling belly-down in the leaf-litter toward the cover of trees on the far side of the attack.

Lela and Aria low-crawled together toward the tree where Gregory and Joseph were bound. Suddenly, at a 90-degree angle from where the sniper's rounds were coming from, a machine gun opened up on the wolves who were fleeing, carefully firing in a tight kill zone somewhat to the rear of the tree where Gregory and Joseph hunkered.

Two more wolves, the last of the Pack, fell to the onslaught of the belt-fed SAW (Squad Automatic Weapon) before it fell silent. Wainwright, all unseen, crawled like a slithering eel into the bubbling creek and slipped beneath the water without a sound. Lela and Aria were untying Joseph and Gregory when they heard a twig snap behind them.

Ten yards away, Sully called out to them with his rifle raised to the shoulder. "Step back from those men and put your hands behind your heads, or you'll be dead before you turn."

Joseph stood, "It's alright, Sully. They... They didn't want this."

"Touching, but I take no chances," said Sully.

Lela and Aria interlaced their hands behind their heads and stepped away from Joseph and Gregory. Gregory lay in a crumpled heap, leg busted, ribs badly broken, struggling to breathe and maintain consciousness. From the trees at about a 45-degree angle from where Sully had appeared, Michaelson appeared with his SAW at the high ready and trained on the women.

"Not bad for Logistics, eh?" he said. Michaelson was a kid in his twenties, tall and beanpole thin with round glasses and an oval face, but the *Gladius Dei* had trained him well in what to do if it all went to hell, so to speak (and so it had).

"Glad you thought to bring the hardware, boyo," said Sully.

"Count on supply," said Michaelson, although he didn't sound as brave as he wanted to. Then, in a slightly more tremulous voice, "Did we get all of them?"

"The leader isn't here. We'll check if you got him on the run. I clipped his shoulder."

"What do we do with these two?" asked Michaelson.

"We talk," said Joseph.

"Talk about what?" asked Aria.

"We talk about Frank, for starters," said Joseph.

Gregory coughed, "That's a stubborn asshole you're married to, Lela."

Aria snorted, stifling a laugh.

Lela said, "You came all the way here to tell me that?"

CHAPTER 33:

RECKONING

Near dusk
Washington D.C.

S enator Freedman's stately Virginia home was in the secluded luxury neighborhood of Barnaby Woods in Washington DC. It was a quiet place, away from the rush of the city. Colonials and Cape Cod-style houses stood in unassuming rows on tree-lined streets that spoke of unostentatious affluence. Indeed, this was one of the most expensive and prestigious neighborhoods in a city of elites.

Senator Freedman's career in politics had been lucrative, even by the standards of career politicians. He had been fortunate in his choice of friends. His four story Colonial home bespoke dignity, taste, and (naturally) wealth.

Given the nature of politics, though, the Senator's home had an eye to security, as well. He hired a private security detail of two men per shift for three shifts a day, 24 hours a day, seven days a week. They worked from an outbuilding behind the indoor pool in the expansive backyard grounds. Discreet cameras were set up on the street and around corners and entryways. All entrances and exits were logged and timestamped electronically.

There was a hardened "panic room" in the center of the house that could withstand direct and sustained rifle fire. Nevertheless, the Senator, his lovely (trophy wife) Melissa, and their children, Alice and Jeremy (when they came home from Columbia and Yale, respectively), lived there in considerable peace and comfort, without incident.

The night of the Reckoning, the Senator and his wife were hosting a small dinner party. Among the guests were a junior House Representative from Massachusetts named Hanrahan who had eyes on bigger offices, his wife Arletta Hanrahan-Perez, a famous painter much celebrated of late for her recent gallery opening in New York. Also in attendance were two eager and enthusiastic city councilmen, Smith and Jones, hoping to climb the ladder, and their rather-too-made-up, strikingly Stepford wives Bunny and Barbie. Likewise, there was a police captain named Denise Jackson who wanted a certain investigation into her rookie days to disappear as she was reviewed for Major. There was a television food critic/celebrity fresh out of rehab. Finally, to round out and spice the dinner, there was a somewhat haggard, chain-smoking French-Canadian novelist named Elena Adrienne, and her rather statuesque and rather-too-young lesbian lover, neither of whom were speaking to each other and between whom one could hardly help but observe sizzling, almost dangerous hostility.

One armed guard, Reggie McCoy, was in the command center watching the monitors and doing his crossword. He watched his partner, Louis Partido, crossing the grounds as he patrolled, once around the house and perimeter every hour (as unobtrusively as possible) to ensure no one was there who shouldn't be. After all, cameras and electronics could be fooled.

Both were 20-year veterans of major metropolitan police forces—Louis in New York and Reggie in Atlanta. Both had seen their share of action, had their share of training, and had now settled into a comfortable security gig which they took seriously and treated professionally, but which demanded relatively little and amounted to zero emergencies of any stripe in the years they had been on the night shift.

Inside, a small team of overdressed wait staff served hosts and guests alike with the most pretentious possible menu the fashion would allow. The party discussed the ravages of poverty within the city over sushi-grade black ahi tuna served with wasabi and garlic aioli.

They drank wine of rarified vintage selected by Melissa's personal sommelier, and all the while, the Senator held court: the great man among those he would favor and cultivate as long as they could be useful.

After the dessert course, they retired to smoke cigars in the parlor. And one by one the guests departed until it was just Senator and Mrs. Freedman, alone but for the last of the help clearing up in the kitchen. The congenial atmosphere suddenly turned chilly now that they were alone.

"Successful evening, I thought," he said, pouring himself a third Scotch.

"Mm."

He looked back at her and raised his glass to his lips. "What is it?"

"I was sure all of them knew about your latest..." (She didn't say "whore" though she wanted to) "...and were laughing at me all through dinner."

"We have discussed this. Must we go over it again?" Senator Freedman asked wearily.

"No," she said, "but be careful I don't start cavorting like you do. Might be worse for your image than mine that you can't keep your wife at home."

He slapped her hard, but not hard enough to draw blood. Her face was a commodity. It not being the first time, she did not weep, but rather straightened her posture, and looked away.

"Keep a civil tongue in your head."

"Fine." She walked away, and he sat down on the piano bench and slugged the rest of his Scotch. He listened to the sounds of the staff departing, his wife drawing a bath upstairs. He could picture her there with the flask of vodka she thought he didn't know about in the cabinet by the claw foot tub in her private bathroom, the valium pills she'd be swallowing with it, and sighed.

"Ain't life grand?" he burbled scotchily, considering the merits of another drink, and considering the merits of having a driver take him across town to his 22-year-old mistress in the apartment he kept for her. He certainly could expect to sleep alone tonight, as usual, if he stayed home. Nevertheless, there were risks. If someone from the press caught the scent... He did *try* for discretion.

"What would be your basis for comparison, Senator?" came a voice—a rasping, hollow voice—from the corner of the room.

Senator Freedman fairly leapt from his seat and grabbed a poker from beside the fireplace. "Who are you? How did you get in here?"

An impossibly pale man with very dark eyes in a black turtleneck and dark slacks lounged on the loveseat, playing idly with the edge of a curtain fringe.

"I think you should have a seat, Senator. We have a discussion ahead of us, and at the end of that, you have a choice."

"Get the hell out of my house before I have you arrested!" He approached, raising the poker above his head, nearly taking out the chandelier.

"I think you'll find that hard to do," said the dark man. "You can call me Keller. We need to discuss your change of heart regarding research and development into lycanthropy."

That stopped the drunk man short and went a good way toward sobering him up.

"What do you know about that? I mean, I can't confirm—"

"Sit down, and we can discuss it."

The Senator sat.

"You are going to make a statement, Senator, very soon. A statement that says you are fully and wholly responsible for the testing of human/animal hybrids at your secret site in the Oregon mountains. That you alone gave authorization through back channels and misallocated funds to a private contractor to do the testing. You can expect to be pardoned and for the whole matter to be hushed up afterward in the usual way, but tonight you *will* be making a statement."

"The hell I will. You have no right to—" he leaned forward as if to stand, then froze as he caught the sudden shift in the man's features, the feral, dead eyes of something inhuman staring back at him in the darkness, glimmering with cold malice.

He felt his spine begging to buckle. He, a ranking Senator, a rainmaker, wanted to crawl across the carpet on his face and abase himself, grovel, because he knew somewhere in the muddy, scurrying bottom of his most ancient cortex that this thing was (though he could not have put it into words exactly) going to eat him if he didn't.

"Senator," said Keller, very softly, his voice like the bottom of a very deep grave. "In three minutes, a man from the Federal Bureau of Investigation will knock on your door. You will answer it. I will be listening to every word, watching every gesture, although I will be upstairs with your lovely wife. You will take full responsibility, confess the world, get it on the record, and *make no mention of me*. He does not know it was not your staff who called him for this meeting, and you will not disabuse him of this fact. If you fail in this very simple task, there will be most unpleasant consequences. Do I make myself crystal clear, sir?"

"Yes," said Freedman, his hands clammy, his mouth suddenly very dry.

"Go ahead and have another drink, Senator. I'm going upstairs." Keller stood in a languid motion, more like a panther than a man, and drifted like an ink stain in the darkness toward the stairway. He turned, and favored the trembling Senator with a lurid, fang-baring smile that made him look positively demonic. A living nightmare in shadow and white stone. He ascended the stairs without a sound. Senator Freedman stood, his heart pounding, mouth agape, unable to move or think. There was a loud knock at the front door.

On unsteady legs, Freedman wobbled to the door and checked the peephole. He opened the door on a tall man in a dark peacoat and Irish cap. "Senator? I'm Bill Crow. I'm here because you said you needed to speak to me urgently."

"Please come in, sir." Freedman opened the door, flicking on the foyer light.

Bill stepped in, eyes cool but not unfriendly. The Senator ushered him into the parlor, still pale but beginning to recover some of his charm. He poured a tall

Glenmorangie and, half-turning, asked, "Glass of something for you, Mr. Crow?"

"Not for me, thanks." Bill sat exactly where Keller had lounged not a moment before, straight and solid and true where Keller had been a lounging black nightmare.

Senator Freedman pictured Keller upstairs, hovering over the reclining figure of his trophy wife. He involuntarily shivered as if dead fingers were dancing up his spine.

He belted his scotch, turned, then sat. "I asked for you because I wanted to make a clean breast of what I've decided was a bad decision."

"This is a little irregular, Senator. Generally even members of the Select Committee on Intelligence can't call up Bureau brass for a house visit, but it sounded like this was important."

"It is." Freedman sighed, then plunged. "For some time now I've been uneasy about steps I took to funnel government funds through a biotech firm, ProGen Global, in the service of illegal human experiments around militarizing human/animal hybrids. It's called the War Dogs Program. I... we need to shut down the program. I will take full responsibility for making this happen, but it needs to be stopped. Dismantled. It's gone too far."

Bill Crow listened, and Senator Freedman talked, and the longer Freedman talked, the deeper grew Crow's frown. Details were divulged. By the time Crow was back on the sidewalk, he was racing for his car.

Freedman watched him go, and when his car was safely away, he turned and looked with terror up the stairway, then slowly walked up on shaking legs. His bedroom was at the top of the stairs. He pushed the door open to darkness, flicked on the light, and no over-heads glowed. The room remained dark. Like an unholy moon, Keller's face drifted in front of his own in the darkness, somehow luminous. His eyes were so sunken and dark they appeared almost hollow.

"That was well done," said Keller in a sinister whisper.

"Where is Melissa?"

"What? I'm here," she said, her voice strong in the dark. She clicked on her bedside lamp. Keller, like an evil apparition, had vanished in the light.

"A-are you alright?" he asked, the scotch beginning to rise into slurred syllables.

"I'm fine," she said, her eyes hard. Reproach rose in her face at his drunken intrusion.

"I—" but he had no words to explain.

She sat up in bed, strangely erect, her head cocked in hostility. It startled him, but he did not know why.

"I've just been lying here thinking, Terence," she said. There was a rawness to her voice that frightened him. It reminded him of something he could not place. He eased himself into a chair, not trusting his legs.

"I've just been thinking that you've kept me in a prison, a very lovely prison, all these years. And I've been complicit in it. I've *let you* keep me here. I've had the key all along, and just never saw it for what it is."

"A-are we talking about divorce again?" he was suddenly weary. "I have to go to my room. I need... I'll... maybe another drink. I'll cancel appointments tomorrow... I can't...maybe..."

She stood, her voice building.

"It was strange. Like a voice in my head telling me the way out. The way to fix this terrible wasteland of a marriage. You see, Terence, the problem with us is you."

That's when she raised the gun. It was a .32. He'd insisted she keep it for security reasons "just in case." In case. The irony nearly made him laugh, but it strangled in his throat.

"Melissa, I can...if you want to leave, we can make sure you're comfortable. No need for—"

"No, no. You'd twist it. You'd lie in wait. You'd *find a way* to punish me. Humiliate me. You'd take revenge on me for wanting, for *having* my freedom, Terry. That's what you do. That's who you are. I had...I had a long conversation with myself about it just before you came in. This is the way. The only way."

There was dawning horror on his face as he realized what was about to happen, but as he tried to rise, hands out, a word (and who knows what word) half-formed in his lying throat, Melissa Freedman shot him three times in the heart. She watched him slump against the wall and slither to the floor. She watched with cool detachment, her eyes as hollow as those of a marionette.

When the security team burst into the room, she was still sitting there on the bed looking down at his corpse with unseeing eyes.

CHAPTER 34:

DANALOV'S GAMBIT

Night
Saturday, 24 June, 2017
Site Bravo

Back at Site Bravo, immediately after Marlowe McCoy's escape down the sewers, Danalov's entire team of *Gladius Dei* operatives moved tactically up the long south corridor of Site Bravo toward the central security office. To the left and right in the south corridor were rows of doors that led to offices and server rooms and banks of cubicles: the administrative nerve center of the complex where data was entered and retained, where logistics to keep Site B running were overseen. They were all dark now, empty, and locked, although their dark windows were like sinister eyes watching the *Gladius Dei*'s gunmen pass with vacant menace. Their objective was to take Central Security, lock down the facility entirely, and then destroy specimens, research, and DNA samples by section. The corridor was thus far empty, and the emergency lighting sent strange yellow shadows skittering up the walls to signal a security breach. Procedure throughout the complex would be that all staff would shelter in place until security was restored.

With Daniels dead, it was only Danalov in command, Angel Lorca as combat medic, Robert Stewart as their tech, Cooke and Markovski as shooters, and Jakes as supply. In emergencies (and their situation certainly counted as one) all could operate in combat conditions as soldiers. They moved as a unit, quickly and smoothly but with measured precision, each scanning his own field of fire. If nothing else, they were warriors for God, Danalov thought. They would die doing His work.

When they arrived at the door to Central Security, Danalov ordered a halt, and everyone took up a defensive position while he advanced to the door. The problem with breaching the Central Security door using a plastique shape charge was that at some point in the very near future Danalov might very much want a hardened steel door between his team (not to mention his de facto command center) and Site Bravo's jackbooted security force. Without the luxury of time, though, it couldn't be helped. He needed to connect with the *Gladius Dei* chain of command and advise them of the breach, contain and neutralize (hopefully without loss of life) the Site Bravo Security Force, and start systematically destroying the research Site Bravo had accrued.

All this was in keeping with his original orders about what to do if it all got out of hand, and it had all gotten, he felt confident in saying, *quite out of hand*. It crossed the line, he felt his superiors would agree, when they accidentally/deliberately released a werewolf that killed his intelligence officer and tried to murder him. That, also, would need an answer. However, he considered that personal business, and it could be attended to when his official orders were fulfilled.

Danalov waved Robert Stewart, his Tech expert over to his position. Stewart hustled over and crouched, weapon toward the security door.

"Can you breach the door without destroying it? We may need it soon."

"I can try to hack in. No promises. How long do I have?"

"Minutes, at best."

"Right." Stewart took a knee behind Danalov, back to back, and slung his weapon, then pulled out a middle-sized black tablet. He switched it on, and green light washed his face. He began to type furiously.

At that moment, they heard footsteps echoing down the hall.

"Shit," said Stewart.

"Keep on it. We have another minute," said Danalov. "Cooke, Markovski, set them a welcome."

Cooke and Markovski peeled from their defensive positions and raced down the hallway. They kicked open one of the office doors, cleared the small office, and stacked up, one high and one low, prepared to fire as the Site Bravo Security Force came around the corner.

Danalov kicked open another locked office door adjacent to their position and shoved Stewart (who never stopped typing away) inside. Lorca and Jakes took up positions in the office across from Danalov and Stewart and farther down, so that Cooke and Markovski were at a 45-degree angle to their front, Danalov and Stewart at a 45-degree angle to their rear.

"Stewart?" asked Danalov.

"Working on it."

"Work faster."

The footfalls slowed, then fell silent as the Site Bravo Security Forces stacked on the far corner of the south Corridor, not yet visible to the *Gladius Dei* team, but assuredly there preparing their assault.

"Stewart?" asked Danalov.

"Thirty seconds."

"We don't have—"

From down the hall came a well-modulated voice. Weynman was on the far end of the hall, hidden behind the corner and behind his squads.

"Mister Danalov, please put down your weapons and step out. I would hate for anything untoward to happen to you and your men."

"Keep him talking," said Stewart quietly. "I'm almost there."

Danalov yelled into the hallway.

"You sent your dog. It killed my Intelligence Officer. Something untoward? We are past this."

"I can certainly appreciate your position, but given the fact that you are outnumbered and trapped, why not save the men that remain to you by surrendering?"

"What terms are you offering?"

"You are in no position to demand terms. I will only promise you your lives," came Weynman's response.

"How many of your men want to die for you? All of mine swore to die at my order. Our souls are ready for Judgment. Can you say the same?"

"I won't ask again. Surrender, Mister Danalov, and we can work out this unfortunate misunderstanding. One of our specimens is loose in the complex. Perhaps you can help us hunt it down?"

"Misunderstanding? Sure. Mister Weynman, let us into Central Security, and we can help you locate your lost lycanthrope."

"I see you doubt my sincerity," said Weynman.

"You doubt mine?" asked Danalov, staring down his rifle's sights at the corner where he expected to see a black helmet and a rifle appear any second.

Several things happened in the same split second.

Stewart said, "Got it."

A few yards away, the door to Central Security opened. Over the GD team's radio channel, Danalov said, "We're in."

And Hell broke loose in the hall.

Cooke started shooting streams of suppressive fire down the hall to keep the Security Force's heads down. Markovski dropped a smoke grenade to screen them, and they began a tactical peel backward toward the gaping black doorway of Central Security.

The Security Force's point men opened fire down the hall, only their rifles visible, and sprayed angry swarms of supersonic automatic fire down the corridor. Markovski went down as a round ripped through his ankle and another shot through the meat of his thigh.

From where he stood in the doorway of the opposite office, Lorca, their combat medic, launched out, low and fast, as Jakes fired on full automatic down the hallway. He raced to Markovski and rolled him over his shoulder in a diving fireman's carry, then slammed into the opposite office doorway, splintering it open. Cooke followed, laying down further suppressive fire and then stacking on the office door. Lorca had triaged Markovski in seconds, even as bullets whizzed by outside.

"Sons of bitches," spat Markovski.

"Thigh wound went through and through and missed the arteries. Ankle's shot, though. Looks like the round shattered the bone," said Lorca into the radio.

"Roger," said Danalov. "Can you get him here?"

"Damn right," said Cooke.

"Make it happen. We'll clear Central Security."

"Yes, boss," said Cooke. He looked over at Markovski and said, "They've just about pissed me off now." He drew a fragmentation grenade from a pouch, pulled the pin, counted two, and hurled it as hard as he could against the far wall where the Security Force was stacked, then he jumped on top of Markovski and Lorca, covering them with his body.

In the second and a half it took for the grenade to land at the feet of the Security Force point man who was stacked on the east corner, Danalov and Stewart darted quickly into Central Security, weapons at the ready for anyone they might find inside. There were two men there, one behind a low counter and one, predictably, in the corner. Danalov's round penetrated the security man's skull just above the hairline as he crouched there. He turned to take the man in the corner, but Stewart was already firing. The man took three rounds to the torso and one to the neck, twitched, and fell as he jerked the trigger of his rifle and a round lodged itself into the ceiling above Danalov's head.

Then, a deafening explosion rocked the corridor, sucked the air out of their lungs, and for a moment the lights flickered and died.

When he could breathe, Danalov coughed into the radio.

"Cooke? Was that a damned frag?"

His ears were ringing almost to the point of deafness. Gradually he began to make out the sounds of dying men on the far side of the corridor.

"Yes, sir. Yes it was."

"Report?"

"Lorca and I are up," said Cooke. "Markovski is going to be fine. Jakes, you good?"

"I'm good here," said Jakes.

Danalov picked himself up off the floor, "Regroup inside Central Security now."

CHAPTER 35:

A FRANK CONVERSATION

3am
Sunday, 25 June 2017
Hutchins, Nebraska

They had found a diner on the outskirts of Hutchins. Lela and Aria sat at a red booth across from Joseph and a hastily patched-up Gregory, each one of them deeply aware of the irony of the situation. After all, this was Lorne Hutchins' hometown, and had he not run such a diner as this for years on Route 66 in Arizona, and then later in Big Sur, California? Lela and Aria were what they were because of Lorne. For a moment his dark presence seemed, as they sat together, to be leering at them from the darkened windows. The others of the *Gladius Dei* were seated at the counter, near enough if there was trouble but far enough away for discretion, if not privacy.

"So, say what you came to say," said Aria.

"I'm not your enemy," said Joseph. "For starters."

"Doesn't your organization kill people like me?" asked Aria.

"Yes, but—"

"Sounds like we're enemies, then."

"No. Maybe we were. But now I'm not so sure," said Joseph.

"Why is that?" asked Lela.

"Because the bosses are breaking rules," said Gregory, his face a grimace. The fact that he wasn't in the hospital was a testament to his toughness and the medical skills of the *Gladius Dei* operators.

"What rules?" Lela felt suddenly like reaching out and ripping their throats from their necks. The rising aggression was hormonal, but the anger was real. They were killers of her kind. She scratched the table, looking down at her coffee. Fought the murdering urge down.

"You okay?" whispered Aria.

"I'm fine."

"Listen, forgive me. I'm a librarian. A scholar and a historian," said Joseph. "Sometimes a bit of a detective, maybe. Here's what I know: The *Gladius Dei* knows about you two, and the *auto-da-fay* came down for you to be hunted. Fine. Normal enough. It was only a matter of time before you hurt someone, kill someone, or infected someone. But we have very old rules about this sort of thing. We don't involve anyone who is innocent. We don't involve family without special permissions and in special circumstances. Like, for example, if a husband might know where a wife is hiding, we wouldn't scoop him up and interrogate him. We might watch and hope he'd lead us there eventually, but we would be at pains not to harm him or interfere with him. That's a rule, and we take it very seriously."

"Very *noble*," Aria grumbled.

"So, it was strange that we had to snatch up Frank, but that was the order from high up. At first, we thought maybe it was because we'd missed something. Maybe you'd infected him. Sexual contact can often be a vector for your particular strain of werewolfism. But he isn't infected."

"You *snatched up* my Frank?" Lela rose from the table. The other *Gladius Dei* at the counter all stood up, reaching into their jackets.

"I did," said Gregory quietly. "Now sit down."

For a tense moment, the diner was silent. Lela sat.

"Continue," she said.

"Lela, there's more, but you should try to be calm, okay?" said Joseph.

She nodded curtly.

"Frank wouldn't give us any information. I guess you already know you married a hard case," said Gregory.

"I'm surprised he didn't kill you," Lela said.

"Well, one thing we could have done is used him as bait. I mean, that's how you hunt big game, isn't it? But that's not what they wanted. The bosses broke another rule: we are a secret organization. If you're not *in* our world, we don't *bring* you in. We don't share. We don't admit. But the bosses had us do a handoff with a third party organization. We gave Frank to another outfit on orders. Unheard of," said Gregory.

"Who?" asked Lela icily.

"Men in black."

"G-men?" asked Aria.

"I'd guess contractors," said Gregory.

"Contractors?"

Joseph nodded. "I'm thinking maybe the bosses are working with some other outfit, maybe the government...and the reason they want Frank is because they want you alive. And the only reason to want you alive, no offense, is because they want what any government would want. To weaponize you. Or to weaponize the Diana Strain."

"Where is Frank now?" asked Lela.

"I don't know," said Joseph.

"I do," said Aria.

Everyone looked at her. She pointed to the muted television in the far corner of the diner. Grainy helicopter footage showed Frank running down the Strip after a huge hairy biped in the middle of the Las Vegas Strip, and beneath it ran a ribbon of text: "WEREWOLF IN VEGAS? DOZENS KILLED".

"Oh my God," said Joseph.

CHAPTER 36:

CROW AT YGGDRASIL

The World Tree
Outside of time

I n the heights of the World Tree, Nob clutched a branch in the shadow of Crow.

You do not know that wolves and crows were twins of woe, once. But they were. The children of Wolf and mine were at every battle, every war, for millennia. We came for the dead. We all came for the Dead. But Fenris, Loki's child, changed things. A pack of wolves can eat much, but Fenris wanted to eat all things. He was Hunger given teeth. Foolishly, you tried to reason with him. Do you remember? You cannot reason with him. He and his children will consume all, and the war of Ragnarok will decide if he succeeds or not. But now Fenris has lost Mani, the God of the Moon, and his own daughters have turned from him, following you as we planned. I spy our chance to weaken him before Ragnarok begins in earnest.

"What more can be done?" asked Nob.

They know it not, but Mani's blessings will shield them from the weaknesses of their kind, yet the price will be terrible, for the Moon is a changing thing, and they will be changed likewise. Their power must be turned toward stopping the powers and principalities from making Rannulf's Blood a spear to wield in their wars. Freki's curse was given by Fenris, made to do vengeance and wrought in murder and blood. No hand is safe that uses a cursed blade. Direct them thither to the sanctum, their brewing place, that cauldron of Death. Aid them. If the human doctors succeed in harnessing the Curse, so, too, does Fenris succeed in raising an army and beginning Ragnarok, and the ending of all things between his black jaws.

"As you say," said Nob. He slipped from the dark branches of the World Tree, sailing down toward the Earth, a cloud of black wings and shadow.

CHAPTER 37:

CHARLIE CONTINGENCY

Late Afternoon
Sunday, 25 June 2017
Site Bravo

here would be no more war, not because Man could now split atoms, but because Man could manipulate the double-helix. No man more so than Doctor Robert Lannon. They would call him, in the Millennia to come, "The Peace Bringer."

His image would replace Christ, the Buddha, and all those old forms of superstition. Instead, Robert Lannon would dwarf even Mendel and Darwin, and stride across the future of the Human Species as the purest Savior and deliverer of Science and Truth ever to be revealed in the Cosmos.

This he knew. This he understood as few Great Men ever fully grasp. Doctor Lannon would conceive and deliver an Age without disease, without war, without need. All it would take was sacrifice.

Weynman was dead. The fool had tangled with the *Gladius Dei* on *their* terms and lost. Now the zealots had taken Central Security. Lannon spoke softly to Meyers, his newly promoted Chief of Security, as the last one was now in pieces on a slab in Site Bravo's morgue.

"Meyers, I want my site back, and I want all research safeguarded, and I want those fanatics stopped before they do any more damage."

Meyers, who couldn't have been out of his 20s, nodded. "Yes, sir. I have clearance to use Contingency Charlie?"

"You do. But this must not get out. And do be careful...it's nasty stuff."

"Understood, sir."

"You may go."

Meyers left Lannon's laboratory, took a deep breath in the darkened hall with its swirling emergency lighting, and keyed the mic on the radio handset on his left shoulder. "This is Meyers. We are go for Contingency Charlie. MOPP up. I say again, go for Charlie Contingency. MOPP up. All personnel in Sectors Four through Ten get into MOPP Gear. We are releasing in ten minutes. Evacuate the south Corridor and pop the breakers to Security Control."

He released the mic, wiped the beading sweat from his forehead, and picked up a double time to the utility room that controlled ventilation.

Danalov, of course, was monitoring the radio traffic as best he could from inside Central Security. It was difficult because Cooke's grenade had done serious damage to their ability to hear well. Nevertheless, Danalov heard Meyers give the order. Whatever this Charlie Contingency was, it wasn't anything they had briefed *Gladius Dei* about. Had he said MOPP? That was a military term for Nuclear, Biological, and Chemical protective gear. It's what soldiers put on when they think someone's fighting *dirty*.

"Sounds like an incoming chemical attack," said Cooke.

"And us without our biohazard gear..." said Lorca grimly.

"Time to go, then," said Danalov. "We can come back and scrub the site, but we have to survive to do that. Get ready to move. Cooke, I don't want this security room to be functional when they get it back. It should slow things for them."

"Roger."

Every monitor went dark, and the emergency backup lights kicked on.

"They've cut the power," said Cooke. "How novel. Why didn't I think of that?"

"Let's move," said Danalov.

CHAPTER 38:
THE MARSHALL'S CHOICE

Evening
Washington D.C.

The Cathedral of St. Matthew the Apostle, Seat of the Archbishop of the Roman Catholic Archdiocese of Washington D.C., was quiet at that hour of dusk. Inside the immense red brick structure, Cardinal Donovan Frye, was sitting quietly at his enormous desk, watching the light fail outside his window. In theory, Cardinal Frye was meant to be reviewing expense and attrition reports prepared by the High Justices and High Inquisitors of his Order operating in the United States just now, but his mind kept wandering.

He was one of the seven Marshalls of the secret Holy Order of *Gladius Dei*, who answered only to the Grand Marshall, Adolfo Conditti, in Rome, and easily one of the most powerful men in the world. He commanded the wealth of the Roman Catholic Church, the respect (if not the love) of the College of Cardinals, and a paramilitary fighting force capable of (and busily employed in) bringing down superhuman enemies. Tonight, though, the Cardinal was concerned.

Rumblings had begun that his alliance with ProGen, his allowances for their research, was unsettling some of his more important underlings. Would they go to the Grand Marshall? He would have to silence the disloyal before that could occur. He turned it over in his mind.

It could be said he had betrayed the Order by striking the Devil's bargain that he had with Weynman, Lannon, and Senator Freedman. But Cardinal Frye considered it a necessary step in transforming the *Gladius Dei* from a relic to something more potent. His decision to trade a Diana Strain corpse for fighting men that could replenish the flagging ranks of the Order was...yes, it had been necessary. The Grand Marshall, if he learned it, could not deny the logic of it. But even as Frye confirmed this to himself, he looked down at his trembling hand and steadied it on the cool smoothness of the poisonwood desk.

At 70, he was still a fit man. His time as a crusader in the Order taught him the value of maintaining readiness. He had been a boy in Philadelphia when he had first encountered a malevolent spirit, and that encounter had led him, ultimately, to a confessional where he divulged all in his terror. The priest, Father Morley, had directed the attention of the Order toward young Donovan Frye.

He mused on this, his beginnings. His early fears became a determination to fight back against the dark. Had he betrayed the Order in his efforts to save it? Again, that question.

"No," he said aloud to the empty room. His office door opened and Marcus, his bodyguard, looked in. He was built like a linebacker with a barrel chest, thick arms, and a boxy torso, but wore a tailored suit, clip-on tie and an almost perfectly hidden high caliber pistol. Senator Freedman's political friendship had many years ago purchased, among other things, licensing for *Gladius Dei* operatives to carry firearms in the city of Washington D.C.

"Your Eminence? Did you need something?"

"Marcus, I'm sorry. I'm afraid old men talk to themselves sometimes. I'll be ready to leave shortly." He gave it up for a bad job and closed the manila folder whose contents totted up, in columns of black and white, the human and monetary costs of killing monsters professionally. Standing, stretching, and yawning, the Cardinal then slipped the folder into a recessed filing cabinet.

"Yes, Your Eminence. I'll have them pull the car around." Marcus closed the door softly behind him.

"Thank you." Frye's smile failed him. "Have I betrayed the men who protect me? Have I sold us out?" he wondered aloud.

The question trailed him out the door, down the hall and the stairway, and into the waiting gray Jaguar—following like a shadow.

"To the Castle, please, Marcus."

"Yes, Your Eminence."

The Castle was an 11,000 square foot Georgian manor house forty minutes out of Washington near the Potomac River front. It was surrounded by 400 acres of woodland grounds and a fifteen foot brick wall. Within the *Gladius Dei*, it was known as "The Castle" or "The Courthouse." It was the place where those who broke with *Gladius Dei* law or defied direct orders were offered a hearing and either exonerated or sanctioned by a jury of their peers.

During the drive, Cardinal Frye switched on the radio and the news channel reported two rather shocking pieces of news: one, Senator Freedman had been shot and killed in his home by his own wife, and two, a bipedal wolf-like animal had apparently rampaged through the Las Vegas Strip, killing multiple victims before it was brought down by a man that authorities were now confirming was former Monterey County Sheriff's Deputy Frank Crow.

Frye's face went white. He picked up his cell phone, then thought better of it.

"Get us there fast. I need to make a call from a secure line. God help us..."

Marcus put the pedal on the floor, the Jaguar's engine went from a purr to a growl, and they slid into the deep darkness of the nighttime trees a few miles from The Castle.

In another mile on the twisting road, a large deer slammed into the windshield. The front end of the speeding Jaguar crumpled like a Coke can and went into a spin as Marcus fought for control. They spun off the road in milliseconds and slammed full force into a tree. The airbags did not deploy, and although both men were wearing seatbelts, they slammed their heads into the dashboard and steering wheel, respectively. Darkness swallowed Cardinal Frye.

When he came to, the pain was excruciating. Concussion, almost certainly. He vomited, then looked around, his eyes clouded over with dancing points of white light, then slowly beginning to clear.

"M-Marcus?"

"Marcus is dead, Your Eminence," came a very deep voice from somewhere outside the crippled vehicle.

Frye looked to Marcus in the driver's seat and saw that it was true. Marcus' neck was broken, and his head hung at a strange and grotesque angle. Groggily, he turned to look in the direction of the voice, but his neck screamed in protest. He winced, then reached out and shakily opened the passenger door, staggering out and keeping his hand on the roof of the car for support. His knees threatened to buckle.

"W-who are you?"

"Nothing. No one," came the voice again. "But you may call me Keller, if it pleases you."

There was a blur of darkness between two trees nearby that Cardinal Frye suspected might be the shape of a man with a smudge of deathly pale flesh where his face should be. *Vampire.* Almost certainly. Frye thought about Marcus's holstered gun inside the Jaguar's cab. It seemed miles away, while his death was only inches distant.

"You gave up secrets you should have kept, Your Eminence."

Frye's breath caught. "What do you know about it?"

"Enough. I know enough. You must pay for it. As you are a man of God, I will allow you to pray before your death. It is more mercy than your Order has extended to my kind in hundreds of years."

"You threw that deer at the windshield, didn't you? It was already dead. They'll check that. No one in the Order will believe this was a car accident. They'll see it for what it was."

"Oh, perhaps. That's not relevant anymore. Or, rather, you can discuss it all with God when you meet Him."

"I'm surprised a being like you can bear to speak of the Lord."

"I have my own Lords to serve. Pray, or I will begin."

Frye nodded, and turned toward the vehicle, kneeling like a penitent on the passenger door. He put his hands together in prayer, eyes fixed on the gun on poor dead Marcus's right hip. His hands were two feet away.

He felt, rather than heard, Keller approaching. He lunged for the gun, retrieved it from its holster, and turned the gun toward Keller.

The impossibly pale wraith arched an eyebrow.

"I don't think that will help you."

Frye shot him twice in the heart. Keller staggered backward, growled, and stood again, his eyes going from pools of black to blood red, his long fangs gleaming in the lurid red of the Jaguar's rear lights.

"Now you'll suffer," said Keller, striding forward.

The Cardinal shook his head, a soft smile on his lips as Keller lifted him by the lapels off the ground with casual ease.

"The *Gladius Dei* will end your suffering, vampire. Mine is over. When they come for you, tell them I am sorry for what I did." Frye raised the gun and shot himself in the head.

The loud report echoed through the trees. Keller watched the light disappear from Cardinal Frye's eyes impassively, then dropped the body. The old man's body crumpled awkwardly at his feet, the bullet hole in its head still smoking.

"I will tell them," said Keller. Then he was gone.

CHAPTER 39:

FRANK AT MERCY HOSPITAL

Late Afternoon
Sunday, 26 June, 2017
Las Vegas, Nevada

Before he opened his eyes, Frank was dreaming of Lela's face as he remembered it back when they first fell in love. If anything, she had grown more beautiful to his eyes in the days and years since. But in his dream, they were together on the grass looking out over Second Sister Lake in Ann Arbor. She was telling him of beautiful libraries like the Clementinum in Prague and the Malfa in Portugal. Frank was watching her face in the sunlight, electrified by ideas of these places he had never guessed at and about which she was passionate. He said, "I love you." Her face, in that moment, was frozen in his mind. If there is a heaven, he had thought, angels look like this…

But Frank awakened to pain. Fluorescent light flickered down at him, sickly and green, and there was a dull white humming of machines and distant voices against bare walls, someone crying softly in another room, people speaking in hushed tones. Beneath him was a firm bed, and as he looked down, he saw IVs up and down his arms. He saw handcuffs fixing his right arm to the metal bar of the bed. Hospital.

The squawk of a radio muted by an earbud outside the door, probably the cop tasked with guarding him. This room looked out on city light—third story he guessed. His head felt foggy. The werewolf hadn't scratched him, had it? His stomach lurched. And yet, if he was infected, maybe he and Lela could reconcile.

Horror and longing warred in his heart as he searched quietly for claw marks down his arms, chest, and legs, all the while very careful not to use his right hand or let the handcuffs clink against the metal bar of the bed. He went slowly. Methodically. He was bruised, and had some cuts from broken glass, but he found no immediate signs of teeth or claws. It was, at best, a question mark. He looked left, then right slowly, trying to determine a way out.

He heard brisk footsteps in the hall coming toward his room. Then, a familiar voice spoke to the cop guarding his room.

"Frank Crow's room?"

"Yes, sir."

"This is for you." The sounds of paperwork exchanging hands.

"Yes sir," said the cop.

Frank's brother Bill stepped in, looking every inch the haggard G-Man living on bad coffee, little sleep, and two packs a day. In his right hand was a briefcase. He smiled at Frank.

"Hey, Bill," said Frank, more relieved than he would ever admit. "What kept you?"

"Hey, Frankie. You look like I feel."

Bill moved to the side of the hospital bed and produced a handcuff key, "I have special authorization to take you into protective custody."

"That sounds very official and important," said Frank.

Bill unhooked the cuff from Frank's wrist and said, "Your tax dollars at work, laddybuck."

Frank got up slowly and stiffly, grimacing.

Bill opened his briefcase on the hospital bed and threw a change of clothes to Frank.

"Hope these are your size."

Frank stepped gingerly into the jeans and cracked and popped as he lifted the t-shirt over his head. His boots were in the corner of the room in a plastic bag, still blood-splattered. He winced as he bent to pull them on.

"Where are we headed?" asked Frank.

"Oregon. But we have a lot to talk about. I need you to brief the Hostage Rescue Team about, uh, you know… werewolves."

"Yeah. I guess I know a little bit about that subject. Speaking of which, that werewolf's body, the one I shot, who has it now?" asked Frank.

"I have a team collecting it now downstairs."

Frank collected his last effects, and they slipped out into the hallway, past the elevator, and toward the stairs. Moving with effort, Frank followed Bill, but instead of heading down the stairs, they went upward.

"We're not going down?"

"No," said Bill. "And hurry up."

Frank followed, out of breath as they reached the roof. A Blackhawk the color of night was just beginning to spin up for liftoff on the helipad with a squad of FBI H.R.T. operators inside.

"You're much too competent for government work, Bill," Frank said over the wind.

Bill just grinned. They moved quickly across the roof and into the waiting chopper, Frank's muscles protesting the whole way. As soon as they were aboard, the Blackhawk ascended, turned northward, and disappeared into the dark.

Frank and Bill rode side-by-side in the chopper, high above the Nevada desert and into nightfall.

"We'll need to stop and refuel and take on a team," said Bill above the roar of engine and rotor.

"How far?" asked Frank.

In answer, Bill extended his hand toward a point of light on the horizon Frank could just make out as a military base, its perimeter fence line lit by the strange orange glow of sodium lamps. It didn't take long for the helicopter to land on the dark tarmac of an airfield surrounded by hangars.

Both men disembarked, crouching low, at 90 degrees from the cockpit. They moved toward a hangar where a platoon of men in black fatigues waited in formation, rifles at port arms. Bill met the uniformed officer at the front of the formation, and Frank instinctively moved to the rear, and fought down the instinct to move to the position of parade rest as the men before him were doing.

"Gentlemen, I am Special Agent Bill Crow," Bill said to the platoon. "I am here to brief you and to accompany you on this op. With me is a subject matter expert on the animals we are going to be dealing with. First, let me say that there is a possibility of contamination and infection, so you'll go in MOPPed up. If a man is scratched or bitten, he must self-report as soon as practicable. I cannot stress how important this is for your safety and the safety of the Unit. Our objective this evening is to seize control of an underground bioweapons complex known as Site Bravo. We do not know if their experiments have been successful—we do know they have a dead specimen. Hopefully they have not been able to afflict any test subject with the disease. Here to tell you more about this is Frank Crow, our subject matter expert, He is a decorated Marine Corps veteran, a former Detective for the Monterey County Sheriff's Office in California."

Frank stepped to the front of the formation and said, "I'm standing here with you because I have personally lived with two infected for nearly a year. I engaged the one that infected my wife in battle and killed one of the escaped test subjects from Site Bravo several hours ago. It would have killed me had it not been for the intervention of a third party. Here's what I know: these things are capable of changing from an extraordinarily strong human shape to that of a nearly invulnerable bipedal wolf-human hybrid standing between ten and twelve feet tall, with increased speed, six-inch claws, jaws capable of potentially bending steel, opposable thumbs, animal ferocity, and a human ability to strategize. During these changes, an afflicted person will be prone to fits of bloodlust and may attack people that otherwise they would not. They can eat an adult human entirely in less than fifteen minutes."

A hand went up, and Frank called on the man who raised it.

"Sir, how the hell do we kill them?"

"They have a severe allergy to silver, which will burn the skin like acid with increasing severity depending on the purity of the silver. They heal very quickly from most wounds but not those inflicted by silver, and they can probably be burned to death in a seriously hot fire."

One of the sergeants raised a hand. Frank called on him.

"You mean to tell me there's such a thing as werewolves, sir?" he asked.

Some of the men chuckled.

Bill cleared his throat and spoke up. "In folklore, these creatures were known as werewolves, but our official designation for infected people at present is Whiskey SS. Wolf, shape-shifter. Upon encountering one, if they have indeed successfully infected a live subject, your Rules of Engagement are to kill on sight. Secondarily, once the facility is secured all contaminated genetic material is to be burned. Civilian personnel will be secured and quarantined back here at Camp P for not less than thirty days for observation. If you are exposed to the disease, report it immediately through your chain of command. In any event, the objective is to secure the facility. Is that clear?"

"Yes, sir. It's all just a little unbelievable," responded the sergeant.

"You think I'm up here for my health?" asked Frank, his eyes narrowing. There was a long silence.

"No, sir," said the sergeant.

"You'd better get your head around what's about to happen and what you are facing, because you're on track to fuck this up by doubting what I've learned from bitter experience, Sergeant," said Frank, his voice heating. Bill put a warning hand on his brother's shoulder.

"Easy," he said quietly in Frank's ear.

"Roger, that. My mistake, sir," said the sergeant.

Bill began again. "There are two ways into the facility that we know of. The first is the main entrance, which is an access control point, and the second is a subway tunnel. A frontal assault would be costly and so we will drill into the subway a few clicks out from the objective and make tactical movement with no sound into the subway station of Site Bravo. First Platoon will secure the station as a fallback point. Second Platoon will assault and secure the ACP from the rear. Third Platoon will secure the Facility control room. Fourth Platoon will remain in reserve in the Subway tunnel, securing First Platoon's flank and, if necessary, to peel off squads and reinforce any unit that calls for backup. Are there questions?"

No one spoke.

"Then get prepped. Birds go up in 60 minutes. Secure your gear, check your weapons, Sergeants check your squads and then wait on the flight line for further. Fall out, gentlemen."

The men fell out of their formation and began moving in all directions like a human ant hill suddenly disturbed.

An agent walked up to Bill and handed him a dossier. Bill reviewed it with a frown.

"Ahh, shit."

"What?" asked Frank. "Or what now, anyway?"

"Two Whiskeys are wanted in connection with a massacre in the desert near the Arizona line. State troopers stopped them, then signs of an animal attack and their vehicles were set on fire. It's Lela and Aria, Frank."

Frank grimaced.

"So, they're on foot in the desert somewhere between New Mexico and Arizona?"

"There's a manhunt ongoing. They'll likely be found."

Frank turned to Bill with fire in his eyes.

"I'd like to see an armory."

"You're not really a shooter on this op, Frank."

"I'd like. To see. An armory, Bill."

Bill looked at Frank, looked at the sky and sighed.

"You need to understand, this thing is extremely sensitive. The Director, hell, the Intelligence Oversight Committee, even the President is likely to be briefed on what happens on this one," said Bill.

"Bill, I want a weapon. You can either show me where to get one, or turn your back for a few minutes and make it deniable, but one way or the other I'm going to be armed."

Bill considered that for a moment as the men of the Hostage Rescue team buzzed hither and thither, their calls and talk loud and urgent as any pre-op ever is.

"Stubborn," said Bill, finally. He gestured toward the rear of the hangar and turned back toward the chopper, pretending not to see his brother slip away amid the bustle and confusion.

Frank walked with grim purpose back toward the armory, which ended up being a large cage. He entered and took stock. His body was bruised, sore, and tired. He hadn't slept properly in some days. By rights he shouldn't be going into a potential combat situation. He surveyed the weapons on hand and opted for a Mossberg 12 gauge shotgun, a SigSauer 9mm pistol, and a silenced H&K PSG1 sniper rifle. He threw ammunition and extra magazines into a black duffel bag, and wheeled out of the cage back toward the chopper.

In the air, Bill briefed him.

"You are strictly coming along as an advisor. You are not a door-kicker on this op, Frank. I need to make that clear. You are being authorized to carry self-defense weapons as it is a hostile environment, but you should only use your weapons as a last resort if your life is in immediate danger. Is that understood?"

"Understood," said Frank. "I just want to be there to make sure this curse doesn't ruin anyone else's life."

Bill nodded his understanding. They both watched the darkness below them for a time, as the chopper sped northwards. Frank wondered where Lela was and hoped she was safe. Bill looked over at his brother with concern, and wondered if this was all a big mistake. The moon above them glowed, a pale sliver on its secret way across the sky.

CHAPTER 40:

CROSSROADS

Morning.
Sunday, 27 June, 2017.
Somewhere in Wyoming.

They were driving west in the Cadillac with the top down. Lela, Aria, Gregory and Joseph cruised into the day, silent and blood-splattered. Gregory dozed, and Joseph watched the countryside go by as Aria drove and Lela looked inward.

After a long time, Lela sighed. "We've been going about this all wrong," she said.

"What do you mean?" Aria asked.

"We have both been hoping there's a cure. That if we went back far enough there would be a cure. There is no cure. This is it."

"How do you know that?"

"Because this is a spiritual affliction," said Lela. "A curse from Fenris."

"No one has ever been cured that we know of," said Joseph helpfully. Both ladies gave him a look.

"Thank you, Joseph," said Lela. "My point is, there's no sense in hunting for a cure."

"I think I agree," said Aria.

After a long time, Lela said, "The thing to do is die."

Aria looked at her sharply.

"I am not planning on dying anytime soon."

"Plan? You didn't plan on any of this, did you? In falling for Billy Hatfield, in becoming a werewolf, in killing several state troopers, in meeting a wolf god the size of a building?"

"I didn't die during any of that. I don't mean to jump on the death cult wagon because you've decided we are cursed."

"I haven't decided we are cursed. We *are* cursed. And the only way to be sure we don't spread the curse is to die."

"You're talking about throwing away an amazing gift," said Aria.

"Oh, yes? Really? A gift? Are you kidding?"

"This can be survived," said Aria. "We can take steps. We can make arrangements. We can practice greater control when the Change is on us. We can be around people like Frank who will protect us when we need protecting. We can—"

"This isn't some alternative lifestyle into which we might develop a subculture. It's not like sexual orientation or something. We are killers and sooner or later we will kill again."

"A lot of people deserve killing," said Aria sullenly.

"And you're going to arbitrate that?" Lela asked.

"It has been given to us to use this power."

"That's all wrong. We haven't earned this power. It's not like we spent years disciplining ourselves to master something—because that breeds discretion and maturity. We are unhinged by this power. We *eat people*. Unearned, undisciplined power is dangerous to everyone, including whoever wields it."

"We can go get Frank, fix things, set up some kind of system, target specific people like drug dealers and pedophiles and mobsters…"

"You're dreaming, Aria. We aren't superheroes."

"Then why are we driving west?" Aria shot back.

"Because Frank needs—"

The morning light disappeared on the prairie like a flicked switch makes a dark room. There was only black beyond their headlights. There, in the center of a crossroad, stood the tall, dark figure of Nob.

Aria pulled over, screeching to a halt, and both women got out. Gregory awoke wincing and drew a pistol. Joseph sat in the rear of the Caddie, watching silently.

"Nob?" Lela said, approaching him. Then both women doubled over, their bodies beginning to contort and change. The surface of their skins began to glow. When they had changed fully, they sat very still. From the glowing shoulder tattoo of the moon on Lela's skin emerged the bent form of Mani, the God of the Moon. They lay beside him, their eyes empty.

"We meet at last, Mani," said Nob. "I am an emissary of Crow."

"I could smell it on you," said Mani.

"I come to offer aid."

"These daughters of mine must thwart Fenris's plan to emerge and begin Ragnarok. They go to save one they love, but their purpose is greater than this. How do you propose to help?" asked Mani.

"I can open a gateway, but what they face will require greater power than they now possess," said Nob.

"I am with them. Much will I do to strengthen them, but it must wait until nightfall."

"Very well. It shall be so. We will take the fight to the enemy at dusk," said Nob.

The wolf women growled, curling around Mani's sides.

Then daylight blinked back into the world, and both women lay naked on the road, and Nob and Mani were gone, and Joseph and Gregory wondered, unremembering, why they had stopped at all.

CHAPTER 41:
ASSAULT ON SITE BRAVO

Evening.
Sunday, 25 June, 2017.
Site Bravo.

Danalov took point as they ran through the abandoned corridors toward the exit, trying to escape before whatever hell brew they had cooked up could hit the ventilation system. Cooke and Lorca carried Markovski while Jakes and Stewart brought up the rear.

Then the gas poured in, flooding the hall. They began to choke immediately, and fell writhing on the floor.

Above their choked screams of agony, Doctor Lannon's voice piped in over the intercom.

"In fact, what you are experiencing may be our greatest achievement, my friends. You see, if gas like this were deployed in a populated area, we calculate the mortality rate would be something like 85 percent, give or take.

Danalov, meanwhile, felt his limbs contorting, joints cracking, skin burning, his system going into what, if he could think, he would recognize as shock. Lorca and Markovski were shrieking in voices not quite human as their muscles seized and bulged grotesquely, bones breaking as they lengthened and rolled beneath their skins. Cooke, Jakes, and Stewart had ceased moving entirely, their bodies frozen in a rictus of pain, necks snapped, hearts burst, tendons snapped like broken piano wires.

"The reason for the high mortality rate is relatively straightforward. It takes a woman roughly nine months or so for her body to undergo the necessary changes to pass a child from her womb. It is incremental, you see. But if she were to go from insemination to labor in minutes, she would almost certainly die. It is no different with our friend, the lycanthrope. It takes at least one lunar cycle to prepare the body for the first change, after which the necessary hormones continue to build until he or she can change more or less at will, and sometimes without meaning to in heightened situations. But to change all at once, at the moment of infection? Well, you can see for yourselves . . ."

Danalov saw his team dying. Their screams had ceased and the gas had stopped flowing. They gasped out their last, laboring like lungfish stranded in black mud of a dry pool under a searing African sun. His skin was an inferno as tufts of black hair sprouted in patches. His lungs were bellows in a forger's fire. His mouth frothed with white foam as he twisted, his body's transformation impossibly painful.

"You see," continued Doctor Lannon over the intercom, "the wonders of this weapon are also that whatever survivors are left will become agents of chaos and contagion, and as far as we can tell, the higher mental faculties of lycanthropized survivors are almost entirely diminished; they are dumb animals, incapable of reverting back to a human form. Do you feel your mind beginning to slip away, Mister Danalov? Do you feel the Wolf Mind growing to replace what you used to be?"

Danalov couldn't really hear, and certainly was in no state to answer, but the last sane thought in his head, the last *human* thought, was a prayer for death.

Keller slipped unseen into Site Bravo moments before Danalov raised his head as a wolfman and howled for the first time in animal rage and pain. Keller had emerged as a shadow from the rear entrance of the mountain. As his Masters wished, Senator Freedman and Cardinal Frye were dead, although unfortunately Cardinal Frye's death would not appear to be an accident as Keller had intended. Nevertheless, nothing in Frye's apparent suicide pointed to any supernatural cause that officials could investigate.

The thrice-damned *Gladius Dei* would know better, of course, but they wouldn't know precisely what took place. In any case, Keller was not even a rumor. He was a shadow, and even if they were looking, they would not find him unless he wanted to be found. Tonight, he was here for Doctor Lannon, and for any evidence of the supernatural that would need to be purged before the authorities arrived.

He moved from shadow to shadow, down the dark hallways of Site Bravo toward the Director's office. He watched from a distance as the *Gladius Dei* team gasped their last breaths in the anguish of horrible metamorphosis. He listened to Lannon's explanation of the weaponized gas.

Keller disappeared into the air ducts as the beast that had been Danalov began to sniff the air for the scent of prey, and began stalking the halls with murderous stealth. If the monster had scented Keller, he made no sign of it as he disappeared down the long corridor.

In time, Keller found his way through the labyrinthine air handling of Site Bravo to the safe room where Doctor Lannon and his personal security detail of six men were hunkered. Keller, the shadow, slipped like vapor into the room from the air ducts.

The room was something like a cross between a hotel suite and a command center. Two men guarded the entrance, and one monitored the wall of screens that displayed comprehensive closed-circuit surveillance of the entire site. What remained of site security—about forty men—was sweeping room to room and hallway to hallway, looking for Danalov. Presumably they had silver ammunition.

The beast that had been Danalov wasn't on any of the monitors. Where Danalov had gone was a question of some urgency and the radio chatter between the security element and the man monitoring the camera feeds reflected this urgency. The other three bodyguards in the panic room were standing within five feet of Lannon in a loose triangle, looking outward and holding slung Submachine guns at the low ready.

Keller, all but invisible, watched from the shadows of the adjoining restroom. He watched and waited.

"There!" said the guard manning the surveillance station, jabbing a finger at a particular monitor. He began speaking into the radio, "Sweep team Bravo, this is Control. The target is in the train station, heading down the south rail line!"

The FBI's Hostage Rescue team put down several kilometers from Site Bravo and began to drill into the subterranean subway system. Above them the winds kicked up and black clouds brooded over the distant mountains, blotting out the stars.

At about three feet down, they dropped in a shape charge and pulled back. Upon detonation, the explosion punched a hole straight down into the subway tunnel wide enough for them to rappel, one by one, onto the tracks of the dead train whose smoldering wreckage still smoked in North Las Vegas.

They moved with tactical precision, establishing a perimeter as man after man rappelled down into the darkness. Bill and Frank waited in the stack beside the other men as the darkness deepened. There was a sudden flash of blue light followed by a deafening crash and the rains began to pelt down and the winds began to howl.

Presently Frank and Bill rappelled down, one after the other. They cleared the landing area for the men behind them, stacking into the 360-degree security perimeter. Their night vision goggles turned the dark subway tunnel a grainy green with white beams tracing across the walls where the team's Infrared sights stabbed into shadow.

When both platoons were in position on the tunnel floor, the commander, Agent Hendricks, gave the order to move out. They peeled off by squads, First Platoon's first squad taking point in a wedge across the tunnel, second and third squads in files just off the right and left walls, and fourth squad in a wedge behind first squad as backup.

They moved with purpose, efficient but careful and quiet.

And then, from ahead in the tunnel, lower than the faint rumble of thunder, came an animal growl that sent razorblades of ice up the back of Frank's neck. He switched the selector of his rifle to "FIRE." Beside him, the men of the Hostage Rescue team did the same.

Aria, Lela, Greg, and Joseph arrived, much to their surprise, in a whirl of black feathers before the main entrance of Site Bravo. Greg's wounds had all but disappeared, and Lela and Aria covered their nakedness with long cloaks of black feathers.

"Nob?" Lela asked, looking around. No answer came.

The entrance to Site Bravo didn't look like much: a clear perimeter cut from the forest, the rutted path in a mere disused logging road, a ten foot electric fence, concertina wire on top, small guard booth slumped at the base of the mountain, a set of closed heavy steel doors barring entry to the site, cameras, and two armed guards huddling in the guard booth against the rain. The sky was black and roiling, the winds tore at their clothing and pulled at their hair. Suddenly from above, the darkness was raked with jagged blue spears of lightning as thunder cracked the night.

"Where are we?" Greg asked above the wind. They hunkered beneath the trees, just off the road that ran along the edge of the security perimeter.

"This must be the place where they are doing their experiments," Joseph replied. "This is where they were taking Frank, if I had to guess."

"How did we get here?" asked Greg.

"Nob brought us here somehow," said Aria, examining the black feathers of her cloak.

"Frank is here. I don't know how I know that, but he is," Lela said, her voice deepening as she shifted into wolf form. Her cloak slid to the ground, momentarily showing the glint of a tattoo in the shape of a sword glowing on her back, and she stood to her full height as a wolf woman, 12 feet of her. Lela covered the distance to the fence with blinding speed, covered by the darkness and the rain.

"Oh, shit," said Aria, pulling her cloak off to momentarily reveal a glowing moon tattoo on her shoulder and shifting to wolf woman form, as well. She disappeared into the trees in the opposite direction, fading into the forest.

Joseph looked at Gregory as lightning shattered the darkness above them and thunder hammered in reply.

"What do we do next?" he asked.

"Strike team," said Gregory.

Joseph looked at him with frightened eyes. "Are you sure?"

"Has to be done," said Gregory, pulling his cell phone from his pocket.

Meanwhile, Lela had charged the guard shack. The guards didn't see her coming until she was upon them. In one smooth motion, she grabbed both men by the throat, jerked them off their feet, and slammed their heads together with a sickening crunch. She dropped them and both men fell twitching to the ground, their skulls crushed in. Aria returned from the forest with a huge log, newly fallen in the storm or ripped from the ground, Joseph couldn't tell, and carried it to the electrified fence, then half slammed, half dropped it on the gate, denting it on the first hit, and obliterating it by the third. She laid the splintered tree across the twisted steel and motioned for Gregory and Joseph to follow.

Inside the guard shack, Lela was growling in fury. There was no switch to open the great doors. Apparently, it was opened by someone on the inside. She loped out and up to the doors, then stopped abruptly. Aria came alongside her, and they looked at the same point, understanding dawning for both of them.

A dead crow lay before the doors, its blood smeared across the lenses of the cameras monitoring the front entrance. Inside they could hear the high, discordant sound of thousands of claws scratching against steel, loud even above the raging storm. Then the mighty doors bucked and broke open, and the air was black with crows.

They flew like a midnight cloud, spiraling into the sky. From the darkness of the broken doors stepped Nob in a black-feathered cloak. He was more gaunt than before, and more pale, but still at his great height of seven feet with broad shoulders and powerful arms. His eyes were without whites or irises, but seemingly just great drowning pools of pupil.

"Mani's Daughters, Frank is here," said Nob. "But here also is another power; Fenris plans to enter the world tonight. He must be stopped. I can lead you to the fight, but you will have to be the ones to fight it."

Both wolf women approached him, and they seemed to speak together without words for a time as if taking counsel.

Gregory and Joseph looked on, then moved to the guard shed and stripped the guards of their weapons, bullet-proof vests, radios, and ammunition. They broke into a standing locker and found additional ammo, then stepped out to find the wolf women and the crow man already gone into the depths of the mountain.

"How long until the Strike team arrives?" asked Joseph.

Gregory racked a round into his newly-acquired rifle and said, "His vengeance comes, and that right soon."

A specter, freshly dead, came before the high throne of Fenris, and Fenris spoke its name.

"Marlowe McCoy," came the booming voice.

The specter, the new wolf wraith, howled his presence to his Lord.

"You will go back to Midgard and prepare a way for my coming. The Ritual will bring me forth into the world of men, and there we shall feast on blood and bone. You will command my legions there, for your appetite is a shadow of my own, Marlowe McCoy."

Marlowe McCoy, wolf wraith of Fenris, grinned a razorblade grin and looked forward with great joy and unspeakable hunger to the taste of human flesh.

Within about sixty meters into the southern Tunnel from the underground subway station at Site Bravo, the ProGen Security Force platoon established a perimeter. They took cover behind quick-deployment portable barriers they brought up. The men, uniformly dressed in black and armored in cut-resistant armor, moved with drilled efficiency. Then they lit the area with spotlight-bright flashlights and began a high-frequency sonic bombardment of the tunnel designed to incapacitate Danalov and any other creature capable of hearing high-frequency sounds.

Within seconds, they heard animal cries of anguish deeper into the tunnel, and a tactical team moved in, lights blazing, toward the noise. The werewolf was writhing in agony, claws clamped over its ears. It was champing its jaws with terrible force and frothing madly.

The ProGen tactical team moved in to collect Danalov. One of them detached from the stack and uncapped a very large syringe, kneeling to administer it he froze. A beam of light from the dark side of the tunnel blinded him.

"ProGen Security, drop your weapons and surrender. This is the FBI! This facility is conducting illegal experiments and all materials are now government evidence. Do not attempt to resist." This came from the Commander.

Frank muttered to Bill under his breath, "He couldn't have waited until the guy sedated the goddamn werewolf?"

The ProGen Commander was speaking quickly into a radio asking for orders. There was a tense moment in which no one spoke. Danalov's writhing continued; he heaved and tossed himself upward in rage and pain, knocking the ProGen guard flying and sending the syringe with whatever hell brew sedative it contained spiraling into the dark.

It all happened so fast that one of the ProGen guards back at the barricades must have assumed the FBI, or whoever they were, had opened fire. He fired the first shot down the hallway and initiated the firefight to come.

H.R.T. returned fire, diving behind cover. A round struck the high-frequency transmitter, which died an instant later. The stack of ProGen operatives between

Danalov and the barricades began firing blindly down the hallway as they leapfrogged rearward toward relative safety.

Danalov roared out of the darkness in mindless, berserker fury. He snatched one of the operators up by throat with his teeth, twisting him like a human wrecking ball into his comrades. Then he danced backward with blinding speed into the shadows.

Everyone started firing, the tunnel magnifying and echoing explosion after explosion as rounds ricocheted and careened off steel and shattered concrete.

The H.R.T. aimed precise shots at the ProGen agents. The ProGen agents poured machine gun fire down the tunnel like furious swarms of wasps, and somewhere in the space between, Danalov hid. Frank was down in the prone position behind the raised hummock of the subway tracks, searching desperately down the night vision scope of his sniper rifle for the werewolf. Bill was beside Frank in the dust, firing his rifle at the ProGen guards as they popped up to shoot, and dropping them one by one.

Suddenly, in the middle of the firefight, the great form of Danalov the werewolf crawled from the tracks to where Frank and Bill were sheltered. He saw them and hissed, drawing its great mouth back to reveal huge and bloody fangs.

Doctor Lannon felt ill. He watched the firefight from his panic room with growing alarm, and his stomach began to churn. He bent double, then scrambled to the bathroom, pushing past his bodyguards and slamming the door behind him. Lannon vomited in the toilet.

The bodyguard was calling at the door, "Sir? Are you alright?"

Lannon spat the last of the bile from his mouth and between dry heaves, said, "Yeah, fine. Give me a few minutes."

Keller slipped from the corner of the bathroom in total silence, raising a clawed hand toward Lannon, but as he passed the mirror something peculiar caught his eye. He looked and there in the glass was a huge, black, wolfen shape with green baleful eyes grinning back at him from the other side of the mirror.

A wraith.

"Don't touch him," it said in a terrible voice. "He belongs to us."

Keller was stunned, but turned to kill Lannon anyway when a huge arm shot from the mirror, shattering it, and took the vampire's torso in its massive grip, slamming him into the wall so hard it cratered. Lannon looked up and screamed. Then the wolf wraith that was Marlowe McCoy was in the room, filling the space with his massive body that smelled of the charnel pits of Hell.

Keller, with his supernatural strength and speed, could not break free from Marlowe's grip though he struggled mightily against it. The bodyguards kicked open the bathroom door, rifles raised, and gaped, openmouthed, before opening fire on Marlowe. The bullets seemed to pass through him, pitting the white tiles of the bathroom shower that crashed, splintering down where Lannon cowered behind the toilet.

The bullets may not have hurt Marlowe, but they loosened his grip sufficiently that Keller slipped from beneath the massive paw pinning him to the wall, and he became a black shadow that disappeared into the vents.

McCoy picked up Lannon like a doll and turned to the guards, grinned madly. "We'll be going now, boys," he said gleefully. "The doctor has things to do. You're not qualified to keep him safe."

With a swipe of his clawed hand, he slashed long, deep gashes down to the bone into the guards as he passed and the five of them fell at once, bleeding their lives onto the blackening carpet. Marlowe took a moment at the wall of monitors, smiled madly, and boiled out of the panic room and into the facility with Doctor Lannon limp and catatonic in his paw.

Keller, like a shadow, followed them.

Lela and Aria, both still in wolf woman form, loped along on all fours behind Nob who walked as a man in a black-feathered cloak. They went into the smashed laboratory off the hall where Danalov's *Gladius Dei* team still lay in misshapen postures of agony and half-transformation.

"Who?" asked Aria in a growl, gesturing to the corpses.

"*Gladius Dei*, I think," said Nob. "But this that killed them was transforming them, too. A gas that kills as it transforms. Imagine in a big city. Survivors become *varulv* servitors of Fenris. Part of his Ragnarok army."

Lela stood over them a moment and shivered.

"This is part of why you are here. To stop this," said Nob.

Aria sniffed the air and growled, baring her teeth. Lela raised her snout and sniffed and slipped quietly into the laboratory.

"Wolf wraith? Here?" Aria growled to Nob.

Nob put his finger to his lips and said, "We'll follow. Hide for now."

Seconds later, Marlowe McCoy filled the hallway, his footfalls shaking the ground with each stride, his green eyes burning like putrescent geysers, his reek filling the place with the stink of sulfur and decay, his great, black claw closed around Doctor Lannon's chest, covering him from neck to waist. The wraith's skin seemed to shimmer like hot asphalt in the desert. Then he stopped dead at the door of the laboratory and took in a deep breath, his great lungs sounded like a hydraulic air pump, and he growled.

"Someone here?" he called. "I can smell you. Come on out, I won't hurt you. Much."

Lela crouched among the shattered beakers and broken test tubes, hidden behind the lab table in the center of the room. The great head of Marlowe McCoy barely fit through the door as he eased in for another sniff. Nearby, behind another table, Aria fought the urge to leap on the wraith and attack.

Her heartbeat quickened even as she hoped he couldn't to hear it. Lela heard it. Where Nob had gone, they had not seen, but they heard his voice as if from a great distance. Marlowe's head snapped back into the hallway, and he was moving again.

"I'll find you later," Marlowe roared as he carried Lannon deeper into the bowels of the facility. The sound of his footfalls died away.

Lela and Aria crawled out from where they hid. Nob appeared and said, "He goes to perform the ritual that will bring Fenris here. He must be stopped."

"Where's Frank?" asked Lela, her voice guttural and rough over the words.

Nob bowed his head, "Lela, this is bigger than—"

She stood to her full height over him and screamed, "Where's *Frank*?"

Nob sighed and pointed down the hall opposite where Marlowe and Lannon had disappeared.

"Frank is that way. But we need you. I have never been tested against a wolf wraith, and this one is imbued with terrible power."

Lela was in motion. Aria watched her go with something like pain on her face, but said nothing. There was nothing to say that would change things. Aria and Nob followed Marlowe and Lannon down one hallway. Lela ran toward the firefight in the subway, and toward Frank down the opposite hallway.

As the firefight raged around them between the FBI's Hostage Rescue team and the ProGen Security Force for Site Bravo, Frank was rising to a kneeling position and firing into Danalov's face. But the monster just kept coming. Whatever the silver content in the government-issued special ammunition, it wasn't pure enough, apparently, to put down one of Lannon's werewolves. If anything, the wolfman that had been Danalov only seemed more enraged with each bullet, but not weakened.

Frank emptied the rifle's magazine into the werewolf before it swiped his rifle away with one powerful blow. Bill was firing, too, but the beast only seemed to have eyes for Frank as it came on. Frank drew his sidearm as bullets from the firefight sizzled around them and emptied the magazine into Danalov's chest.

Flowers of red bloomed on the werewolf's fur in the half light, but Danalov reared back and tackled Frank to the ground. Bill was there then, standing over Danalov, using his empty rifle as a club again and again, yet the werewolf barely noticed, opening his jaws to crush Frank's torso with a roar of animal madness and pain, his eyes vacant of sanity or human feeling. The good man, the hunter of evil, was gone. Replaced by this monstrosity.

Lela crashed into Danalov from the side. She ripped him up and away from Frank and into the concrete wall of the tunnel with a snarl of outrage. Danalov was on his feet again instantly, circling in the darkness.

The cries of injured and dying men echoed in the tunnel as the firefight slowed. There were fallen bodies strewn across the tunnel in the half-light. The beasts circled each other snarling, then Danalov leaped for her throat and Lela ducked and raked her claws across his form from face to groin as he passed above her, nearly disemboweling him. He landed in a heap yowling and whimpering in animal pain, but was already visibly healing, rising and drawing back to give himself time to close his wounds. He healed much faster than any normal werewolf, she realized.

"Lela?" Frank was standing now, clutching ribs he was sure were broken. Bill was also standing, and they both reloaded their weapons.

Lela knew she shouldn't take her eyes off Danalov even as she did it to see her husband's face. She wanted to shift back down to human form, to go to him, to hold his body against her and pretend none of this had ever happened. Then Danalov was on her, ripping at her shoulder with his jaws. The pain was terrible, but she could not scream. Could not make a sound. She felt cold as if she had fallen face first into a black and icy sea.

Frank cried out to her. She was falling, fighting, struggling to throw Danalov off even as her strength ebbed. Frank and Bill were scrambling to her aid, but it all seemed so far away, suddenly.

Frank shoved his Ka-Bar knife directly into Danalov's spine at the base of the skull and pushed with all his might. The werewolf spasmed, threw Frank off and reached in vain to pull the knife off. Danalov fell to the ground making terrible whimpering sounds.

Lela lay there, her human form again, naked and staring up at the ceiling as blood pooled black around her.

Bill walked up to the twitching form of the werewolf that Danalov had become. Bill gingerly placed the barrel of a discovered shotgun to Danalov's temple and pulled the trigger, then fired again, then again, then again. There was nothing left but a red stain on the concrete floor.

Frank crawled to Lela and took her in his arms and kissed her softly.

"Baby?" she said, almost in a whisper. She reached up to touch his hands.

"Hey," he said softly, fingering a stray lock of bloody hair out of her face. "Hey, beautiful." He coughed and spat blood away from her. Something was broken inside him. He could feel it.

Bill knelt beside them and began to triage Lela. "Why isn't she healing?"

"I don't know," said Frank, turning to spit blood again. Her shoulder and neck were badly mauled, and she was bleeding profusely. "Staunch the bleeding."

Bill began to rip his shirt into strips and apply them as field dressings. "Lela, honey, will you heal?" he asked.

"Hi, Bill," she said with a faint smile. "Frank, Bill's here. That's nice."

Then there was a blinding light as pale as the surface of the moon flooding the tunnel, emanating from the tattoo on Lela's back but so bright it illuminated the tunnel for hundreds of yards in every direction. An old man was there suddenly, seemingly made of moonlight. He was bent over Lela and Frank with a frown on his face.

"The Son of Fenris who wounded them both has death in his claws. She cannot heal."

"Who are you?" asked Bill.

"My name is Mani." He stroked Lela's head gently. Her eyes lost all focus, and her breathing was slowing. Frank slumped against her, fighting to stay conscious. "This was my daughter."

"Lela?" Frank whispered.

"Love you," she said, stroking Frank's hair gently.

"Can't you do something?" asked Bill, his eyes clouding, and he cradled his brother and sister-in-law.

"I can't take death and make it life, but I can offer them some comfort," Mani said, putting a hand on Bill's shoulder.

"Please. Anything," said Bill.

Then the light grew brighter and brighter and brighter still until it was unbearable.

Frank and Lela awoke in their bed at the house in Monterey. He held her and she held him. It was early morning with pale blue light just pushing into the darkness of their bedroom. A light rain pattered on the rooftops, the gutters, and the windowsills.

She leaned in and kissed him "What's for breakfast?"

"Am I allowed to say bacon?" Frank said, nuzzling into her neck.

"Will you cry if I say grapefruit is better for your health?"

"I'm going to turn into a cranky old guy early if I eat grapefruit for breakfast once too often."

"We can't have that," she said, caressing his back.

They kissed, and they whispered together, and they made love. They lay long together in the quiet of the morning and listened to the rain.

The light began to grow brighter in the windows. The day had truly begun.

"This can't last, can it?" she said, at last.

"No," he said. "But I love you. I guess that will have to be enough."

"I love you," she said, holding him closer.

They rose together and opened the curtains to the light, holding hands as it filled the room, and they were lost in it together.

CHAPTER 42:
RAGNAROK

Night.
Sunday, 25 June, 2017.
Site Bravo.

"See, you've been leading a charmed life," said Marlowe to a now-seated Doctor Lannon.

Lannon stared at the floor in terror and said nothing.

They were in the control room of the storage unit that housed Doctor Lannon's weaponized gas. This was high in the mountains. The room itself was large and round like an amphitheater with a massive skylight above it which could open for ventilation. The storm outside pounded on the glass and lightning shafts threw crazy shadows on the floor of the control room.

Marlowe McCoy had seated Doctor Lannon at a long ebony table before the control panel and now crouched beside him, his massive wolf's head and burning green eyes still towering over his prisoner.

"Y'see, Doc, you were born to midwife Ragnarok. Your good work here will bring Fenris into the world and then we'll *really* get to play. He's been watching you, guiding you, helping you along from the minute you drew your first breath. Ever notice how easy it was to get into the best schools? How money was never a problem? How you always ended up working with the best? You think that was just good luck. Naw, the Wolf God had a plan for you, my friend." Marlowe reached out a clawed hand and tapped at a pressure gauge on the control panel wall.

"This is the stuff, boy, let me tell you," Marlowe chuckled.

"I don't understand. Why would he need me at all?" asked Lannon.

"There are rules. What one god does another god can do. So, if that puke moon god, Mani, is carried out into the world by a mortal, so can Fenris be. That would be you. He's going to join you very soon."

"Join me?"

"Yes, soon he will be with you, in you, carried on your skin. And then, buddy, the world is ours to eat. The whole world is one big buffet."

Marlowe McCoy took a clawed hand and raised it as if in demonstration before Lannon's eyes.

"Long time ago there was a Viking, see? This one was a berserker. Called 'em *Berskr*. Bear shirts. They wore the skins of beasts and they would become like beasts themselves. Well, this one fella, Rannulf the Red, he has a score to settle with another Viking. Some blood feud, see?

"And he goes to a witch-doctor to get the power to kill his enemy, and the witch-doctor makes Rannulf kill himself a wolf and skin it. Then that fella does some hoodoo, mixes up a poultice and spreads it all over the wolf skin. Then he makes Rannulf sleep in the wolf skin. When Rannulf wakes up, he's a werewolf, see? Great Fenris told me this story. Told me to tell you so you'd know.

"That magic the old witch-doctor cast on Rannulf summoned the patronage of Fenris Himself. He granted that men could become his Sons and women, his Daughters. He forged it, but he didn't do it alone. His magic was mixed up and mingled with Mani's, that Viking moon god of no account. There's been this tug-of-war ever since between 'em. We're gonna settle it, though. Fix that Mani up good and Fenrir will eat the moon before it's all over. You watch and see."

"Why does Fenris care that I know this?" asked Lannon, his eyes wide with fear.

"Oh, well I's just comin' to that," said Marlowe with a savage grin. He raised up his claw and traced it from the top of his head down to his groin, over the legs, over one arm, then another, and as black blood splashed and pooled over the floor, sizzling and smoking as it burned into the concrete, Marlowe McCoy skinned himself alive and pulled off his own flesh to reveal the black bones, bloody tissue, and greasy entrails beneath.

When he had finished, his skin lay like a huge black wetsuit lay on the floor. Marlowe shambled forward, advancing on Lannon. The movement of his muscles rippling visibly was almost hypnotic. He wrapped Lannon in his own skin as Lannon screamed and thrashed, then went rigid and deadly still.

Marlowe McCoy, his body one great wound, began almost immediately to clot over as his torn flesh began to repair itself.

The door at the far end of the room opened and Nob walked in.

"You?" Marlowe snapped, rising to his full height. "Crow's little lackey. Run back and tell him he failed. Fenris rises tonight."

"That shall not be," said Nob.

Marlowe grinned, his fangs incandescent, his eyes mad. "Fighting words."

There was great stillness in the room before the chaos.

Marlowe moved so fast he almost seemed to blink from one place to another. One second, he was standing on the other side of the room, the next he was upon Nob, ripping and biting. Nob's form dissipated into a black cloud of thousands of crows which lifted the roaring Marlowe into the air and up, ripping through the skylight with a crash that sent the torrential rain and shattered glass down on the floor below.

Marlowe and Nob continued to rise into the sky, surrounded by lightning and buffeted by the storm's violent winds. They rose higher, Marlowe clawing and mauling—dead crows falling in ones and twos as the cloud pecked and raked his blackened flesh.

Then the cloud of crows released him, and he fell down, down and landed in a bloody heap at the very summit of the mountain. Nob reformed as a man before him.

"More, dog?" he asked. "Or will you return to the labyrinth and forego this madness?"

Marlowe rose and growled. "Now you will bleed." He lunged, howling, for Nob's throat as lightning filled the sky and the hard rain fell.

Below, Aria, human in appearance now and wearing the crow-feathered cloak, was in the control room. She had waited, as Nob asked her to do, for him to take Marlowe out of the equation.

"Doctor Lannon?" she called, her voice high against the storm's rage.

Lannon looked out from under the blanket of flesh, black blood thick in his hair and on his face. "Who are you?"

"I'm here to make you stop," she said.

Lannon stood, suddenly and threw off the skin with a crunch of broken glass underfoot.

"Stop?" he laughed. "Nothing stops." He began to loosen his tie, pulled it from his neck then threw it to the ground. Reaching down he ripped open his button down shirt to reveal the dark impression, almost a brand, of a great wolf's head, eyes alive with malice and hunger. "*He* has come. *He* is with us now."

Ice unspooled in Aria's belly, and she shifted into the wolf form, reaching back to pull the great silver sword from her back, which moments before had only been a glowing tattoo. Her hand sizzled and she yelped in pain, but kept a hold of it and moved in on Lannon.

"Down on your belly," Lannon growled in a deep and horrible voice not his own.

Aria felt her legs go weak, felt the sword slip from her hands as if she were watching herself from above.

"N-no." She felt herself slip on unsteady feet to the ground.

"I am the Lord of Werewolves, child. You are *my* creature," came the voice of Fenris from Lannon's mouth.

"No," she whispered, even as she sank to the glass-littered floor. Even as it bit into her skin, she felt the weight of a cruel and invisible weight pressing her down. She felt she might be crushed by it. It was closing in on her mind and body. The crushing will of Fenris was collapsing her own.

"You will learn your place by suffering, little one."

Aria howled in pain and fear, dangerously close to panic as she writhed on the floor.

Keller stepped out from the shadows and picked up the silver sword.

"I was rather hoping she'd end you so I wouldn't have to," he said. "Ah well, if you want something done right and all that."

"A leech? You think you can stop Ragnarok? Why? So, your masters can hide from the light like the bloated old cowards they have always been? I am Fenris. You are nothing to me."

"I've come to do a job," said Keller with cold indifference. He moved faster than any eye could follow, the arc of the silver sword like a band of light flying straight for Lannon-that-was-Fenris.

Aria was in the air then, clawing at Keller and pulling him down. She hurled him away from Lannon-that-was-Fenris. Her eyes now strange and vacant, tinged with darkness.

Keller tucked and landed lightly on the opposite wall. Standing in defiance of gravity at 90 degrees, he bared his fangs and opened his fist to reveal long translucent claws as sharp as diamond razor blades. In the other hand he still held the silver sword.

"Kill the leech," ordered Fenris.

"Yes, Lord," came Aria's growling reply. She lunged for him, but Keller was already moving.

He swung the silver sword in an arc which halted her approach, then, like a striking serpent he performed a perfect fencer's thrust and caught the very edge of the silver blade directly into her left eye, slicing and searing it and bringing a roar of pain and rage from Aria as she clutched at her dead eye. Keller leaped over her and kicked her hard in the middle of the back and she felt it give. Aria fell to the ground, her broken spine beginning to heal almost instantly while she twitched and contorted in agony.

Keller stood over her and raised the silver sword.

"Stop!" came a voice from the doorway. Curiously, Keller did stop. Mani and Bill stood in the entryway of the room, Bill with his rifle raised, Mani standing in the doorway wearing chainmail armor and a glimmering silver shield. Mani looked younger and stronger, his hair like silver fire and his shoulders broad and strong as a Viking of old.

Bill walked across the room, leveling his rifle at Lannon-that-was-Fenris.

"You're under arrest, Doctor Lannon."

"You dare…" Fenris hissed.

"That is *my* sword, vampire," said Mani to Keller. It shimmered and disappeared from Keller's hand, reappearing in Mani's.

"And that is *my* daughter. Not yours, Fenris. You shall not have her. I am here to ensure you return to the City of Bones."

Keller turned to face Mani and said, "If you're here to kill Lannon and destroy this place so that the werewolves remain only a story to humans, then we have the same idea."

"I would stop the Sons of Fenris, and welcome my own children to greater freedom," said Mani.

Mani walked over to Aria and, kneeling, placed a hand on her head. She felt instant relief from the pain, but no light returned to her ruined eye. She stood and looked back at Fenris with fury. Mani placed the silver sword in her clawed hand, but it did not burn her.

"Never again," she growled, starting towards him.

High above on the mountaintop, embroiled in the storm, Nob and Marlowe McCoy spun together in a deadly spiral of black feathers and claws. The white snow of the summit was littered with black ruins of dead crows and smeared with the red of their blood.

Marlowe's body was almost without skin and oozing red, yet he fought on as the black cloud that was Nob slowly diminished. Marlowe felt himself being lifted again and hurled down, smashed against the stones of the mountaintop over and over and over, tumbling up and being smashed down until the wet slap of his body on rock was distant and his vision darkened. Nob lifted him again and this time hurled him off the top of the mountain and down into the valley below. Marlowe met his second end this way, impaled on a treetop a thousand feet below.

Nob reformed into a human shape, bloodied, battered, and weak. He knelt on the mountain and cried out to Crow, then eased gently into the snow, closed his eyes, and slept.

The *Gladius Dei* Strike team came in black helicopters and fast-roped down at the main entrance of Site Bravo where Gregory and Joseph waited. There were a hundred crusaders in full battle gear, and they came loaded for werewolf.

The Commander was a Justice named Daedalus Hall. His body armor was black, his helmet black, and around his neck was a golden crucifix. Daedalus, a legend in his own time, was tall and dark-eyed with silver hair and a lantern jaw.

His shoulders were broad and his hips narrow as a swimmer's, with a barrel chest and wiry arms. He met with Gregory and Joseph just under the sheltering stone eaves of the front entrance, out of the pounding rain, as the *Gladius Dei* troops formed ranks and awaited orders under the raging storm.

"Gregory," he said, nodding a hello. "What do I need to know?"

"They're weaponizing the Diana Strain in there. There are werewolves on site, at least two, and some kind of spirit guiding them called Mani," said Gregory.

"That correlates to a Norse moon god. Minor deity in that pantheon. There is also some kind of sorcerer manifesting with crows," said Joseph.

"Biological weapons out of satanic curses. That's... about right, actually," said Hall. "This is a government thing?"

"I think it's a contractor, but yes, essentially," said Joseph.

"You will both fall in with my personal guard in case I need intel. I won't lie to you, there have been questions as to your whereabouts and conduct. The fact that I would have to come down here for your emergency knowing so few details, or that the full might of Strike team would be authorized on your say-so...well, this is no small thing. But what you're alleging is of utmost seriousness and the Order seems to have been culpable in some of it."

"We have acted in the spirit of the true Order, sir," said Joseph. "I will swear as much before a tribunal if need be."

"Sir?" asked Gregory. "The Order is culpable in what way?"

"Cardinal Frye is dead. Murdered, apparently, though it is made to look like suicide. It looks like he may have provided a specimen to these people. An inquiry is ongoing, but that's what we know so far. As to why, it looks as if he meant to open up the U.S. military as a recruiting ground for the Order. All he had to do was sell his soul."

Joseph and Gregory looked at each other for a moment and then Joseph said, "That explains a lot."

Aria charged, silver sword upraised. Lannon dodged, his muscles rippling, clothes ripping. He grew massive, dwarfing Aria even, the massive and terrible Fenris roared and Bill doubled over in pain, one eardrum ruptured.

Aria slashed upward at Fenris, biting deep into his arm at the wrist, but not cutting through. Fenris slashed back at her, and she flew against the far wall. Fenris stalked toward where she lay crumpled, but Mani stepped in the way and raised his silver shield. It glowed with intensifying light, ever brighter, ever hotter, until Fenris staggered, stepped back, shielded his eyes. Aria was up then, rushing him, she slammed into him with her shoulder at full force, staggering him. She chopped downward and cut into one of his legs, forcing him to kneel.

Bill, shaking and pale but back in the fight, emptied his rifle into Fenris' face. Keller raced forward with impossible speed, kicking Fenris full in the chest. Fenris fell. Aria came on with blinding speed and put the sword through his heart, impaling him to the hilt. Fenris clamped his jaws down on Aria's leg, then let go as she fell.

Fenris screamed. His great body thrashing so hard that shockwaves throbbed through the building. The wolf god roared and howled even above the howl of the raging storm outside, and his cries continued even as the silver burned him away to ashes. Then he was gone.

The floor began to rumble beneath them, then fissures spiderwebbed the cement floor, and suddenly a long black chasm opened nearly under their feet. The gas storage meters began to sound the alarm. The tanks ruptured and the gas was expanding. An explosion deafened them and rocked the groaning structure as they fled.

Mani ran to where Aria knelt and became a silver mark of the moon on her flesh. Keller flew up and out of the skylight, into the storm above.

Bill and Aria ran for the door, and the hallway beyond as the floor fell away, and the chasm yawned, trying to swallow them. Far below she saw the sickly green light that illuminated the City of Bones and the huge, sprawling form of Fenris, prone and unconscious—a wreckage across the length of the labyrinth. He was far from dead. Only unhorsed from his mortal vessel.

They ran like drunken stumblers through the hallways toward the rear exit, even as Site Bravo rocked and decayed around them as the earthquake continued. The gas was surging high into the air and swirling into dissipation on the winds of the thunderstorm. Floors fell in on lower floors, the chasm ever yawning, swallowing the mountain.

"Where's Lela?" asked Aria frantically. "Where's Frank?"

"They're gone" Bill's voice caught.

Aria froze. "No." Devastation pulled Aria out of the wolf form, and she was just a naked girl—pale and wounded, one eye socket black and empty.

Bill shook his head in sorrow.

The earthquake was intensifying, everywhere was the sound of steel twisting, fire burning, glass shattering, and scientists dying in their locked shelters."We have to go." Bill said over the death throes of Site Bravo, pulling her up.

She took a deep breath, nodded, and began to run with him, his arm on her hers. They cleared the abandoned gate and kept running. The mountain above began to truly topple into itself. The raging storm covered them as they disappeared into the safety of the trees.

The Strike team pulled back as the mountain imploded. By morning there was only rubble and a black lake where the mountain had been. They established a perimeter and tried to find a way into the site, but it was gone completely. They extracted by helicopter, unsure of what had happened. When reports were written,

Joseph and Gregory were credited, rather than castigated, for their steadfast devotion to the principles of the Order.

Privately, Joseph questioned if this was merited. They had allowed Lela and Aria to live, even to kill. Gregory just shrugged and told his friend that war makes strange bedfellows. Whatever they were after was worse, and it looks like they beat it. All's well that ends.

Joseph wonders. For many nights to come, he wonders.

CHAPTER 43:
WHO IS NOT DEAD

Elsewhere.
After

"And so, the war is over? Fenris is defeated?" asks Nob, his bent form scarred and slowly mending. "The first battle is over. We have lost," Crow answers from his perch high above the World.

"Lost?"

"Lost."

"I don't understand."

"Look." Crow gestures downward, and Nob sees.

What Nob sees is a package being delivered by courier at the Russian Embassy in Washington D.C. Inside this package is an aerosol can and detailed chemical breakdowns of Doctor Lannon's work. Schematics. There is a data stick with all experiments, all findings, all the information a scientist would need to reproduce the serum that brings on lycanthropy. This serum comes both as a stable compound that will enable werewolf soldiers to be developed without the possibility of death at transformation, and also an unstable version that will kill 90% of the people that come in contact with it. It will drive the rest into animal frenzies of madness after transformation. A perfect way to destabilize an enemy nation.

Nob sees the functionaries of the embassy take delivery of this package, and Crow shows him identical packages at the Chinese embassy, at the British embassy, and even at the American State Department. The technology for engineering enhanced werewolves to serve military purposes, and to bioweaponize lycanthropy are now available to the world powers thanks to the research at Site Bravo and the genius of Dr. Robert Lannon.

"Ragnarok has begun. Fenris will move again. His hunger is unsleeping," said Crow.

"Is there no hope?"

"There is hope in Mani's Daughter. She is not Fenris' creature the way these abominations infected by the altered Curse are. Her doom is certain, but for the time being she and those like her are the soldiers of Mani against Fenris. Her victory will be the survival of men. We will aid her in this. Rest. Heal. I have much for you to do."

Nob nods, curls into himself, and sleeps as a crow sleeps, but his dreams are those of a man.

Keller kneels before the throne of Master Alexei again, his forehead pressed to the floor by the weight of his Lord's will.

"You have failed us, Keller," the Master's voice sings dangerously low and soft.

"The doctor responsible is dead, my Lord. The site is destroyed. Please, how have I displeased you?"

"My spies tell me the mortal governments have the secret of Rannulf the Red. They know how to make wolves do their bidding. They will propagate them."

"I offer my lifeblood, Lord. I have no answer for how this happened."

There is a long silence. Master Alexei rises from his throne and strides to where Keller lies prostrate. He reaches down with a long, pale, spider-like finger and touches the back of Keller's head with his long claw.

"It is long since I have feasted on a servant of your age and power," Master Alexei hisses, "though it is still feeble childhood to such as ourselves.

"All I have is yours to command, Lord."

Master Alexei straightens and says, "I think not. I have other business for you. You shall extend my invitation to the other Masters. We must meet in council to discuss what will be done. Our kind is now vulnerable to exposure. It may be time for an army of our own."

"Yes, Lord." Keller sighs relief despite the needlessness of breathing.

"Go," says Master Alexei. "First to Master Silas. He has the ear of the others. He sleeps in Cairo."

"As you command, Lord." Keller, thus dismissed, stands, backing away and disappearing up the stairs and out into the silent tunnels far below the sleepless city.

Bill and Aria sit at the table in silence. She wears an eye patch now and still isn't used to it. Dinner cleared away, they sit together and listen to the forest outside. The weeks-long journey has been difficult. Bill has used every piece of tradecraft he knows to keep Aria—keep them both—from popping up on anyone's radar. So far as anyone knows, he perished along with the rest of the men of the Hostage Rescue Team and Aria remains at large.

Anonymously traveling back down to Frank's old cabin in Big Sur has required a little thievery, a lot of discomfort, a good deal of stowing away, and sometimes long walks in the dark. Now they are here, and no one knows it.

After a time, she says, "You aren't worried?"

"Full moon tomorrow, you mean?"

"Yes, that."

"You seem to be able to control it now."

"It's a lot easier than it was. I guess that's Mani's doing. Still, I don't want…"

"I'm not worried," he says. "I trust you, Lela, and Frank trusted you."

She doesn't say, "And look what happened to them." She just sighs because the pain is so raw and so close to the surface. This is probably why they haven't left each other. These two strangers are the only people each knows the other can trust. The only stay against being completely alone in the world is the one looking back from the opposite chair.

It isn't romantic, though it could be, and it isn't physical yet, if it is ever going to be. There are dangers in that, as Aria knows only too well. Her brief affair with Billy Hatfield had given her this life. This curse.

"Lela was right," she says finally. "It is a curse. If you hang around long enough, it will ruin you, too."

"That's possible," says Bill. "But what if it already has? No point in being alone and damned if you're damned anyway."

"You won't go back then? To the FBI? To your life?"

"The FBI was my life. But the government funded this thing. *My* government. I'm betting Lannon and Weynman had backups. I'm betting the people behind this don't want loose ends. So, we watch. We wait. And in time we do what needs doing to stop them."

"Fenris will try again," says Aria. "Mani tells me things sometimes. He's sure of it."

"We'd better be ready, then. I know the shadow world pretty well. I know the players. We can get by. I have a pretty deep address book."

Aria laughs for the first time in a long while, "Address book? Man, you're really dating yourself with that one."

He smiles. "No school like the old school."

"Now you sound like Frank."

"Well, I taught him everything he knows. Knew." This chases the smile away from both of them.

"I'm sorry," he says.

"Me, too," she says, putting a hand on his.

"But they didn't die for nothing," he says. "They died fighting for each other. For warriors, this is a good death."

"A good death. I guess that's what's up ahead, right? A fight. Maybe we win, maybe we don't, but if we're lucky we have the courage to die well," Aria says.

He nods once.

"But not tonight."

"No," she says. "Not tonight."

To Be Concluded in *Sons of Fenris*.

Made in the USA
Columbia, SC
13 November 2021